Rumena Bužarovska

I'M NOT GOING ANYWHERE

Translated from the Macedonian by the author
and Steve Bradbury

DALKEY ARCHIVE PRESS
Dallas / Dublin

Originally published in Macedonian as *Не одам никаде* by ili-ili

Copyright © 2018 by Rumena Bužarovska
Translation © 2023 by Rumena Bužarovska and Steve Bradbury

First edition

ISBN Paperback: 978-1-62897-454-6
ISBN Ebook: 978-1-62897-481-2

Library of Congress Cataloging-in-Publication Data: Available.

Cover design by Kayla E.
Interior design by Anuj Mathur
Cover image © BuZar (Buzarovski Archive)

"The Young Housewife" by William Carlos Williams, 1916
"Rain" by William Carlos Williams, from THE COLLECTED
POEMS: VOLUME I, 1909-1939, copyright ©1938 by New
Directions Publishing Corp. Reprinted by permission of New
Directions Publishing Corp.

Dalkey Archive Press
www.dalkeyarchive.com
Dallas/Dublin

Printed on permanent/durable acid-free paper.

PRAISE FOR *MY HUSBAND*

"The Macedonian writer, born in 1981, shatters pretenses with a sense of humor that spares not a single character. With an acid pen, she depicts situations that are pathetic, at times even tragic, to allow laughter to open the way to liberation." —*Le Monde*

"This Macedonian writer has a sharp tongue. If the men are stupid and vain, unfaithful and chauvinist, the women are naïve, replete with their own weaknesses. Rumena Bužarovska plays on the blurred, shifting ground of relationships, the slippery moments that give rise to fantasy, or to those, especially uncomfortable, that trigger doubt, regret, and feelings of frustration." —*Lire*

"[Her] prose is rhythmic, with a sharp sense of theater and cinematic montage … leaving space for things left unsaid, for semblances, for the materiality of the flesh, for romantic failure, for burlesque." —**Philippe Petit**, *Marianne*

"Bužarovska's literary strength lies in the weaknesses of her characters . . . whose words are never what they think, whose thoughts are never what they feel . . . [in] an eternal struggle for attention and recognition that is never satisfied nor ever granted to another soul. In the end, both men and women receive their just deserts by reason of their emotional ineptitude and emotional sloppiness. [But] Bužarovska is never cynical, for between the lines she reveals the battles that everyone is forced to wage within themselves." —*Falter*

"Carnage, yes, but of the most hilarious variety." —*L'Express*

"In the eleven stories that make up *My Husband*, the institution of marriage is at the center of each petty cruelty, each profound disappointment, each quietly cutting comment and abrasive fight… Bužarovska points out a key constraining fact with which every woman is intimately familiar: patriarchy breeds cruelty... It makes sense that Bužarovska was largely responsible for pioneering the Macedonian version of the #MeToo hashtag. Who else would be bold enough to take on the institution—the system—of marriage?" —Eva Dunsky, *Los Angeles Review*

"[A writer of] formidable intelligence, cruelty, and talent for the tragicomic." —**Astrid De Larminat,** *Le Figaro*

"[Her] stories treat the abysmal with defiant comedy." —*Die Welt*

*You'll always end up in this city. Don't hope for things
elsewhere: there's no ship for you, there's no road.*

C.P. Cavafy

Contents

THE VASE

They want to give us the grand tour of the apartment, at least that's how Tanja and Kire put it. "We just moved in last week and we're almost done with everything," Tanja is speaking so loudly into the receiver I have to hold the phone away from my ear. I can hear Kire yapping in the background. Something I really hate: I'm on the phone and someone can't stop yammering and doesn't give a shit that I'm trying to have a conversation. "Have them come early, before it gets dark!" Kire barks, which is swiftly followed by Tanja's loud repetition, "Yes, come early, come at seven, before it gets dark!"

Nino is sitting next to me, puzzling through a crossword. I nudge him and roll my eyes. He shrugs and then finally sniffs. "Alright then, we'll see you soon!" I say, happy to hang up.

"God," I groan. "She ruptured my eardrum. You could hear her, right?"

Nino nods.

"I hate housewarmings. Nino, are you listening? We need to get them something. It's tomorrow."

"Well, you know, we're not exactly swimming in money," he says without taking his eyes off the puzzle. The reading glasses he bought at the farmer's market a month ago are poised at the tip of his nose. He only wears them at home

1

because he doesn't want people to know he's growing old.

"I know," I say, thinking of the thousand-denar bill I keep hidden in the side pocket of my purse in case I need to go for a drink or have the urge to buy something. And, of course, there are those three hundred euros I keep in a separate account. You never know what can come up. Nino doesn't think about these things. Sometimes I wonder if he actually knows I've set aside a little something and is at ease because he believes this money is for the two of us, for hard times, God forbid. "This means we're going to have to tighten our belts," I add.

I wince at the thought of all the potato-stew, beans, and lentil soup we'll be forced to eat for days on end. And there'll be no more going out for drinks or coffee, even on the weekend, which is just around the corner. And we can't invite anyone over for drinks, unless they were to bring their own liquor, which we could never ask them to do, because it would be so embarrassing. Not that any of our friends are much better off. Sometimes I feel they only want to come over to get a free drink.

We sit there in silence until I blurt, "But we've got to get them something."

"Do we have to?" Nino asks. I've always found his disregard for social conventions annoying.

"Yes, we *have* to. We could drop by JYSK tomorrow on the way to their place," I say, knowing the store is on the pricey side. But the fact is, I just want to go there. I dream the day when I will be able to purchase those fluffy pillows, those colorful doormats, those elegant bathroom soap dispensers and toothbrush holders, which I don't really have any place to put because our sink is so wobbly.

"So what do they need?" he asks, filling in the crossword puzzle with his big, messy letters sprawling out of the boxes.

He sometimes rips the page with its tip, pressing the pen so hard it makes a pop that gives me goosebumps.

"How would I know? I just don't get it. You go to somebody's home for the first time and you're supposed to bring a housewarming gift, but you have no idea what to get them because you've never been there before and you don't know what they're missing, and of course you can't ask them what they need, because they'll just lie and say, we don't need anything! Stupid phony Macedonian humility, that's all that is," I grumble.

"M-hm," Nino peers at me over the rim of his glasses, which is his way of saying he agrees. Then he takes them off and becomes lost in thought. "Yes," he finally says, and falls silent again. It always takes him ages to say what he's thinking. At the beginning of our relationship, his pauses impressed me, especially considering the words simply tumble out of my mouth as fast as I can think them up. But after a few years together, the silences are really starting to get on my nerves. "Yes," he repeats. "You remember when we moved in here, and Tom and Lydia gave us that vase?"

We both look at it, which is easy in a living room as small as ours. The one big wall is barricaded by a block of square white cabinets with round brown handles. Some of the handles have fallen off, leaving behind holes that look just like a pig snout. Several cabinet doors are loose, exposing threads of cheap plywood. Whoever designed this place had two shelves cut into the wall, which is where we keep our books. These are mostly books from our childhood, sets of Serbian translations we took from our homes. We don't have a lot of new books. Because you know, we're always saying Macedonian translations are so crappy, and the Serbian versions so expensive, there's nothing to read anyway. The shelves used to have glass doors but for some reason the landlord took them off. In the middle of the wall there is a deep hole meant for a TV set. Ours is pretty small, albeit large enough for a room like this, so we put Tom and Lydia's vase beside it. This vase, the nicest thing we own.

It's a classic Greek-style amphora. Not those that are long and narrow, but with a fat belly, smaller than the ones you typically see in museums. It's not brown and doesn't have any Greek motifs. Rather, it's a deep vibrant green. In fact, if you look up close, it's got a mixture of different shades of green that all blend into each other and a fine web of thin cracks that give it a kind of rough texture, as if it were made of stone. Looking at this vase calms me. They gave it to us about a year ago, and come to think of it, we haven't gotten together with them since. Even when we're watching TV I'll glance at it. Then I'll think of Tom and Lydia and a warm feeling comes over me.

I probably get this feeling because of their perfumes. It's not that they wear a lot, but every time Lydia would swish her scarf or Tom came up close, the fragrance would hit me: his sharp, yet fresh, hers more flowery, more like the smell of some expensive hand cream. Lydia always smells like all the women with painted nails and jangling bracelets who used to come over to our house when I was a child and stroke my hair and pinch my cheeks. Tom is the kind of guy you could easily fall for, with his olive skin and hazel eyes, sitting elegantly in his chair with his legs crossed, one athletic arm dangling from the armrest, the other holding a perpetual cigarette in its hand.

"Jade-colored," that's what Lydia said as she removed the vase from the box to present it to us. Jade. I didn't really know what color jade was, but I liked the sound of it.

"It's our housewarming gift," said Tom in his husky voice.

"But dis is not our apartment," Nino explained in the hard Slavic accent he was not the least ashamed of.

"Well, think of it as a step in the right direction," said Lydia as she gently held it out to us. The textured gold rings on her strong and slender pianist fingers stood out against the vase's deep greens. I thanked them in my somewhat broken English, trying to echo Tom and Lydia's perfect British accent, knowing full well I overextend my vowels and sometimes confuse the "th" sound with "d" and "t." I explained that what Nino meant was this wasn't our permanent home. We were only living here until we got back on our feet, until we settled some inheritance issues. They didn't say a word, seeing I'd dived into waters they were not prepared to swim in, at least not while they were sober. It annoyed me that I was making more excuses than Nino. But nonetheless I kept digging myself deeper into a hole, saying the apartment was much too small for us, it was very old. But the location was great—

"Yes, it's a fantastic location!" Tom chimed in, happy to change the subject.

"And new location of dis beautiful vase is?" Nino asked, returning attention to the gift, for which I was grateful. But my gratitude was short-lived. Because all this did was make Tom and Lydia look around the apartment and realize we were barricaded by cabinets, that the sofa and armchairs we were sitting in were old and mismatched and camouflaged by decorative covers, and that the stained and beat-up coffee table crammed between them barely left room for our legs.

"We'll find a good place for it," I said, just before Lydia suggested, "Maybe you could put it in the bedroom?" not knowing that we didn't have one, that we slept on the two-seater sofa bed we could barely open even after wedging the coffee table into the corner of the room, so I just pretended I hadn't heard what she'd said and asked, "Is it from Greece?"

Indeed, it was. They had bought it from a "perfectly charming" little shop in one of those picture postcard villages with the whitewashed houses and blue-shuttered windows, the balconies draped with bougainvillea, and narrow, cobbled lanes that meandered to hidden squares lined with cafes where one can have a cool glass of water and savor a spoonful of homemade preserves.

The vase was made by a local but internationally acclaimed artist. "The certificate is inside the box. You can read more about her later," Tom cut in, eager to tell us about their Aegean island cruise, about the fresh octopus they had grilled, the dolphins leaping around the prow of their boat. The crystal-clear blue of the deep sea where you can bathe nude. Where the water is so salty it seems to lick your skin. ("It makes love to you!" Lydia exclaimed and her head nearly lolled back in ecstasy.) And then once again about the dreamy little villages. The hospitality of the locals. The homemade specialties they had tasted. "The moussaka!" Lydia sighed.

"Svetlana makes very good moussaka," Nino said, clambering to his feet. We hadn't yet offered them anything to drink. "But for food we have only meze with cold homemade rakija or white wine," Nino stooped as he was offering these "homemade specialties," which Tom and Lydia later dubbed the tomatoes, peppers, cheese, and liquor Nino had lugged back from his uncle's village.

"I wouldn't drink whiskey or eat seafood while I'm in Macedonia," Lydia said as she savored a pepper. Even this homely thing looked distinguished between her elegant fingers.

We'd heard Lydia play once. She had stopped performing regularly a while back, but agreed to give one recital. Tom was an art historian visiting on a university research scholarship and, without a job of her own, Lydia had little to do. Despite Nino, who works at the National Opera and Ballet, I know next to nothing about classical music, and really, it's not something he enjoys either. Regardless, I was enchanted by the way she moved her body as she played: her elbows flaring, her back arching with the rhythm and the music, her torso swaying in circles, her head turned so that her silvery hair hung across her eyes. She had striking fingers: strong, angular, nimble as a spider. I became so enthralled I clapped when I wasn't supposed to. The elderly lady I sat next to shushed me angrily. We were in the first row and Lydia must have noticed, Tom too.

I was just as embarrassed as we sat in our tiny living room, crowded with cabinets. It seemed like Nino didn't give a damn. He kept topping up his glass of rakija, sweating in the sudden stuffiness of the room. We opened the balcony door leading to the miniature kitchenette, but still couldn't get a breeze. It was hot and the four of us were smoking, me more than ever, nervous that I had invited Tom and Lydia to this dump. I shifted my to foot to cover what looked like a crusty ketchup stain on the carpet I hadn't noticed before. My embarrassment grew with the increasing realization of how stupid it was to invite them over. But we had no money and we wanted so much to hang out with them. We were flattered that they wanted to drink with us and tell stories about their dazzling past. We were flattered they chose us as their audience, flattered by how they looked, long and lean, in loose white flannel that outlined their sinewy figures and highlighted their sun-bronzed skin.

We're not too bad ourselves. Maybe our apartment is awful, maybe we don't have the money to move into a better one, but we look impeccable, especially me. That evening, even as I covered up the carpet stain, I couldn't help but admire how beautiful my heels were, how my sandals complemented my slender feet, how my red toe-nails glittered like wild strawberries. I was sure that we also smelled good and that if anyone

came into the room, they'd notice the crisp mix of the fra-
grances we wore and the aroma of the cigarettes we smoked.
But Nino had started to sweat. Beads had formed on his forehead and there were big wet patches under his armpits. He
was clearly drunk and wouldn't shut up.

"We're working toward saving up to get a bigger apartment. We'd like to have children. We're trying," he said, his
eyes a little crossed from all that rakija.

"We don't have any children either," Tom said, his head
cocked back as he took a dramatic puff of his cigarette. "We
don't know why. It was nature's way. We never bothered to
get it checked out."

"Some people are so inconsiderate," Lydia added, "they'll
ask you right up front: what's wrong with you? I remember
this particularly brazen couple who asked me that and I said:
what, do you mean physically or mentally?"

We tsk-tsked and then fell silent. I could tell Nino was
getting emotional, like he always does when he's drunk. He
slapped both palms on his knees, as if finally mustering up
the courage to do something grand: "Can I play someting?"
he asked. Tom and Lydia shifted excitedly.

"Of course! Why in the world didn't we think of that
sooner . . . what a pleasure that would be," their voices over-
lapped. Nino took out the violin from the case he kept behind
the door.

"Someting traditional," he announced, leaving room for
Tom and Lydia's sighs of satisfaction. He then improvised a
jazzed-up version of *Kaži, kaži, libe Stano*, tears welling up
in the corners of his eyes. To my taste, this song was too slow
and sad, and it had too many grace notes. Honestly, I thought
it was trite, but at the end of his little recital, Tom and Lydia
gave him an encouraging applause.

"It's about couple which can't have keeds," he began to

explain. "D' men says to d' women: do you need anyting? Mannie or cloths? She says, no, I have everyting, but I don't have child. D' men says to d' women: I'm gonna go to Greece and getchoo golden child. She says, golden child can't call me dear mami. Very sad."

"Oh, it's heartbreaking," Lydia said, raising the rakija glass to her lips and accidentally hitting a tooth. Meanwhile, Tom unintentionally slammed his glass on the table and covered his face with his large hands. "Oh, oh," he moaned, "Oh." We all knew what was next. He always cried when he got hammered. Once he cried for an hour over the tsunami in Indonesia, but that was nothing compared to the way he blubbered over the war in Bosnia. It was like he wasn't sure what was wrong with the human race. He insisted the world was falling apart, that the apocalypse was nigh.

"Things fall apart! The centre cannot hold!" he declared. I later found out he had been quoting a famous Irish poet whose name I can't remember. "To make a child a man, a man a child!" he said with a solemnity that made me suspect this was a meaningful and well-known line. Lydia looked at him compassionately, while Nino and I didn't know what to say. Tom and Lydia knew so many things and had traveled everywhere. They were incredibly open-minded and educated. We didn't know anyone like them. True, they drank an awful lot and always got plastered, but it's not like Nino and I are exactly lightweights. Lydia stroked Tom's neck as he sank his face into his hands in a sweet, inspired state of despair. Watching this display of emotion somehow pleased me, but what was even more appealing was how Tom snuggled up to Lydia and gently laid his cheek upon her breast. His hand reached around her waist while his other hand cupped her breast, as Lydia toyed with his thick strands of ash-blonde hair. Cuddling his face against her chest, he rose up and kissed her throat, softly moaning. Lydia whispered in return, "My darling, my darling, it's all right." I saw her gently nip his earlobe.

Seeing people intimate in public usually makes me uncomfortable. But watching Tom and Lydia like this, in our apartment, got me excited. There was a warmth stirring inside me, rising from my groin. I couldn't say a word for fear of falling softly apart. Lydia looked around and said that perhaps it was time for them to go. Tom shook himself out of his reverie and began to say, still choked up, that we were terrific hosts, that they had had such a wonderful time with us.

"Come back," Nino replied, his eyes droopy as if he were about to fall asleep. For some reason he did not get up from his chair. Tom and Lydia bent down to give him a goodbye kiss. I took the four steps to the door to see them off, where they embraced me, their perfume lingering on my skin. Tom left a wet streak of tears on my cheek. As I closed the door, I didn't want to wipe it off.

Nino was still sprawled in the armchair. I had to virtually step over him to get back to my seat in the cramped space, and as I did, he grabbed me. He pulled me down on his lap and I felt he was hard. He kissed me on the throat, he wrenched my shirt off, he licked and squeezed my breasts, then pushed me over on the two-seater and in one brisk move he stripped off my panties and shoved his penis inside me. I was so aroused at first that I forgot about everything, which is hardly ever the case. I melted into a pool of flesh. But after a bit Nino began to falter and went a little limp. My ears suddenly switched on again and I could hear the rhythmic squeaking of the sofa, like a creaky old swing about to break. I opened my eyes and saw all the little pig snout holes in the cabinets peering down at us from the wall and then Nino just stopped.

"My knee's numb. I keep hitting it against a loose spring," he complained. Pity and shame swept over me. It was like we were in high school, fucking in my little brother's bed.

"Fuck me on the table," I said, not knowing where these words were coming from. I'd never spoken like that before. I wanted him to lift me as I was and carry me to the little dining room table adjoining the hall that pretended to be a kitchen, but that would never occur to him, so we strolled half-naked to our destination. I got up on the table and we continued unsteadily. This time I decided to keep my eyes closed. I imagined Nino was Tom, and that Lydia was sitting on the two-seater where Nino and I had just been fucking, watching Tom's copper buns thrusting between my legs. "Shoot your load!" I said, again saying something I had never said before, and I felt sugar running through my thighs and Nino letting go inside me. After this I felt nauseous all night long.

The next morning I realized it'd been one of my fertile days. If it's a boy, I thought, I'll call him Tomislav. If it's a girl, I'll name her Lydia. I told Nino. He looked puzzled. "Why?" he asked. It dawned on me we hadn't experienced the same thing. "They're just pretty names," I lied, but Nino isn't stupid.

But no, I didn't get pregnant. Not that time, nor any other time Nino and I had sex. The doctors kept assuring us that, anatomically, we were fine and shouldn't have a problem conceiving. Which is why I got more and more annoyed when I chanced to see a cradle in a furniture store window, and those dangly things you hang above them, those tiny wardrobes painted pink or blue. Not only were those kiddy things a painful reminder that sex was becoming more and more exasperating because we just couldn't make a baby, but it also drove home the fact that we were stuck in a one-room apartment so jammed with cabinets there wasn't room for a cradle anyway. There wasn't room for anything.

This might be why, when I get to JYSK, I feel like going into the children's section with all the stacked-up cradles and the fluffy kiddie pillows piled on the floor and just mess them up. It's all I can do not to go there. So, like usual, I go to see the shelves with the colorful cushions. But one cushion (hey, a single cushion!) costs six hundred denars, and I only have a thousand. I also don't want to get them anything I deeply desire for myself. I'm not so crazy about furniture. What I really want are accessories.

So, I then stroll to the bedding section. Not that I can afford to buy Kire and Tanja matching sheets, nor do I know how big their bed is. No, I go there because our sheets are ugly. Nino has this inexplicable fondness for stripes. In fact, he once came home with matching Auschwitz pajamas and bedsheets.

I finally stumble on a selection of clocks on sale, some of which have unusually odd shapes. But then I think that maybe giving a married couple a clock isn't such a great idea. If someone gave me a clock, I'd think they were telling me I was growing old and my clock was ticking. Maybe they would think that I was saying: "Your time is up!" But then again, maybe the opposite: "May you live forever!" Right. This is what I'll say when I give them this stylish clock that probably won't match their furniture.

I have just twelve denars left. It's such a pitiful amount, I decide to spend it. I walk into the nearest shop and buy matches for eight denars. Out of sheer contrariness, I drop the remaining coins one by one as I walk out. "Madam, madam! You dropped something!" two responsible citizens call after me. I turn and look them straight in the eye, then cast a disdainful glance toward the metal on the ground, as if to say *here, it's yours*. As I wait for Nino by the curb outside, I take out the matches and light them one after the other, letting them fall at my feet when they are half burnt. When Nino arrives, it looks like I'm standing in the middle of a small pyre.

I hate our car. Whenever we go to Ohrid for vacation, I can barely endure the two-and-a-half-hour drive that feels like I'm riding a busted exhaust pipe. Not only is it outrageously loud and draughty as hell, but it rattles and shakes, and has that cheap plastic smell. Our car is like a toy, like something not meant for adults.

Nino has just come from a rehearsal at the Opera. On our way to Kire and Tanja's for the housewarming, he looks lost in thought.

"You don't care what I got them?" I shout over the clanking of our wreck, which rattles like a can whenever we hit a pothole on the streets of Skopje.

"Huh?" he says. It's like I've shaken him out of a dream. "Sorry. What did you get them?"

He's apologized, but too late. I feel the need to punish him. He didn't even notice my symbolic little pyre.

"It's supposed to be from *both* of us. It will be embarrassing if you don't know what's in the box."

"Yes, you're right," he says. I can tell he's trying to shut me up.

"Ok, it's one thing not to go shopping with me, but to not even care what I got." I know I'm pushing it, but I want to see how far I can go.

"Right. Please tell me what you got them. I really want to know. Really," he adds in a soothing tone, as he stares straight ahead. I look at his silhouette. He's got this extremely large, beak-like nose. When we first met, I found it sexy. Now it just makes him look more "whatever you say, dear," which gets on my nerves.

"A clock. A *cool* clock. If it doesn't match their furniture, they can regift it, because I didn't know what else to get them."

"That's ok. A clock is fine. It's the gesture that matters anyway, not the actual gift. The act of paying attention. You know how excited they are to have finally found a place. You know how long they looked," Nino says calmly, as if it isn't the two of us who are stuck in a rut. "Here we are. I think that's the right door," he says, parking in front of an apartment block straight out of the 70s.

It's definitely not a new building. That's good, I think. Because now there are these nice new ones, with cute little porches, flashy doorways and intercoms, marble staircases with elaborate banisters. The walls at these places smell fresh. On the other hand, new buildings are really flimsy. If there's an earthquake, they're more liable to collapse and kill everyone inside. Which is why it's better to live in an old building like ours, especially the sturdy ones that don't just fall apart. Still, I gloat as we climb the stairs, because it smells of piss. As we huff and puff our way up, I relish the thought of Tanja and Kire having to lug all their groceries and the stroller and the baby up all these stairs, panting under the weight of all the bottled water you have to keep buying because the tap water in Skopje tastes like rust. The higher the floor, the cheaper the place. But that's not going to happen to us. All we need is for Nino's mother to die. Just let her die.

"This is it," says Nino and rings the bell next to a shiny new white door with the plate *Trpeski* inscribed in gold. Look at my friend Tanja, the great feminist, taking her husband's name, I think to myself. I could understand it if she had some peasant-sounding last name. But no. She just had to go for the hillbilly *Trpeski*.

They both meet us at the door, their mouths stretched wide in gleaming grins that reveal all their teeth. The scent of baby hits my face. The foyer smells of baby, they both smell of baby. "Where's the little one?" I ask. I haven't seen her since shortly after she was born.

"She's asleep," Kire half-whispers. "We'd better go into the living room. We don't want to wake her. But first I'm going to have to ask you to take your shoes off. Babies like to crawl, you know." So we take them off, which Nino isn't too happy about. He's always getting holes on his socks, and his feet tend to stink. Fortunately, Tanja and Kire have slippers. They don't gloat over the grandeur of their entryway, probably because they don't want us to linger there. As for us, we don't even have an entryway. Just a place where we pile our shoes, in front of the little bathroom where Nino had to shove the washing machine under the rusty old water heater that breaks down every six months and rumbles like an empty stomach whenever we turn it on.

Here there is ample room for four people. We can comfortably take off our shoes and marvel at the circular patterns on the floor tiling, just like the one in Tito's mausoleum in Belgrade. There is room for coat hangers. There's a shoe cabinet with a row of drawers and a stone bowl for depositing loose change, like the change I threw out earlier that day. Atop the coins, their car fob gleams. I can see my figure in the hallway mirror. It's one of those mirrors that makes you look thinner.

Tanja doesn't need a mirror like that to feel good about herself. She looks incredible for someone who gave birth less than a year ago. She doesn't even have those puffy eyebags you see on new mothers. I examine her from head to foot as she guides us into the living room. Her hips are as slender as ever. It's if she'd never even had a baby.

They usher us into the living room. I can't disguise my admiration. Neither can Nino. Nino, who had the nerve to buy Auschwitz pajamas and bedding, could actually see the place was really nice. Matching armchairs and two-seater sofas complement the turquoise wooden coffee table that occupies the middle of the spacious room. A single peach-scented candle adorns the table. An enormous abstract painting in pastel hues fills one whole wall. "This is one of our favorite things," Tanja says, "a painting by Nevena Maksimovska," a name that means nothing to me. I nod, as if I know who she's talking about, while Nino just stands there. "We asked her to make the painting just to cover that wall, and it turned out to be a masterpiece!"

"Yes, it matches your furniture," I say, knowing Tanja won't appreciate the remark. "Maybe what we got you won't fit in so well in this room, but I'm sure you can find a place for it," I say, handing her the gift-wrapped clock.

"Oh, you really shouldn't have," Tanja says. She and Kire give each other a look and smile courteously. Come on, unwrap this clock that has nothing to do with your living room, that looks like we picked it up at a flea market, I think to myself. "A clock!" Tanja exclaims. "Thank you, it really is beautiful. I'm sure we'll find a place for it," she adds.

I've forgotten my lines about time and eternity, so I just stand there with a stupid grin on my face. Nino steps in at the right moment, complimenting the floor to ceiling bookcase next to the painting. "Oh yes, we also had that made," says Tanja, setting the clock down on the coffee table. She walks to the bookcase, stokes one of the shelves, and says, "Baltic birch," as if we're supposed to know what that is.

"You get a lot of sunlight in here, don't you?" says Nino, just for the sake of saying something.

"That's the best thing about this apartment," Tanja replies, slowly turning in a circle with her arms extended, as if she's showcasing the place for sale. Coming to a stop, she gestures at the bay window across from the bookcase. We follow her out onto the balcony with green tiles just like the ones in the foyer. "And this is Kire's project," she says, showing us the lush potted flowers in bloom lining little shelves and hanging from handrails.

"Dude, I would've gotten you some flowers if I knew you were so into them," Nino turns to Kire and slaps him on the back. Kire's back is rather huge. In fact, he's a big guy all around and doesn't come across as a guy who likes flowers.

"What a great place for your dining room table," I say as we step back inside, admiring the alcove by the bay window.

"The light bathes us in the morning when we sit down to breakfast with the sun," Tanja waves a hand toward the windows like a flight attendant indicating the nearest emergency exit.

I make a note of this remark so I will remember to make fun of it to Nino later. When Tanja first got together with Kire, she would write him love poems. I don't know how he could stand it. But then again Tanja has an amazing body, so Kire puts up with her sentimental shit. From the sunlit dining area, she takes us into the kitchen. "It's got a pantry and natural ventilation," Tanja says.

"You sound like a real estate agent," Kire adds. We all laugh.

"The kitchen didn't cost us that much," Tanja continues. "It's small, but efficient. We weren't going for anything flashy."

Yes, the room is nothing out of the ordinary. Just a plain white kitchen, like any other, except that everything is brand new. The sink and faucet have a silvery gleam. Our faucet has long since turned green with bacteria and buildup, but I have no intention of cleaning or replacing it. Our landlord never invests in anything. He just waits for us to fix something when it breaks down. And he has a way of screwing us over. He's cross-eyed so he pretends he's slow. We never know what he's looking at, and whenever we ask him something, he seems disoriented. "I can't argue with him. He's not right in the head," Nino says every time he spends our own money to fix the water heater or what not.

"We've got two more rooms," Tanja says. "It's just that Anfisa is asleep, so we'll have to be quick. And quiet. Is that ok?"

Anfisa Trpeski. What a name. A grand display of petty bourgeois sentiment. "We don't have to go in there if you're afraid we might wake her up," I say. I've had enough. It's all I can do to refrain from looking down to see what kind of tiles they have in the kitchen floor. If there's something I admire, it's nice tiles. And king-sized beds. If they have one and it has a pretty coverlet, I may well burst into tears.

We all tiptoe into a long hallway, to the left of which is a built-in closet with mirrored sliding doors. Train-like, we move one behind the other: Tanja up front, dressed in an unassuming, yet costly white cardigan, her spine erect, obviously proud as a peacock to show us what she has created. Close behind her, Kire, like her bodyguard. Then Nino, thin as a rail in comparison to Kire, and finally me, bringing up the rear.

"This room is empty. We haven't furnished it yet. It's for Anfisa, when she gets a little older," Tanja says. She opens the first door in the hallway, slides her hand in and gently flicks on a light. We catch a glimpse of pinkish walls.

"And now, the bedroom. Shhh," Tanja whispers and opens the next door.

The scent of baby—of diaper cream, sweet and sticky— grows stronger as we move further along the hallway. And when Tanja opens this last door, it hits us like a wave. The room is pretty big. Anfisa's elaborate crib is decked with those dangly toys floating around her head. A lamp atop a corner bedside table gives the room an orange glow.

Nino backs out. "There's too many of us," he whispers after stretching his neck like a turkey to get a peak at the child. Not that he's really into kids. Even the cutest baby will rarely change the composure of his face. "Isn't it adorable?"

I'll occasionally say when we see a baby. He'll just nod and force a smile. That's it.

In fact, sometimes I'll ask him, "Are you sure you want kids?" And he'll respond, "I do," in a flat voice. Never, "Oh, you have *no* idea how much I do. It would be so nice to have a baby snuggle up between us."

I'm so stupid—we don't even have the room for a baby on that godawful two-seater. And here's Tanja and Kire's bed, which could easily fit three people. It's humongous. I'm sure Anfisa will sleep in the middle once she gets a little older.

Kire follows Nino out of the room, leaving Tanja and me alone with the baby. "Let me have a peek at her," I whisper, trying to ignore the bedsheets and covers and the rows of fluffy pillows. Right then, I just want to watch Anfisa sleep. I want to hold my head over that cloud of baby scent and close my eyes in the near darkness. I don't want Tanja to see this. But she is right next to me, invading my space by shoving her head into it. All I can smell now is her heavy perfume. The sight of her shiny long earing distracts me. *Move away. Move away, bitch*, I imagine telling her. Right then she places her hot palm on the small of my back, as if in sympathy, which makes me sick to my stomach.

"She's beautiful," I say in an unsteady voice. Then I take in a last breath of that scent rising from the crib before I straighten up and follow Tanja out of the room.

"And here's our bathroom," Tanja whispers after sound-lessly closing the bedroom door behind her. I know I'll have to use the bathroom before we leave, so I really don't want to witness the latest feats of toilet designmanship, now, with her watching. I pray it's just an average bathroom. But it's surprisingly large, with a brand-new washing machine and a great big tub that houses a smaller, red tub for Anfisa. With its turquoise tiles, it's oceany and smells of baby-soap.

"Really nice," I mutter, eyeing the matching soap dispenser and toothbrush holder. "Where did you get these?" I ask.

"IKEA," she answers quietly. "It's gotten so expensive lately. What am I saying! It's not that IKEA has gotten expensive, it's our standard of living that keeps falling. We can't afford things the way we used to. Even for me this cost too much. But they are beautiful, aren't they?" she gently runs the long, polished nail of her index finger along the neck of the soap dispenser.

In the living room Nino and Kire are deep in conversation, drinking whiskey. There is a bottle on the table and a bowl full of ice.

"Your apartment is wonderful," I say.

"Yes, your apartment is wonderful," Nino parrots after me. He's going to just keep on repeating what I say because he's clueless as far as apartments go. If they lived in a shack, he wouldn't know the difference.

"You've really done a great job with the interior design. Great taste. Functional and cozy," I continue, more emphatically.

"That's all wifey's doing," Kire chimes in. Tanja's face lights up. But just like any other well-mannered lady, she attempts to diminish the value of her accomplishments.

"Oh, come on. Anyone can do this. I just had extra time on my hands to spend on the apartment. The agency found it right off the bat. The moment I saw it, I just knew. This is it. This is where I want to live," she says, clasping Kire's hand. They look like a commercial for housing loans.

"It must be rough, though, carrying the stroller up all those stairs," I delight in saying.

"Oh my, yes. I'm not saying this apartment doesn't have its faults," Tanja admits, which bothers me.

"Faults? Come on. Why do you think she has such a great butt? She's lived on the top floor her entire life," Nino says, pointing to me.

"Yes, it definitely does help with one's figure," Kire inter-venes, stupid as ever.

"It's a pity you don't live on the top floor. But you know how hot it was at Mimi's place because they were right under the roof? You get so hot, you don't want to eat and so you get the best figure ever," I say. "And eating nothing but beans and lentils four times a week? And climbing those stairs? Beat that, Kate Moss," I say, knocking back the glass of whiskey Kire poured me. The tension I've created magically revives me. It's as if my head has cleared. I motion to Kire to pour me another glass. Whiskey is such a rarity for Nino and me that I have every intention of getting wasted. I'm not going to be the one to drive our junk heap home. I'd rather be the drunk one, I think, downing my second glass. Nino is quietly chewing ice, trying not to look at me. He's not stupid and knows exactly what I'm up to.

"Look," Tanja says, "living up here definitely helps if you want to get rid of those post-pregnancy love handles."

"Post-pregnancy love handles!" Kire says. "Don't give me that. I'm the one with the love handles!" he laughs.

"You're such a teddy bear," Nino adds and the three of them laugh and laugh. What an amazing sense of humor, I think.

"And you know once she starts walking she'll run you rag-ged!" I say with a sarcasm that goes right over their heads.

"True, she hasn't started walking yet," Tanja says. "But she can stand up! Though most of the time she crawls all over the place."

"Is that so?" I say, pouring myself another whiskey. Nino looks at me, still chewing on his ice. He doesn't want to argue in public. In fact, he never wants to argue, which drives me nuts.

"Yes, and she's so fast!" Kire says. "And of course she'll put anything within reach in her mouth."

"She's very cute," Nino says.

"How do *you* know that?" I snap. "You've never really seen her."

"I've seen a picture of her."

"Liar," I say. "You're just showing off your manners."

"I'm *not* lying," he shoots back. "There's a picture of her over there by the TV set. As for manners, we all know who lacks them," he says and gulps down the rest of his whiskey. But there was no way he is catching up with me. I am already on my third. With every drink I am getting more and more pissed at him, and at his mother for not dying. The idea that she is sitting there all sick and hideous in her living room like a neglected houseplant, watching stupid soap operas all day, enrages me. If I ever turn out like her that, kill me, just kill me.

"Well, thank you, Nino. I know you think we're partial because she's our daughter, but she really *is* cute," Tanja says.

"We hope that things finally work out for you guys, too," Kire blurts out indelicately. I would be livid if Tanja said this, but Kire clearly means well. He's just one of those dumb males who unintentionally says things that hurt people.

I wonder if I should hold my tongue. But why? If I do, they'll never learn that they can't talk shit in front of people who can't have kids, people who don't have a space to raise a kid, people who barely have the space to fuck in.

"I doubt it. Your friend Nino here shoots blanks."

Nino finally loses his composure.

"What did you say?" Nino turns toward me, his expression dark.

There is a terrific silence and tension you could cut with a knife, as they say.

"Just like that. Boom, boom. Nada, zilch, zero," I say, bursting into laughter.

"Hey, this is a little too intimate," Kire says. Tanja would never say something like that, unless she could benefit from it. She's savvy, unlike her husband. But he brings home good money, and they are annoyingly functional as a family. They take holidays together, then show us pictures of the azure beaches where they got great value for their money.

"Oh, come on, that's not intimate," I say. "I was just inside your bedroom. I saw your baby sleeping. Now *that's* what I call intimate."

"You're mean and you're a bitch, and you always have been," Nino spits. "The doctors said I was just fine," he says to Tanja and Kire, articulating every word. His face is transformed, which scares me a little. I like that. So, I knock back my whiskey and decide to egg him on.

"Yes, your male doctors in their male world of medicine. Your balls could be rotten and full of rice pudding and they'd still say it's my fault."

"Here we go again with that feminist shit of yours," he says.

"Feminist shit? Thanks for reminding me I need to use the john," I say, staggering to my feet. And then I see it on the TV table, the very same vase Tom and Lydia gave us. I am sure. I know that vase so well from seeing it so often. They gave both of us the identical vase.

"Wow, what a nice vase!" I say. "Where'd you get it?"

Tanja's reply was cautious. "It's by a Greek artist from the island of Paros. Tom and Lydia gave it to us after they came back from cruising the Aegean last year. Tom and Lydia—you remember them?"

"Why, of course we do," I say, giving Nino a sideways glance. He can't take his eyes off the vase, which I am now holding in my hands. The air is so heavy with anticipation I'm afraid to breathe. "It's a beautiful vase," I say, beginning to turn it over as if to inspect it. "What the name of the artist?"

"Anfisa Papadopoulou? Was it Papadopoulou?" Tanja turns toward Kire, who shrugs.

"Anfisa?"

"Yes, we loved that name. They said it means *child of the flower.*"

"Wonderful!" I say, as if I was exhilarated. "Are you still in touch with Tom and Lydia?"

"Of course," Kire says. "They're here, in Skopje. They're back for another semester. They arrived two months ago, I think. You haven't seen each other yet?"

I shake my head, glad I'm not going to have a child called Lydia.

"Nino, look. Our vase is just a bit different than theirs. Because it's handmade."

"You've got one too?"

I don't respond. I let them sit in silent dread, wondering what I'm going to do next.

"Hey Nino, catch!" I call and pretended to throw the vase. Nino jolts and makes as if to catch it, then drops his hands. That's when I toss it at him.

The vase hits the parquet floor and shatters into little jade shards. As it breaks, it's as if it releases the dusty stench of all the flattering hopes that Tom and Lydia, in their refined exoticism, raised in us.

Stone-faced, Kire and Tanja stare at the shards, as if they are imagining Anfisa crawling among the remains of her Greek namesake.

"We're leaving," Nino snaps. "Get your stuff." He springs up and moves gingerly across the floor. There is no running away from this.

"She's crying," Tanja says, jumping to her feet. It's only then that we hear Anfisa's piercing little voice in the other room, Tanja's excuse for leaving this mess. Deer-like, she leaps across the room and vanishes, depriving me of the pleasure of seeing her burst into tears, of telling me to go to hell, of screaming at the top of her voice, of just losing control. As she disappears, I catch her throwing Nino a look of compassion. Nino moves toward me, his slippers crunching the little bits of vase. He grabs me by the elbow and shoves me toward the entryway. "Come on. Let's go."

I turn toward Kire. "I would like to extend my deepest apologies," I say, "for my unsensitive clumsiness. I mean, insensitive clumsiness. As you know, we have the same vase and Nino will drop it off tomorrow. Which provides you with the perfect opportunity to give us back the clock, which I am sure you don't want anyway." Nino snatches my jacket from the coat hanger, shoves it in my hand and tries to push me out the door.

"Dude, I'm sorry about this," I hear him whisper.

"Hey, and I'm sorry about all the cleaning you'll have to do," I say over his shoulder, my voice echoing down the staircase. "And I'm really really sorry if I woke up Amanfisa," I add.

Kire shuts the door and Nino races down the stairs without waiting for me.

"Hey, wait a minute! You don't want me to trip and fall, do you?" I say, trying to keep up with him. But he obviously isn't listening. By the time I get to the street, he's smoking a cigarette at some distance. When he hears the glass door closing, he turns to face me, but does not approach.

"What, you're running away from me? So where are you going to go?" I say.

"Wherever I want!" he yells.

"Wherever you want? Maybe your mom's, huh?"

"At least I have some place to go. Where are you going to go?"

"Go to hell if you want. I'm not going anywhere. I'm staying right here. You think I want to get into that crappy car of yours? Go ahead!" I scream, and he really does go. I hear the engine coughing to life, and the rumble of our car fading in the distance.

I sit on the edge of a concrete flower bed and stare at the pedestrian crossing. I'm just going to sit here doing nothing, I reason. Not a thing. I'm not going to get up, I'm not going to budge. I'm going to wait for something to happen, anything. But I'm not leaving this place. I imagine Nino driving home, his hawkish profile silhouetted against the car window, and feel a stabbing sorrow. I remember him playing *Kaži, kaži libe Stano* for Tom and Lydia. I remembered how gently and how well he played, not the least bit embarrassed for performing in front of a musician like Lydia, and how his beautiful, unrepentant playing made no difference because he was just going to go lie down on our two-seater bed and wait for his mother to die so we could be happy.

I lie on the concrete wall even though I'm wearing a short skirt. I might get some kind of ovarian inflammation from the cold, I worry. And someone could rape me. Who cares. Nothing was going to grow inside me. *Nothing will come of nothing*, Lydia and Tom had repeated that night, as if we were supposed to know what that meant. I roll the words in my mouth, expecting to see our junk car approaching with its cool darkness inside, and the outline of Nino's nose and scruffy hair, and then me, snuggling up against him, laying my cheek on his violin hickey, feeling his graying stubble brushing my eyelids.

BLACKBERRIES

Everything is in shambles. I try to fit the rusty old key into the lock, and it sticks when I turn it. I worry the door won't open. The key slips from my sweaty, shaking hand. Chips of brown paint and dusty strings of spiderweb cling to my blouse. A cold wave of panic sweeps over me, down my arms and up my throat and across my face. In spite of all this, I realize that if by chance I'm unable to unlock the door, I'll simply drive back home and nothing will have happened. My panic subsides. I draw in a deep breath, dry my hands on my trousers, and brush the paint and spiderwebs from my sleeves. I calmly turn the key and watch the door open.

The scent of my grandparents hits me: lavender, pine, and nettles. Their summer house, damp, cool, and dark, is like an abandoned museum. I manage to pry open one of the crooked wooden window shutters despite its rusty hinges, and shafts of light lance the room. Thousands and thousands of dust motes awakened by my entrance dance in the air. Now to find the switch box and the water valve.

"How are you going to manage?" I can hear Gorazd say, with his eyebrow cocked. "You know you can't," he would add, or my father would. "You're such a klutz," Gorazd would say, as always. "I'd better come along," my father would say.

"You'll never be able to do this on your own," he would add and insist on coming with me.

A cold wave sweeps over me again. I can picture my grandmother when she came here alone, or, alone with me, because I don't really count. I can see her big behind sticking out from under the sink, and then her ruddy, pleased face when she turns the tap and watches the water run, as if it were a miracle.

I kneel under the sink and gingerly place a clammy hand on the valve, but for the life of me I can't remember which way to turn it. I close my eyes and picture a hand turning a faucet, then tentatively turn my own to the right and feel the valve give. I rise to my feet and twist the tap, watching it tremble and splutter before gushing out its first jet of water in three dry years.

I sigh with relief as the water flows down the drain, but now I have to find the switch box. I can see my grandmother go to the cupboard by the window and grab a wooden rolling pin, then hobble toward the entrance. I do the same and see the switchbox high above the door. *Snap—snap—snap*, I can feel each switch give as I push the end of the rolling pin against them. My hands are still sweaty as I flick on the living room light: it works. I flick on all the light switches: everything is working; nothing is amiss. But it can't be, I say to myself. Nothing is ever right. That's just how it looks.

I pull the sheets off the couches. The dance of the dust motes in the light becomes even livelier as I plop myself down, wondering what I should do next. Everything needs cleaning, and I should go up into the attic to make sure there isn't something dead up there. I should get rid of all these spiderwebs. I should replace the sheets with the ones I brought from home. God knows, the clothes in the closets must be rotting with mold.

"It's an absolute mess up there," my mother's voice flows through me. "It's unfit to live in," she says, reluctantly handing me the key to the house. My father is supposed to give it to me, but he's angry I'm going. He and Mila are reading a picture book in the backyard, his way of showing me he's a better parent than I am.

"Everything is falling apart," my mother adds even though the key is in my hand. They are well aware that I always change my mind, and that whenever I do make a decision, I'm left with painful doubts. And if they don't like my choice, they make it hurt even more.

I remain silent as a first line of defense, something that, because it rattles them, I've been doing ever since I was a little girl.

"You know what your father thinks about this," she says. "On top of everything else, there isn't anyone up there. You'll be all alone in the mountains. You'll freeze to death. What will you eat?"

"I'm thirty-three, and I'm a mother," I remind her. Though I look frail and insecure, whenever I say I'm a mother, people take me more seriously.

My mother sighs. It's summer and they're hoping they can have Mila longer. They want this because they think, among other things, that I'm not a good mother, considering all that's happened to me.

"As you wish," she says, while actually meaning the opposite.

"I'm off now," I say, putting my arms around her. "I don't want Mila to see me leaving."

"I worry about you, sweetheart," my mother says in a weepy voice, as if I were going off to war and not to a summer house in the mountains.

"Come on, mom. I'm just going there to relax—clear my head."

"I know, honey. But why can't you just stay here with us? It'll be so much better for you. I'll do all the cooking. And it's clean here. No one has been up there in years. How in the world are you going to manage?" she asks with a troubled stare. "I feel so sorry for you." I can feel her getting on my nerves.

"OK, I'm off," I say.

"You're not saying goodbye to dad?"

"He's with Mila. Let them be."

"As you wish," she says.

I'm barely out the door when I call my friend Ilina. I often wonder how she puts up with me. She knows I rarely call unless I'm feeling insecure about something and want reassurance. Ilina is in a meeting. "I can't talk right now!" she says in a loud whisper. "You should just go and call me when you get there!" Even this helps a bit. I repeat Ilina's advice, which always starts, just like my parents, with "You should." "You should go there on your own." "You should be alone." "You should learn to cope with what's happened." "You shouldn't be afraid." You should, you shouldn't, you should, you shouldn't.

I should learn to manage things and not be afraid, I say to myself. OK, I'm managing, egging myself on: the water and electricity are working, the windows and shutters are open, the sheets are off the furniture. But my bags are still in the hallway. And yet I don't move. I only stare out at the fir trees slowly swaying left and right, like hands playing a waltz on a piano.

I turn my gaze to the framed photo next to the broken-down TV from the 80s. The photo shows us seated for dinner in the yard outside. The table is a cornucopia of my grandmother's specialties. My grandfather sits at the head of the table. He is grinning, and his gold incisor glitters in the sunlight. My grandmother stands beside him, proud, a smile on her face, looking grand in her apron. Her hands are resting on her hips, pleased at the thought of feeding the family. My mother has allowed my father to put his arm around her stooped shoulders. In his other hand is a tall sweating glass of beer. My mother looks like she's missing her left arm. A fork dangles from her right hand. She's not looking at the camera, but somewhere to the side. My brother is already absorbed in the food on his plate. He seems oblivious that we're taking a family photo. I'm at the far end of the table. I look as if I'm trying to hide behind my brother, though I'm actually sitting in front of him. The sun in my eyes makes me look worried. My mouth is slightly open. I look frail and thin, as conspicuous as a half-starved street urchin. The fact is, every time I see that photo, I feel a wave of pity, pity for myself.

I've often felt, long before Mila was born, a kind of paralysis, a desire for everything to miraculously pass so that I can finally have a wish and desire of my own. I know I need to make myself do something, but I can't imagine what. It's all I can do *not* to call Ilina, so I repeat what she said: "You should go for a walk. Long walks are good for the mind. It'll clear your head; it'll be good for your body. You shouldn't lock yourself up like this. You should be out in nature more." You should, you shouldn't, you should, you shouldn't.

It's that hour of the evening when the elderly and I step out for a stroll. I'll watch them tottering down the lanes and alleys, leaning on canes they've carved themselves. The children will have been out playing all day long. They'll scamper around the old men and women, hide behind bushes or disappear into the woods, their cries ringing out, now close, now far.

I step out onto the path in front of the house, peering up and down, but I don't see a soul. None of the neighboring houses show the least sign of life. All their shutters are closed tight, their facades crumbling, their yards overgrown with weeds. Sani's house is among the most derelict. The garden beds are a riot of ferns, goldenrod, and wild roses littering the yard with petals. Tufts of weeds jut from cracks in the walls. Here and there a tiny fir tree has sprung from the earth, and in a corner grows a lush maple sapling. The backyard of the house leads into the forest. Along a steep trail, through tunnels of rustling beech trees, Sani would lead me to a clearing where blackberries grew rampant.

Sani had a younger sister, Andrijana, who was always clinging to us. Before going off to pick blackberries, Sani would chase her sister off, telling her she was too little to be tagging along, whereupon Andrijana would cry, and I would feel all grown up.

Sani always took the lead. She was fearless, fast, and nimble. Both of us were scrawny little things, but while I looked frail, Sani seemed strong and supple as a hazel switch. She moved through the trees like something feral, while I lagged behind, afraid of slipping on the patches of moss. She would leap over anything in her way, and if she happened to fall, she would spring up at once, as though she felt no pain. And she would plunge into the blackberry bushes just so. The first time I followed her, I did the same, since it seemed painless. The thorns drew blood and I began to cry. I wanted to leave, but I didn't know the way home and was afraid of wandering through the forest alone. As I stood there whimpering, Sani picked mouthfuls of the jet-black fruit, indifferent to the thorns scratching her skin and then turned home, her lips and teeth purpled, her arms bleeding. I trailed behind her, still whimpering, though it wasn't the thorns that hurt as much as the feeling that I wasn't there.

The next time we scrambled up the forest trail I told Sani what my folks had been saying about her family. I wanted to be the first to tell her, feeling that this would add to my importance.

"Sani," I said, not even knowing what that meant, "your parents are getting a divorce."

She didn't say a thing. She just pressed on into the woods.

"Your dad caught your mom in bed with someone else," I said, though I didn't know what that meant, either.

"Fine," she said.

We didn't utter a word until we got to the blackberries. She plunged into the bushes again. "Want some?" she asked.

"I'm not really hungry," I lied, pretending I was interested in a cluster of mushrooms whose caps I'd knocked over.

"They're really good. You gotta come and try some," she said several times, her mouth blackening. "Mmm," she moaned, closing her eyes.

I went over and reached for a nearby blackberry and scratched my hand. This time I didn't cry out, though I became afraid when the thorn wouldn't give, pulling on my skin as if wanting to take it off. I placed the blackberry on my tongue and bit it. The sweetness hit the back of my ears and glided down my throat, and as it did, my whole body went sweet.

"I don't know," I said. "They're not that great," I lied, seeing the other blackberries were deep among the thorns.

"As you wish," Sani said.

Turning back Sani said she wanted to go home and clean herself up. Her forearms were bloody with scratches. Her shirt was torn in several places, her lips and teeth dyed dark blue, her tongue black. There was a scratch under her left eye. We headed straight to the bathroom and she began washing her arms. Whirls of pink water disappeared down the sink. Then her father, Chichko Krsto, barged into the bathroom. It was too small for the three of us. I leaned back toward the tub.

"Picking blackberries again, you little rat?" I'd never heard someone say that to anyone before. I tried to make myself smaller.

"Yes!" she snapped back defiantly.

Chichko Krsto slapped her hard across the face. She had to grab the sink to avoid falling.

"You little shit!" he snarled. "Look what you've done to yourself! Why don't you ever listen? So, was it worth it?"

"Yes!" she shot back. "They're delicious," she added and stared him down. He slapped her again, and I fell back into the tub. Which is when Sani's mother burst in. "What have you done to them!" she screamed, pushing him out and scrambling to help me up out of the tub. "Are you okay, honey? Are you hurt anywhere?" I nodded, trying my best not to cry. "You better go now, honey, go home," Sani's mother repeated, edging me toward the front door.

When I got home, I told my parents what had happened.

"Those people are batshit crazy," my father grumbled.

"Insane," my mother agreed. "Those poor girls," she added.

"What do you expect," my father said under his breath. "A nut and a nympho."

The things grownups say in front of their kids, I think to myself, following the old tire tracks on the dirt path. Several times before I witnessed Chichko Krsto hit Sani in the bathroom, he came over and railed that he was going to kick Dijana out. That he'd caught her fucking half the men she worked with. That he should've known she was into fucking that he'd been so fucked over. "She's a nympho. Sick in the head," he'd bark, emphasizing the word *sick*. When Chichko Krsto used the word *fuck* too often, my parents would send me up to my room. But even from there I could hear every word.

The day after Sani got slapped, my grandmother hush-hushed me into the kitchen. "Come here, I have something for you," she whispered. She showed me a plastic container brimming with blackberries that filled my eyes. "Open wide," she said and placed a berry on my tongue. I closed my eyes. Nothing. Then a touch of sweet turned sour. I swallowed, but my body felt no sweetness. "Aren't they good?" she asked. "Yes," I lied. She beamed with pleasure continuing to feed me with her glossy, wrinkled hands. I obediently opened my mouth each time. "Aren't they tasty?" she would say each time she fed me one. "Very," I lied again, knowing she'd bought them just for me.

Before bed, I asked my brother what a nympho was. He laughed at my not knowing. "A nympho is a *whore*. A woman who really likes to fuck."

I can't remember when Sani left, but after that summer she never came back. For years I thought I was responsible for her not returning, and for her getting slapped, since I was the one who told her about her parents getting a divorce. Later I heard from our neighbor Lenka, to whom Chichko Krsto had also ranted about Tetka Dijana being a nympho, that her parents actually did get a divorce. "A divorced man is a fail-ure," I overheard my father saying to my mother, "a man who's failed at life." "Those poor girls," my mother kept repeating. "I've never met a girl as intelligent as Sani," she often said. At times she would even say *hyper*-intelligent. And each time she did I felt like rolling into a little ball. Which is why, once, over dinner years later, I told them that Sani had become a travel writer, a lesbian, and an S&M enthusiast. "Well, with parents like hers, how *could* she have turned out all right," my mother concluded. I added, "She's married to an older woman." "What the hell," my father muttered.

What I didn't tell my parents was that Oxford University

Press had published two of Sani's books, one a political trav-
elogue on her adventures in Papua, the other an account of
the S&M subculture in New York, which she had researched
while working as a *domme*. I scoured the web for negative
reviews and comments, but I couldn't find a single one. But
what I did find was that she'd gotten both a Guggenheim
and American citizenship. I also found out that her wife was
a renowned lesbian poet. They lived in Manhattan, and on a
Texas ranch, as well as "on the road".

    I follow Sani on all the social media. At least once a month
I browse through her Instagram pictures, her Facebook posts,
her political comments, and the countless updates of her
glamourous life on Twitter. But of all the things that pain
me, it's the pictures that hurt most. In every one Sani is clearly
enjoying herself. And oh yes, her name isn't Sani any longer.
It's Alex, Alex Marr—from Markovska. Alex, that is, is enjoying herself in all the photographs, in which she's invariably
half-dressed. One side of her body is covered with tattoos of
cacti and other thorny things. The other is the color of creamy
sand. The down on her light-brown arms is golden. Her teeth
gleam in all the pictures—a double row of perfect tiles. Her
hazel eyes match her complexion. I find a crumb of comfort
in the fact that she's not all that pretty, her nose a little flat, her
cheeks rather chubby for someone as lean and supple as she
is. Her beautiful body is always being touched by someone.
She is passionately touched, with taut fingers sweetly sinking
into her smooth skin. She is touched on her hips, her waist,
her inner thighs, and the thorns adorning her strong body.

    I, too, have photographs where I'm being touched. No one
knows about them except Gorazd, but I'm afraid that one day
Mila will see them, and that'll be the end of me. They were
made seven years ago, exactly nine months before Mila was
born. I'm naked in all of them: pale white, with skin that has

always been hidden behind clothing. I'm spongy, like "old mozzarella," as Gorazd used to say, as if it were an endearment. In the first series he made, the morning-after pill is in the palm of my hand. "Look sassy," he ordered. This was supposed to be another one of his "art projects," all of which were utter failures. He called it, "Documenting the Death of the Idea of Our Child." He also thought of calling it "How I Killed Us." In the second series of photos he took that day, he made me stick my tongue out with the pill ladled on the tip. Gorazd ordered me to stand with my legs spread, seductively tilting my hips forward. In the photos, my breasts hang like pears, my nipples so light, they're barely visible. In the third series Gorazd told me to sit on the bed. He put the camera on auto, knelt down on the mattress and towered over me. He made me open my mouth with the pill still on the tip and spat on it, then commanded me to swallow. He yanked my hair, pulling my head back. With his other hand he squeezed my right breast and pinched the nipple. Breathing heavily, he tilted his head as if to kiss me and then stuck his tongue out. Then he forced his hand between my thighs. This is how it always was. At first I would feel a fire there and a sweetness beneath my tongue, behind my ears. I would be left with the feeling that I was burning, but never burnt up. He grabbed my head again and shoved his penis in my mouth. The camera clicked for twenty minutes or so, which was the time it usually took him to come. First soft, then hard, soft, then hard again, he bucked relentlessly. I never saw the photographs, but I must have looked an awful mess. I tried to stop him, but he wouldn't let me. I could barely breathe. He slapped my hands away, grabbed me by the hair and stuck his penis in my mouth again. He bucked and panted like a horse being broken while his sweat rained down on me, mingled with my tears, snot, and spittle. It was all I could do not to gag. But when he thrust it deep down my throat, gripping my head with both hands, vomit spewed out my nose and the sides of my mouth. Only then did he let me go. I scurried to the window and threw up again. He laughed throughout, which was better than him getting angry. He told me to come back and wipe myself clean with the sheet. Then he ordered me to lie down and open my mouth. He knelt over me again and jerked on his penis until he ejaculated in my mouth and told me to swallow it.

I had vomited up the morning-after pill. It crossed my mind right then that this might have happened, but I didn't have the strength to reenact the "Death of the Idea of our Child" again, because I knew he wanted to get me pregnant. He came inside me intentionally, knowing he shouldn't have, knowing I didn't want it. He knew I was applying for a graduate scholarship in the UK. Then I might have become something.

I finally come to the forest spring where Sani and I used to fetch water. Sani drank directly from the stream. I was afraid of the water touching my face. This is where my grandparents would collect water for cooking and cleaning. The water was never as cold coming from a plastic jug as it was flowing in the stream. It didn't taste as good, either. Sani would take off her shoes and dunk her feet in. "It's so cold!" I'd cry out. "It's cold at first, then it gets good. This water is always flowing. You can put your feet in and still drink it," Sani added.

I take off my shoes and dip my feet. I shudder from the cold at first, but then feel warm all over.

Alex Marr—I often google the name. I get thousands of results. I then type in mine, *Ivana Petrova*. There are many Ivana Petrovas. One is a female weightlifter. A journalist or two. There's Ivana Petrova the lawyer, and a cosmetician who goes by that name as well, and yet another who trades women's wigs. I am none of those Ivanas. I am not on the Internet. I am nothing. Maybe I could have been something. Maybe, if I had gotten another pill and taken it. If I had left.

I'm beginning to grow cold again and lift my feet out of the stream. I haven't called Mila. I haven't called my parents to tell them I've arrived, that I've "managed." The very thought of calling them gives me a feeling of having a hairball in my windpipe. All I want to do is lie down on the moss beside the water and stay there.

I find my way out of the woods and make my way home. Though the sun is sinking below the horizon, I haven't seen a single person, much less a child, but then two elderly women appear on the path before me. They are dressed like the old ladies of my childhood: long, knitted, sleeveless brown sweaters, tubular skirts, dark knee-length stockings, and leather sandals. One of them has her hands clasped behind her back. The other woman, older, smaller, leans on a cane in her right hand while bracing her left upon her hip. They are silent as I approach.

"Good evening," I say.

"Good evening," they reply and stop. The older one squints at me. She seems familiar.

"How are you?" I ask, not knowing what else to say.

"We're fine, somehow managing," the older one says. "And you—which house are you staying in?"

"That one there," I say, pointing with my chin.

"Aren't you Andon's granddaughter?" she asks. "You don't remember me?"

Over the years I've learned to stop feeling guilty at not remembering the grownups of my childhood. But I do remember this woman. We used to play with two of her grandchildren who were just a bit older than Sani and me.

"Tetka Rada?"

"Yes, yes," she nods with a contented smile. "It's been ages since I've seen you here!"

"Ah," exclaims the other woman. "Andon and Gorica's granddaughter! We would come for coffee."

"Gorica made such delicious pies," Tetka Rada says.

"Oh, and the sweets she baked," the other woman adds.

"Those were the days. And now you see us all old and ready to leave the world," Tetka Rada says. Her blue irises sparkle between her wrinkled, nearly lashless eyelids.

"Andon and Gorica left us a long time ago, may God rest their souls," says the other, crossing herself.

"The future is yours, child, it's your turn now," Tetka Rada says, straightening herself.

"But look, look around, there's no one here," the other woman says. "No one comes anymore. And everything is falling apart. It's just us two old biddies and a couple of other old women who wander through the neighborhood like ghosts."

"The times have changed," I say, beginning to sound like them.

"There are no children anymore," the other lady sighs. "We're going to die out."

"What are your folks up to?" Tetka Rada asks.

"They're fine, they've just retired."

"And your brother?"

"He's in Germany."

"He's managed, then," the other lady says. "It's better there now than here," she adds. "So, are you married, do you have children?" she asks as they glance toward my ringless finger.

"I have a seven-year-old daughter."

"So why didn't you bring her along? There's another child further down the road. They could play together, get fresh air."

"The place used to be full of children . . ." Tetka Rada says, looking around disappointedly. "You used to run around, making a racket, causing all kinds of trouble. You'd sneak into the house to steal chocolates."

"I stole your chocolates?" I say, feeling offended.

"Oh, yes," Tetka Rada says with utter certainty. I can see she has no intention of offending me but is just poking fun. "You always figured out where I hid them and ta-da! You'd slip right in and steal a handful. You'd even steal for your friends. You little fox!" she says with a smile on her face.

Her companion laughs.

"Well, I'd better be getting along. I've got work to do," I say.

"How long are you staying?" Tetka Rada asks.

"I don't really know," I reply. And I really don't.

"We hope you stay for a while," the other woman says.

"Yes, stay," Tetka Rada says, chiming in. "And do come by for coffee."

I leave with the contented thought that I had once stolen chocolates. Though I find it difficult to believe. First of all, I don't like chocolate. And second, I've never stolen a thing in my life. Third, I think I would have remembered something like that—or someone else would have. As I open the gate into my overgrown garden I realize with great disappointment that maybe it was another girl who stole her chocolates.

Soon the sun will set behind the mountains. I take out one of the folding chairs Andon and Gorica used to relax in as they drank a glass of wine and watched the colors change and disappear with the sun. They'd listen to the sounds of the forest—the chirping of birds and crickets, the rustling of unseen creatures through the foliage, of frogs and hedgehogs in the grass, of the imagined movement of foxes and bears. I find an old wine bottle in the cupboard above the sink. I take one of my grandmother's ancient, chipped glasses and pour myself a drink, then sink back into the chair as the sun colors me orange. I know I'll have to call my parents soon and talk to Mila before she goes to bed. I take out my phone and lay it on the low concrete wall beside me. Even now I can hear the conversation in my head:

"Hey there, how are you guys doing?" I'll ask casually.

"We're fine," my father will reply. He won't say "How is it up there" because that would be his way of begrudgingly acknowledging my decision.

"How's Mila? How's she doing?" I'll ask.

"Mila? Amazing! What do you expect when she's here with us!" *Psssss*, he will let out a disparaging whiz from between his teeth which means, "well, of course." "She forgot about you ten minutes after you walked out the door." I do my best, since I'm the only parent she has left, but here she is, forgetting about me now as she no doubt will forget me entirely in the future.

Being forgotten happens to me all the time. Even Gorazd has forgotten me, for the most part. He hasn't forgotten about those photographs, or rather, of me in those photographs, photos he would bring up every time I asked him for the child support he never paid. Now he lives with some Gordana. I don't know her. I only feel a malicious pleasure that I'm not the only one who makes mistakes. He never calls Mila. It's as if she doesn't exist. If she asks about him, I tell her that her father is a busy man, always traveling.

I once heard her talking to the neighbors' daughter who's a bit older:

"You got a dad?" the little girl asked.

"I do," Mila replied.

"So, where is he?"

"He's traveling. He's a sailor," Mila said.

"Which sea?"

"The *Atlantic* Sea," my daughter answered.

I wanted to call my parents and ask if they'd ever talked about seas and oceans with Mila, but I knew I'd have to explain why I was asking. I don't need to add to the guilt I feel whenever I see that she's as scrawny as I used to be—her limbs as frail as a dragonfly's wings, her eyes, slanted and heavy-lidded like Gorazd's. And wearing that look of his that meant reproach and contempt, though I'm not sure yet what it means in Mila.

My phone is still on the concrete banister beside me, next to the wine glass. I hear women's voices—a clatter of cries and chiming laughter. I rise unsteadily to my feet and see that there is a group of women in Sani's yard. One of them is thrashing the rampant weeds and ferns with a stick, attempting to clear a path. Three other women stand under the balcony, helping Sani climb up. She eases her way over the rail and rattles the shutters to the entryway. "It's no good. I can't get in!" Sani cries. The woman fencing with the ferns looks up. "No way, huh?" she asks in English. Sani shakes her head. The women help her climb back down and leave together through the newly beaten path. "Watch out for nettles!" one of the women warns. "Too late," another replies. They straddle the fence and disappear somewhere down the road. I'm still half out of my chair, wondering if I should go after them. While I'm thinking, I hear the babble of women's voices and now I see them all standing at my gate. They're waving. "Hey! Hello!" they call. I wave back, gesturing to them to come in because my legs are shaking.

As they climb down the stairs leading to the balcony I rise to my feet, straightening my skirt. I become aware of my greasy hair, my hairy legs. I'm so stunned at their sudden appearance that I blurt out a loud, "hello." I try to keep my eyes off Sani. The first woman to step onto the balcony is older than the rest.

"Hello," she says, "Ivana, is that you?" and I recognize Tetka Dijana, Sani's mother. "Yes, it's me. Dijana?" She nods. Sani reaches out her hand.

"How are you?" she asks, but I can tell by the look in her eyes that she doesn't remember who I am. She looks at me the way celebrities do, or people who have been around the world, or teachers who no longer remember their students: an empty, albeit polite stare.

"Hey, Sani, haven't seen you in ages," the words tumble out of my mouth.

"Yes, yes," she replies, still making an effort to place me.

"Here's Andrijana—remember her?" Tetka Dijana says, pointing at Sani's younger sister. I shake hands with a fairy-like creature with long blonde hair and a porcelain complexion.

"Wow, Andrijana, I haven't seen you since you were a little girl," I blurt, stupidly, realizing that Sani was a little girl when I last saw her, too.

"And these are our friends from America," Sani says and introduces me to the woman who was battling the weeds in the yard. She is silver-haired and wearing a lumberjack shirt, faded gray jeans and square sunglasses with metal rims. She stands aside, examining the green buds of a hazelnut tree.

"This is Lenna. Lenna, say hi to Ivana," Sani says in English. "Hi, Ivana," says Lenna with a crooked smile. Lenna must be the poet, Sani's wife. Sani knows my name, I say to myself. Or else she just heard it from her mother.

"And this is Ashley," Sani says, pointing toward a dark, sinewy tattooed young woman in a sleeveless white shirt and blue jeans. Ashley extends her hand.

"Sani and Andrijana are visiting, so we're traveling around a little," Tetka Dijana tells me.

"Is that so?" I say, pretending I don't know Sani lives in the States. "Do you live overseas?"

"I live in America. Andrijana lives in France."

"My brother lives in Germany," I add just to say something. The rest of the women smile politely.

"Are your parents well? Oh, I heard your grandmother passed away," Tetka Dijana says.

"They're fine," I reply. "They're in Skopje. And yes, my grandmother left us a few years ago."

"Have you seen Krsto?" Sani asks, pointing with her chin toward their house.

"No, but I haven't been up here for quite some time, either."

"It looks run down, like he hasn't been coming around. We tried to get inside. No way," Sani says.

"You and Sani were such great friends when you were little! You played together all the time," Tetka Dijana says.

"Yes," Sani says as if beginning to recall. "We had great times together. So what brings you up here now?"

"Not much. Just came to unwind."

"Are you alone?"

"Yes," I say.

"Atta girl," she says, as if I have done something extraordinary. "There's no one around, and it gets kind of eerie at night," she says, looking about her. "But it sure is beautiful up here. Just smell this air. And look at that view," she adds turning her head toward the sun, as her skin glows golden. Her tawny irises soak up the rays of the sun which illuminate her slinky body through her white linen dress.

"Hey, what's this?" Lenna calls out from behind the hazel tree. Ashley joins her, and Andrijana and Dijana follow.

"Remember how we used to go pick blackberries?" I ask Sani, now that we are more or less alone. "Or rather, you'd pick them, not me."

"Blackberries?" Sani asks, looking blankly at me. "Oh,

right! There were blackberries around here!" Clearly she didn't remember a thing.

"Come on, I thought she'd actually seen something interesting," I can hear Andrijana saying from behind the hazel tree. "They're just a bunch of mushrooms. Hey Sani, what kind of mushrooms are these?" and she throws one at Sani which flops at my feet.

"I have no idea."

"They're just mushrooms," someone says in English.

"Are they magic?" Lenna asks, pretending she's going to put one in her mouth. The others giggle. Again, the chime of their laughter.

"I remember you and me going down to the forest stream," Sani says. "So I wanted to take them there, but the path from my house is overgrown. How do we get there? I can't remember anything. I have the memory of a goldfish," she laughs.

"Just go down the stairs and take a left on the path." I look at her tattoos as I speak. All those thorns, all those plants tattooed on her skin are from some desert overseas. Not a thorn from the forest here.

"Great," Sani says. "I guess we better get going, dip our feet in the water and take off. It's getting dark." She turns toward the others. "Hey, let's go, the sun's going down," she says in English.

"Oh, but I've been such a bad host, not offering you something," I say, trying to keep them from going, though I'm not sure how. "Not that I have anything to offer you, except to share this bottle of wine with me."

"We want to leave before nightfall. We left the car down by the main road. But, hey, yeah, let's have a sip," Sani says, picking up the bottle of wine. "*Vino*, anyone?"

"Vinooouuu," Ashley says, eagerly approaching.

"Wait, let me get some glasses," I say.

"Forget that," Tetka Dijana says. "Let's drink straight from the bottle."

"You go first," Sani says, handing me the bottle.

"*Nazdravje,*" I say, smiling. "*Nazdravje!*" they all cheer, Ashley and Lenna, too. I take a couple of swigs and pass the bottle to Sani. We're all laughing.

"Let's see if someone spills any wine on themselves," Andrijana says, since we're all wiping our lips. We do several rounds, and Tetka Dijana gets the last drop.

"Well, cheers to you, girl!" she says, giving me a firm embrace and then planting a loud smacking kiss on my cheek.

"I'm so glad we saw each other," I say, hugging everyone in turn.

"It's so nice to have met you," Ashley says. Lenna holds my head between her hands and kisses my nose and forehead. Sani is the last to say goodbye.

"You have no idea how happy I am to see you," she says, embracing my waist with one arm, my shoulders with the other. I give her a strong clumsy hug back. She's like a warm, smooth stone.

"Me, too. And to think I just got here," I say. "It's all like a dream."

"Well, this place is a dream," she says, her hand lingering in mine as she walks away.

"Goodbye, honey!" Tetka Dijana calls out.

"Goodbye, Ivana!" Lenna calls, taking a mushroom from a pocket and throwing it in the air. Ashley blows me a kiss, Andrijana waves both hands. I wave back, blow kisses, my laughter ringing in the air.

They vanish among the trees. The air and sky grow cold, but I feel warm. I sit and watch the houses and the trees change their complexions as the colors dim and the shadows thicken. A fleck of light flashes down below on the road. And another. And still more. Fireflies fill the little path to my yard. Then I hear the echo of the women's laughter and the flurry of their footsteps. They run among the fireflies, waving as they pass. I wave back, calling goodbye, goodbye, goodbye.

TSI-TSE

Elena's brother called that night to tell her their father had had a bad stroke and was in the ICU. He called the landline, waking Richard and Eva.

Elena picked up the phone. Richard never got up first. He slept like a rock even when Eva cried. He would say that he was exhausted from having to work so hard. But Elena felt this had nothing to do with being tired, but was simply because there was always someone else—she, of course—to do whatever needed to be done.

"Alo?" she said instead of "hello." It wasn't the first time she had spoken Macedonian in the middle of the night while Richard was present. Richard didn't speak the language. He pretended a few times that he would learn, but after the second lesson he left the textbook face down on the lamp table next to the couch and it had lain there ever since. Whenever Elena spoke Macedonian to Eva, he would grumble: "Talking about me again?"

"Elena, hello, Elena, can you hear me?" Dragan's voice was at the other end, a gentler version of his usual gruff self.

"Hey, what's going on," Elena said, keeping her voice down so she wouldn't wake Eva. But the child was already whimpering, as she always did when she woke up at night. First, she'd make a little moan, then begin whining, and—if Elena didn't

rush to Eva in time to put her nipple in the child's mouth—
she would let out a shriek and, as of late, bang her forehead
on the rail guard of the bed. And all the while Richard would
barely stir.

"I didn't mean to disturb you but . . . daddy had a stroke."

"What do you mean he had a stroke," Elena said, looking
at Richard. His eyes were closed but she could tell he was
awake by his breathing. Eva's whining increased.

"Well, yeah—he had a stroke. He's in the ICU."

"So he's alive?" Elena blurted, exhaling the breath she had
held.

"Yeah, he's alive, but he's in bad shape. I don't know what
to do."

You've never known what to do, Elena thought.

"What do you mean he's in bad shape?" she asked.

"Well, he's just not in good shape." Dragan could evidently
hear Eva's wailing. "Did I wake the baby?" he asked.

"You woke all of us up. It's four o'clock in the morning.
You could've waited."

"I'm sorry. I keep forgetting the time difference. But I don't
know what to do. I just had to tell you."

"What does 'in bad shape' mean, exactly," Elena said and
gave Richard a little shove. His eyelids slowly unglued. She
pointed to Eva and scurried out from under the covers into
the living room, closing the door behind her. Eva was still
shrieking.

"Well, the doctors don't sound too optimistic," he said.
"But you know how they are over here. First of all, they don't
give a shit, because he's old. They think he should die anyway."

Richard opened the bedroom door, stopped in the doorway
and turned. Even now he looked handsome, almost sculpted,
despite his scruffy hair and the leg of his Hawaiian print pajamas riding on his kneecap. Had he been holding Eva, his

sinewy arms would have looked even stronger than they were. But he wasn't holding the child, who was still shrieking in the crib in their bedroom. He gave Elena a puzzled look and raised his hands in the air as if to say, "What's going on?"

Elena pointed toward the bedroom, mouthing "the baby," but then said into the phone "What happened?"

"He was in the shower when it hit him. He managed to get to the living room to call me, I guess, but it sounded like 'fla-fla-fla.' I went over and found him all stiff on the couch. So I called an ambulance. He's in a room now with five other guys like him. One side of his body is all bruised, where he fell, and he's got a bloody wound on his forehead and some scratches on his cheeks."

Eva's screaming got louder.

"He's completely paralyzed on the right side. It's like he can't move at all, and he can barely talk. I can't understand anything he's saying. I'm not sure he can see, either. He may be blind. I don't know."

"What do you mean you don't know?"

"I mean I don't know! I'm going to go there and ask them again. You know what it's like here! No one ever tells you anything."

Richard opened the door and let Eva into the living room. She toddled toward Elena, but tripped on her pajamas and fell at her mother's feet. The shrieking got worse, but Richard did not bat an eye. Elena took the child in her arms and tried to snuggle her, but Eva kept clutching at her breasts.

"Hello, hello?" Dragan kept repeating.

"Yes, I'm here," Elena said, trying to tell Richard with her eyes to take Eva. "What do we do next?"

"Nothing. I really don't know what's going to happen. This may cost money, and I don't have any. You know that. And I'm afraid he might just—you know, kick the bucket or

something. He's getting on. I don't know. I don't know what
to tell you. Hello?" Richard finally picked Eva up and took
her back into the bedroom where the screaming continued.

"I'm here, Dragan."

"I don't know what else to say."

"Call me back later or text me how things are going, okay?"

"Okay then. Talk later."

"When are you going to the hospital?" Elena asked, but
Dragan had already hung up. This was something he always
did. He never waited at the end of their conversations to see if
she had anything else to say. She looked at the phone screen:
4:18 A.M. was noon in Skopje. She figured Dragan would
wait a few hours before going to the hospital, and that's when
she would call him. Richard would be at work then, and she
would be home alone with Eva.

Eva was still screaming. Richard was holding her in one
arm, jiggling her up and down. "It's you she wants. Feed her
and she'll stop," he said.

"You were the one who told me to start weaning her,"
Elena replied, taking the child into her arms. Eva was no longer a baby. She was already an intelligent little person. She had
begun to talk but refused to use a potty or stop breastfeeding.

Richard shrugged and said, "What happened?"

"My father had a stroke."

Richard continued looking at her, as if he was waiting for
something. "And?"

"He's in the hospital," she said. "I'll have to go see him. He
might die," she added, stroking the forehead of the child, who
was ravenously sucking Elena's breast, her face tear-stained
and snotty.

"Well, if you think you should go, then go," Richard said.
"I'm here to support you. Morally and financially," he added,
robotically. Elena used to think statements like these were

a sign of a good upbringing, so radically different from the Balkan savagery she was used to. She later understood that there was something else about his last sentence, that it was a cliché from the phrasebook of investment banking, and that Richard had a habit of addressing her in the same manner as he addressed his clients.

"I appreciate your concern," she replied, wondering if he'd catch the irony in her voice. But of course, he didn't.

After Eva fell asleep drooling on her breast, Elena put her back to bed and opened her laptop. She imagined her father sprawled on a rickety hospital bed in a rundown room with cheap green linoleum flooring and dirty windows, and she broke into a sweat. She turned her attention back to her laptop and realized that, since it was noon, there might be another email from Jovan. If she had a single friend here in the States, she would have asked her: "You think there's something going on here? I've never written letters to anyone like that. I mean, they're not really *special* letters, but still . . . you think there's something going on between us? Why would he write to me? You think he finds me interesting? You think he likes me? He's not on Facebook, so of course he can't see me, and I would feel kind of dumb sending him my pictures . . ." Elena's thoughts ran on as she imagined having this conversation with a girlfriend, any girlfriend. Anastasija was in Australia and the difference in time zones made it difficult to talk. She had a job and a husband who was always taking her on trips. Martina was still in Skopje, but her husband probably had a mistress. Every time they talked, Martina would go on and on about how she felt compelled to check his messages certain he was seeing other women, though she could never prove it. She talked about how horribly amoral such women were. Little whores—that's what she called them. Elena didn't dare tell her that she was writing to—not that frequently, and on a purely friendly basis, of course—Jovan from high school. Jovan was not married, but still, Elena had Richard—what on earth was she doing writing emails to Jovan?

"We used to exchange books in school," she imagined saying to Richard, or Martina, if they ever found out about the correspondence. "Who else has ever given me books? No one. If it wasn't for Jovan, I'd have never read *The Master and Margarita*. I wouldn't know who Pablo Neruda was. Or Rilke, for that matter."

She had recently discovered William Carlos Williams. As a new American, she felt she should be acquainted with his work. She asked Richard if he knew who William Carlos Williams was. And he said that he did. That he was a writer. And that he'd written *Cat on a Hot Tin Roof*. Elena felt a flutter of superiority. She didn't bother to correct Richard. He knew how America worked, and she didn't. Every day he learned something new: he went to work, he talked to clients. If he didn't come home tired from work, he would go to business dinners, and every once in a while they'd hire a babysitter so Elena could join him along with the clients' wives. "I love your accent!" they would always say, grinning mechanically. "Your English is so good!" they would chime in admiration. Wanting to keep something to herself, but also out of spite, she decided not to tell Richard who William Carlos Williams was. Besides, what if he asked her how she knew so much about poetry all of a sudden?

She started sweating again when it occurred to her that instead of thinking about her dying father, her mind was on Jovan. Every time she thought about her father, something gnawed at her. Especially now that he had aged so poorly. His large ears protruded from his balding head like a set of speakers. His head was wreathed by a white circlet of disheveled hair that bristled like barbed wire. A few unruly hairs jutted from his eyebrows in every direction. The two times she had returned to Macedonia to see him, he looked more and more like a lost, sad old man. There was something tragic about how his mouth had begun to shrink and fold into itself like a rotten apricot. She called him twice a week, every Wednesday and Sunday morning, Skopje time, but always needed a good half an hour to summon up the willpower to dial his number.

"Elena! Elena!" her father would shout into the receiver, giggling with joy when he heard her voice. "How are you doing?"

"We're fine, Daddy! How are you?"

"I'm fine, I'm fine! How is my sweet little queen?" he would always say, and she would always answer "She's fine, Daddy, she's growing!"

"Put her on the phone!"

And she would call the child and put the receiver to her ear. "Say something to Dedo. Say: Dedo! Dedo! *Kako si!*" But Eva would push the phone away and let out noises of annoyance.

"Dedo's little sweetheart!" Elena's father would exclaim, regardless of whether the toddler's grunts reached him or not. "Dedo can't wait to pinch your chubby little cheeks!"

"We'll come soon, Daddy, I promise," Elena would say. "It's just that we need to wait for the holidays so that Richard can come with us."

"Yes, darling, of course."

"So how are you, Daddy?"

"I'm doing fine, I'm doing fine!" he would repeat.

"What's new?"

"Same ol', same ol', nothing new. I'm fine! And you?"

The conversation always boiled down to the same tired formula: "How are you? I'm fine. And you? We're fine." Elena could never get anything out of him because, truly, he had nothing to say. But then, he had hardly ever spoken even when her mother was alive.

"So tell me, Dragan, what's dad up to?" she'd ask her brother on occasion.

"Nothing. He's fine," he would reply.

"I'm asking you what he does all day, not how he is," she would insist.

"Nothing. He watches TV, mostly. Sometimes plays chess with the neighbors outside. That's pretty much it," Dragan would say, never taking his eyes off the TV, even though they were talking on Skype. On the computer screen Elena could see his flabby belly bulging across his lap like a blob of Jell-O. She imagined her father sitting hunchbacked on one of the broken old green benches in the little park by his apartment building next to the makeshift grocery store where the owner sold beer after the 7 p.m. ban, staring at the chess board from under his bushy eyebrows. His sweater would be tattered, his trousers so short you could see that his socks were riddled with moth holes. Elena would be overcome with pity, then anger and frustration that she was unable to do a thing to help him. She remembered a letter Jovan had sent her where he had quoted some American writer: "To a sensitive being, pity is not seldom pain." Then there was something about how if there is nothing to be done about this pity, it's only common sense to get rid of it. Jovan was full of such interesting quotes. Which was no coincidence, since he worked at the National Library. He had a degree in geography, but he loved to read, so he had become a clerical worker there. Elena had never seen his office, but she could picture him sitting at his desk and composing emails to her. The desk stands in the middle of a long room and the computer is facing away from the door, so no one can catch him writing her during working hours. Behind him a lofty window looks out onto a cluster of firs, pines, and maples she had never seen in New Mexico. The light dapples through the leaves and throws happy shadows onto a clutter of books, some opened face-down, others closed, with bookmarks jutting from the pages. The walls of the office are lined with glass-fronted cherrywood bookcases filled with vintage editions. The rug is oriental and soft. If they snuck into his office at night and closed the door, they could make love on that rug, in the darkness interrupted by the streetlights seeping through the trees . . . Elena chased the image away, in large part because she was married and had no intention of cheating on her husband. Once she had suggested making love on the American carpet that covered the entire house and the entire country, a carpet that smelled of air-conditioning, sheetrock, and office furniture, but Richard didn't want to and Elena was suddenly embarrassed by her own boldness. But Jovan . . . perhaps he would like this. But no—the only important thing now was the fact that her father was in the hospital. This is what she was supposed to think about. Her father is what she was supposed to think about. If he died and she didn't get to see him, and he didn't get to see Eva, she would be racked with guilt for the rest of her life. She would have to go back for the funeral anyway, which was another thought she tried to chase away for fear that simply to imagine him dead would be tantamount to inviting his death and oh, how terrible it would be if someone—but who? she asked herself—were to think she wanted her father to die. Of course, she didn't want her father to die, she reassured herself as she logged into her email. There were two unread messages in the inbox. The first was from her friend Bibi, who had married a man in Kansas, already had three children and loved to forward jokes. The other was from Jovan.

Dear Ellie, (*Dear! Ellie!*)

I hope I have not offended you with my previous letter. It was not my intention in any manner possible to insinuate you were an unhappy housewife. It is simply a small inopportune ill-judgement on my behalf that I happened to send you that particular poem by Williams!!! I beg you trust me this is exclusively related to my myopic understanding of America and its family dynamics. I learn much more from you than from Williams or any other American poet. I do not know how I can apologize enough and I deeply and sincerely hope that you will find it in your heart to forgive me.

J.

I learn much more from you than from Williams or any other American poet—she was suffused with warmth as she read that sentence. Then she read the email again and again until the warmth subsided. Then she went back to his previous email with the Williams poem:

Ellie,

I simply cannot help but think about Williams Carlos Williams when I read your letters. There is an American quality in them that imperceptibly draws me to the images of American everyday life that Williams so skillfully paints . . . every word is a stroke of his invisible brush . . . what a Master, truly!!!

> *At ten AM the young housewife*
> *moves about in negligee behind*

the wooden walls of her husband's house.
I pass solitary in my car.

Then again she comes to the curb
to call the ice-man, fish-man, and stands
shy, uncorseted, tucking in
stray ends of hair, and I compare her
to a fallen leaf.

The noiseless wheels of my car
rush with a crackling sound over
dried leaves as I bow and pass smiling.

I hope you like it.

Give my greetings to the orange rays of the desert skies.
It is almost spring here and the sky is turning a cool pink.

J.

"A cool pink" . . . "it's almost spring here" . . . those words
moved Elena, as did "negligee" and "uncorseted," along with
the onlooker who smiles at the woman, someone's wife, living in her husband's house. Meanwhile, her lover, wearing
the disguise of an onlooker, noiselessly passes by, just to get a
glimpse of her. Such was Elena's interpretation of the poem.
She saw no sadness in it. Unless it was the sadness of fall? Or
of the fallen leaf? she wondered. Instead, she savored the pleasant feeling aroused by Jovan's apology, which she assumed he
had only made because she had put off emailing him back.

It was Elena's habit, when Richard was at work and Eva
asleep, to read MeAndMyMan.com, where she found the
following advice: *Men are more individualistic than women.*

They're the more selfish of the two sexes, and they really don't like it when you take up their personal space. They'll treat you better if you let them breathe. To avoid making them think you're pushy, don't respond to their messages or call right away. Instead, pretend you're hard to get, and you'll hook him in no time at all! Accordingly, Elena would never respond immediately to Jovan's emails, but, instead, would compose her reply in her head while she was doing dishes or making crepes, or when Eva was playing with toys. But then her mind would drift toward the young housewife in the poem. She went so far as to read other William Carlos Williams poems she found online, thinking she might surprise Jovan with her newly acquired knowledge and prove to him that he had inspired her to learn. Or, alternatively, since he had said that he had learned so much about America from her, she toyed with the idea of describing her everyday life, though she was always at a loss as to what would be worth describing, since apart from housework, her life consisted by and large of trips to the supermarket or the mall. When it wasn't too hot, Richard would drive them in the Buick the size of her mother's kitchen to a sprawling, empty park that left Elena feeling lonely and unsafe. The local TV stations were constantly airing "breaking news" stories of shootings, rapes, and burglaries so that when, for example, she was pushing Eva on the swing set, she would wonder whether the little figures moving in the distance were carrying concealed weapons. Even Richard had a gun he kept hidden in a drawer. Maybe this was something she could tell Jovan about—how unsafe she felt in these desert spaces and how afraid she was to even touch Richard's gun when she put away his freshly pressed Egyptian cotton briefs in the drawer. But she decided to put Jovan off a little longer and let him think she was offended, for when he realized she was not, that the reason she didn't write was because her father had had a stroke, he would be moved. So moved that when they saw each other, soon, in Skopje . . . Feeling drugged from all her daydreaming, Elena closed her laptop and fell asleep on the couch.

Eva's whimpers woke her. As usual, Richard was still out like a light. But unlike Elena, he had a job to get to, which made her feel that she needed to let him sleep a little longer and needed to make him breakfast. Several years earlier, before the baby, when life in America was still new to her, the word "breakfast" carried a fragrant sound, like the breaking of a loaf of warm, crispy bread. Everything felt sweet: the smell of scrambled eggs, hash browns and bacon, of pancakes smothered in maple syrup, even the enormous quantities of watery American coffee she bought mugs for like the ones found in cheap diners. It's just like in the movies, she would think, gazing at Richard in their sunny breakfast nook, his hair wild and golden, his vowels drawled and nasal, his "r"s liquid and low. It's just like in the movies, she thought; my husband is American, he's a *real* American. But she didn't feel that way about breakfast anymore. The ritual had turned into a chore. She was worried it showed that she wasn't as careful in setting the table, that sometimes she forgot to make a pot of coffee, that she didn't smile when he was eating, or even when he was leaving for work. *If you want to keep your man, you need to let him know that everything you do for him, you do with pleasure. Look like you're having fun, even if you're not. Put a smile on that face and forget about how tired you are. You don't want to sour a sweet thing, do you?*

"How's your dad?" Richard asked, his mouth full of eggs.

"I don't know," she replied, sitting across him. "I'm still waiting for my brother to call." Reaching for his plate, she broke off a piece of toast and began chewing absent-mindedly, her gaze on Eva. The child was sitting in a highchair by her father and was intent on eating an apple wedge. "I think

I need to go back home. Even if it's not that serious," Elena
said. "He's my father," she added decidedly.

"Remind me to give you my credit card before I go to
work. Just go ahead and book your flight. And take Eva with
you. You know I can't come."

Elena felt relieved. It occurred to her that then she could
see Jovan, but she chased the thought away and was soon
convinced that such a thought had never entered her mind.

"How about taking a few days off work, like it's for a vacation?" she asked, hoping the answer would be no.

"Don't get me wrong," Richard said with great civility, a
manner she had come to loathe in him and in all Americans,
"but I don't want the little time I'm able to take off work to
be spoiled by, you know, the situation. I don't want to hurt
your feelings," he continued, crunching a slice of bacon, "but
I want our vacations to be quality time. This thing is liable to
cost us a great deal of money, and I could be working overtime." He looked calm, which always unnerved Elena, since
she never knew what he was really thinking. "We'll see how
things go. For now, though, you're my number one priority,
honey. You go, and we'll take it from there," he added, lightly
brushing the back of her hand. In the beginning, she saw such
gestures as a polished politeness. Back in Macedonia people
spat on the streets, cut aggressively into line and always wore
an angry look. Here, everyone smiled and respected your personal space. But you rarely saw anyone out on the street They
all seemed to be locked in their cars and houses.

"Say ciao to Daddy! Ciao, Daddy! Come on sweetie. Say it.
Ciao, Daddy!"

"Da-ddy," Eva said and waved her little hand. Richard
sidled into the driver's seat, shut the door, and blew a kiss as
the car started down the empty street.

Elena turned on the TV and played the *Bushava Azbuka* show for Eva. She wanted the child to learn Macedonian so she would have someone to talk to without feeling the strain of speaking a foreign language. Not that she had many conversationalists in English. She had met a few women in the local mom's club who sometimes arranged playdates together, but all they ever talked about was teething, diapers, and breastfeeding. Helen, a young woman from Connecticut, was the only one to wean her son early, when he was six months old, which the other mothers were not pleased to hear, although they took it with a smile. Having lived in the States three years, Elena could tell when a smile conveyed polite disapproval. "Well, you're not going to see me forcefully weaning my baby. There is nothing healthier and more natural than breast milk," said Dina, a large, pale woman with beady eyes who called the meetings and served as the group's self-proclaimed leader. "Which is not to say I don't appreciate your opinion," she added. The other women nodded approvingly. "All that's good is natural," someone chimed, and they all smiled, revealing perfect rows of whitened teeth. The next time they had a playdate, Helen was conspicuously absent. And though Eva was nearly two, Elena decided to let her wean naturally.

As she absentmindedly stared at the TV screen, she heard the ping of a text message:

dads still not better n i cant get enyone to tell me y not. can u make it overr or not. me n keti cant bc we got work some 1 needs to be there
need help with money n all these bills from the hospital n doctors n all that
can u come tamarrow
if you cant then call me in the am

He's drunk, Elena thought. He's always drunk by 2:00. He starts with one beer and pretends he's not drunk, although you can tell from his messages that he is, and also because he doesn't want to talk on Skype. It had been obvious to her that Dragan wouldn't be able to take care of their father once she left. "You can't sacrifice your own life because of the choices of people around you," Richard would say when they were still in Macedonia, before his contract expired. "You have to be your own priority. You can't help anyone if you're unhappy." "You're going to leave and leave Daddy alone?" her brother snapped after she announced she was marrying Richard and moving to the States. "He's not alone," Elena replied, "You and Keti are here." "It's not the same," Dragan said. "You're his daughter."

She would have to go back and face "the situation." She would buy the ticket now, for tomorrow or the day after, Elena thought as she opened her laptop. She clicked on her browser and it opened to the page with the William Carlos Williams poem she had wanted to send Jovan but lacked the courage. Reading it for the first time, she thought it was a sign that he had intentionally steered her toward this poet to see if she remembered that magic moment they had shared back in high school. They had run into each other on their way to school. It was the first time she had paid him much attention, for he was a quiet boy, a year older than herself, who wore glasses and never caused the slightest trouble. If they bumped into each other in the hall, they would say hello. They had said hello that afternoon on their way to school when they had found themselves awkwardly in step, both conscious of each other's presence, but not knowing how to start a conversation. The silence weighed on her so heavily that she finally asked him what classes he was taking and who his teachers were. Then it began to drizzle and, a moment later, the clouds broke and poured down on them. They started to run, but the rain turned into hail. Jovan said "Quick!" as he wrenched his glasses off, slipped them in his pocket, opened his denim jacket and covered Elena's head. They darted toward a nearby kiosk to take cover under its awning. As they ran, their sneakers filling with rain, their ankles clumsily colliding, her face pressed against his shirt which gave off the soft scent of his sugary sweat. (*Every woman longs for a man who can protect her,* she remembered reading on the advice website for women). The hail stopped as soon as they reached the kiosk. "Hey, let's not be late for class," Jovan said. "This rain could last awhile. Besides, we're drenched anyway." And then, without a word, she ran out into the rain and he followed. They raced each other to the school, splashing their feet in every puddle on the broken sidewalk, and when they reached the gate, went their separate ways. It was the end of May. The air smelled of lilacs and acacia, but they did not see each other again. And now, after many years, he had messaged her on Facebook: "Hello, Elena! I just happened to see you here, so I thought I'd say hello. Greetings from Skopje!" It wasn't long before she had replied, and when she did, he deleted his account, and that's when the emails began.

This was what the poem was about; it just had to be:

As the rain falls
so does
    your love

bathe every
        open
object of the world—

In houses
the priceless dry
    rooms

of illicit love
where we live
hear the wash of the
    rain—

But she didn't send it to him. Instead, she wrote a few lines she hoped would sound urgent: "I'm not mad at you. My father had a stroke. I'm buying a ticket and coming to Skopje. I'll be there for a while . . . who knows for how long."

He immediately replied: "When are you arriving? Drop me a line, it would be great if we could meet up!!!"

* * *

Dragan was picking her up at the airport. She could hardly wait to climb into the back seat and feel the car rushing down the highway. She imagined herself cracking her window and breathing in the cool spring air and feeling the sprinkle of raindrops that were now crawling horizontally across the airplane window. She would close her eyes and soon find herself home, in her old room, where she would sleep with Eva for the first time in her life. But as if to spite her, the conveyor belt refused to spit out her luggage until the very last. Eva lay slumped across her shoulder fast asleep, and Elena could no longer feel her right arm. She had been that way or on Elena's lap the entire twenty-six hours since they had left for the airport. The girl would only watch cartoons if she was in Elena's lap, and of course, it was only in Elena's lap that she would play with her toys. Then she would get bored and begin to whine, "tsi-tse." The passengers in their row avoided all eye contact, smiling coldly if they had to squeeze past them. Whenever Eva screamed, they stuffed their ears with earplugs or covered them with headphones. Once the teenage girl sitting in front of them turned around after Eva had kicked the back of her seat, and hissed "Quit it!" Elena did not apologize and only prayed that one day the girl would have a child of her own and have to travel with it on a long flight.

She barely managed to drag her suitcase off the belt with her free hand. There was hardly anyone left to help her, anyway. All the people who had been pacing nervously around the baggage-claim carrousel were gone, and the few remaining passengers still waiting for their luggage were far too worried about their missing bags to even notice Elena needed help. Somehow she managed to hobble out of the terminal. It wasn't the first time she had to lug something heavy while carrying Eva (*Don't despair! Having to carry a baby* and *groceries will get you back in shape in no time at all!* the website had said). She hoped to find Dragan waiting by the rails at the terminal entrance, but the only person there was a sad-looking sleepy old man holding a sign that said "Mr. Barry." Drivers accosted her from all sides saying, "Taxi, ma'am, need a taxi?" I bet he got drunk and forgot all about me, Elena thought as she wrenched her phone from her pocket and fumbled to turn it on.

"Elena!" she heard a woman's breathless voice behind her. It was Keti, Dragan's wife. "Hurry up!" she shouted, grabbing the suitcase and rushing ahead. "My parking ticket is about to expire and I'll be stuck with an 800 denar fine! Move, quick!" Thirty meters ahead, beside the exit gate, a car was parked with its blinkers flashing. Keti popped the trunk open and levered the suitcase inside. "My God! What do you have in

there, bricks?" she said, slammed the trunk shut and almost
pushed Elena and Eva into the back seat. The running and
shouting had awakened the child who was screaming and
pounding Elena with her fists. Keti started the engine up and
drove quickly to the gate. She slid the ticket into the machine
and the gate rose. "Oh!" she let out a sigh of relief, "In the
nick of time!" Keti's eyes flashed in the rearview mirror as she
looked back at Elena and the child. "Sorry I had to make you
run," she yelled, trying to out-shout Eva, "but I waited forever.
You came out last and parking isn't free after ten minutes. I
had to go round once already," she added. Eva was clearly disoriented and a little frightened, for she was kicking and claw-
ing at her mother. "Oh, my," Keti remarked. Elena slipped her
hand into her bra, eased out her breast and pressed it to Eva's
mouth. The little girl calmed down at once. Elena closed her
eyes and felt the spring air stroke her face, as the car juddered
over every pothole in the road. Then the stream of air stopped
and the juddering and noise of the engine were muted. "I had
to close the window. It's the draft. It'll give me a stiff neck,"
Keti said. "How was your trip?" she finally asked. "Shhhh . . ."
Elena whispered, pointing at Eva, whose soft skin glowed now
and then from the headlights of the approaching cars. Elena
closed her eyes, let her head lie back against the headrest. And
was suddenly awakened as Keti shook her, saying, "Elena,
Elena. We're here."

Keti helped her drag the suitcase up the stairs to the third-
floor apartment where Elena had grown up. She unlocked the
door, then handed her the key, saying Dragan would come
to pick her up at 8:00 in the morning, and left. Opening the
door, Elena was struck by a familiar smell. It was as if her
mother was still alive, napping in her bed. As she walked into
the living room, it seemed to her that nothing had changed;

everything was the same, only older, darker, dingier. The furniture had so faded that it appeared to be covered with dust. All the plants that they had once had, no doubt left to wilt, were gone. The smell of garlic permeated the apartment, since her parents had been in the habit of eating a whole head of garlic with their dinner. She wasn't sure if her father had continued this practice alone, or that the smell had seeped into the very rugs and furniture. The room was dimly lit because of the 40-watt bulbs her father insisted on using believing that this saved electricity. Some were not working. The sink was filled with filthy plates and glasses, and on the counter lay a pair of knives caked with dirt and a cooking pot filled to the brim with greasy water. She opened the refrigerator and found a chunk of dry cheese, a lidless jar of pickles, a stick of margarine, two beers, and half a block of cheap chicken ham. When she stepped into the bathroom, she couldn't help but notice that the tub was lined with a dark black ring, the taps were all begrimed, and the light above the cracked mirror no longer worked. Here and there a tile had dislodged itself from the wall. She recognized the same tattered towels from her childhood hanging by the sink, and she imagined her father stepping from the tub and toweling the sagging, wrinkled skin, with its fleece of wiry white hair that hung from him. She could see him desperately clutching the washing machine as he grew faint; could see him stagger, naked, into the living room and speed dial Dragan's number, then collapse onto the couch, wet and confused, unable to utter a word.

Elena shook herself as if to shake off the image of her helpless father. She ran her fingers gently down the buttons of Eva's spine. The little girl slept with her head cradled on Elena's shoulder. She carried her into the bedroom, tucked the girl between the cold sheets of her parents' rickety bed that still carried the scent of her mother's facial cream and her father's shaving foam, and then lay down beside her. Burying her face in the pillow, Elena fell fast asleep.

They were both awake by the time Dragan arrived. Elena had made Turkish coffee because she couldn't find anything else to drink. Eva was absentmindedly chewing a mash Elena had made of the banana and biscuits she had carried in her purse, staring at her grandfather's television. Dragan's stomach bulged more than ever and when he embraced her, it almost pushed her off her feet. He smelled like a beer barrel, and his stubbly beard scratched her cheek when he bent to kiss her. He tried to take Eva into his arms, but the girl screamed at his touch. "But honey," Elena cooed, "this is your Vujche. You know him from Skype. Vujche! Vujche! Come on sweetie, say Vujche." But the child would not stop crying. She hid her face in her mother's shoulder and refused to budge.

"How's Daddy?" Elena asked after the child had calmed down.

"I saw him yesterday," Dragan said, wiping the spittle that had gathered in the corner of his mouth. "He's the same. Conscious. But he can't talk and one side of his body is completely paralyzed. The other side isn't doing too good, either. He's not well, Elena," he sighed and lit a cigarette. She almost reproached him for smoking in front of the child but remembered this wasn't America.

"Visiting hour is at 3:00," he told her. "I'll take you to our place first. I'm working the evening shift today so I can drive you to the hospital. Did you decide how long you're staying?"

Elena shrugged. They both avoided saying what they were afraid of. "I'll see what the doctors say today."

"Well, don't forget—those guys won't tell you anything."

"It's not their fault," Elena said.

"Sure it is," Dragan replied. "You'll feel like puking the

moment you walk inside the place. Especially after America. Peekaboo!" Dragan said to Eva, who was peering sideways at him with one eye.

"I don't know what's wrong with her," Elena said apologetically. "I mean, I *do* know. We changed time zones. Everything's upside down now. I don't know how I'll manage her."

"You could take her for a walk while the weather's still good. Or maybe take a nap."

A silence fell between them. "May I?" his eyes suggested as he reached for Elena's coffee and took a loud sip as she shifted her seat so that Eva, who was now standing in her lap, could watch TV.

"She's so cute," Dragan said.

"Daddy hasn't seen her in person," Elena said. "You think I should take her with me today?"

"What can I say?" Dragan replied, stubbing the cigarette butt in the saucer. "It's pretty ugly in there. I mean, *real* ugly."

"I don't suppose there's anyone who could look after her."

Dragan did not say a word. Elena was hoping he would suggest something, but, clearly, that was not going to happen. This meant that when she met Jovan, she would have to bring Eva along. Which might not be a bad thing for a first meeting, she thought, trying to dispel her excitement at the thought of seeing him. The only thing to focus on now was her father. Her father is what she was supposed to think about. Not Jovan. The same father who used to say, "Some people have a life, but don't know how to live it," but then, when her mother died, seldom left the house. On the other hand, she thought, returning to herself, Daddy would not want me to spend all my time feeling bad about him and—

"Do you mind staying here?" Dragan said, interrupting her train of thought, "I mean, if that's okay with you?"

"Of course I don't mind. I don't want to bother you, and

there's not enough space at your place anyway," Elena said. "Besides, Eva can be quite a handful. And now with the time zones and all . . . You're going to be a good girl, right honey?" Elena murmured in Eva's ear, but the child continued staring at the TV.

"Perfect," Dragan said. "And if they let Daddy out of the hospital, you can look after him."

"For a while, maybe," Elena replied. She knew what was behind his words: the unuttered accusation, "You left your father alone and ran off to America."

"I'll help you with the groceries and anything else you need. I have a SIM card too, so you can have a cell phone here," he added.

Elena wanted to ask if the card came with internet but said nothing. Jovan must have written in the meantime, arranging a time and place for them to meet.

"Well, let's get going", Dragan said, as he struggled to his feet. "There's no real coffee here, and there's nothing to eat. And no internet, either."

"Yeah, internet," Elena said.

I'm at work every day until 4 P.M. You can visit any day you like. Just ask for me at the front office. They'll telephone me and I'll come and get You. I'll show You the library!!! I'm sure it's not like the libraries in America . . . but, still, You might find this interesting at the given moment. We can have coffee in our cafeteria, and if you want, we can even walk to the old town, where you can remind yourself of the local tastes, he he he.

* * *

Dragan cursed all the way to the hospital. In the States, Richard and Elena took great care never to say words like "fuck" or "shit" in front of Eva, but things were different here. Here there were no rules, and you were expected to put up with all manner of rude behavior. So she ignored the fact that there were no seatbelts in Dragan's car because he had removed them. "They bothered me," was all he said. He had never worn his seatbelt, anyway, even when he was a drunk as a skunk, even when he was driving. He was, in fact, a drunk who loved to drive. He would drive and curse with all the other horrible drivers in the city who went to great efforts to ruthlessly cut each other off and never took their hand off the horn, especially when they were jammed in front of the State Hospital entrance. "I'd forgotten what traffic is like here. My blood pressure just spiked," Elena said, as her heart pounded in her ears. Her palms were sweaty and her arms ached from carrying Eva around for two whole days.

It was 3 P.M. Visiting hours had already started, and their father was still nearly half a mile away from the street they were barely crawling along. "Tell me about it!" Dragan sneered. "This city is full of hicks. Zero level of culture!" he added, flicking his cigarette butt out the window. "I gotta tell you, leaving this shithole was the smartest thing you ever did. Jesus, look at that!" he shouted as he furiously honked at a taxi driver who had stopped in the middle of the entrance to the hospital complex. "Hey, Elena," he asked, "How about you saving me the hassle of going in there and having to pay for parking? Just come out here and give me a call later, okay? Keti should be back by six and said she'd make some dinner, so, I don't know, see about everything with her later," he said, his voice trailing off as he pulled up exactly to where the taxi he had complained about had stopped.

"Can't you watch Eva for ten minutes while I go in to see Daddy?" Elena asked.

"No way, I'm already late for work," he said. "Besides, you may need to stay longer than ten minutes, you haven't seen him in a while. Maybe he needs something. Maybe you need to check with the doctors if he's, you know—"a loud honking from the car behind them interrupted him. The driver made angry faces and gestures behind his windshield. "Okay, talk later," Elena said and scurried out of the car. "Bmmmm, bmmmm," Eva babbled, in imitation of the cars edging past them in the tight narrow line packed with people.

Elena counted her steps as she broke into a run she had to occasionally interrupt in order to hop over the stumps of trees that had once grown there, or to overtake the slower pedestrians weaving through the throng of *gevrek* and pajama vendors and the ragged line of orderlies pushing carts. One-two-three-four, one-two-three-four, she repeated to herself (*If ever you find yourself getting anxious, just try counting to four. It will calm you down. Satisfaction guaranteed!*). She reached the neurology ward at last. "Go up to the second floor and it's the second room on the right. 302, I think," Dragan had told her. "Don't I have to check in with someone?" she had asked. "Have you forgotten where you lived your whole life?" he asked incredulously. "'Course you don't need to check in. Just make sure you get there during visiting hours, so you don't get some pissed off orderly shouting in your face."

She went up the stairs past three broken chairs that had been dumped on the landing. The walls were smudged with mold and the paint was peeling. The banister was warped, the stairs slicked with filth. The doorway to the second-floor ward led to a parlor with nothing but a single TV and a row of plastic chairs from the 80s in which men in pajamas sat watching the news. A plastic door behind them with a missing handle had a sign that read, "Ward Supervisor." Elena panicked at the thought of having brought Eva to this garbage dump of death, but she also knew that there was nowhere she could possibly leave the child. She walked into the room where her father was supposed to be. It contained six facing hospital beds and an additional bed wedged in the middle. Elena prayed that this wasn't the bed her father was in. Then she spotted him in the second bed on the right. He was in a pair of ragged hospital pajamas and had an IV drip in his arm. Half his face was black-and-blue, evidently from the fall; the other half was gray and twisted, his dry wrinkled skin like roughly worked stone.

She sat gingerly down on the edge of the iron bed as Eva stared about her, considering whether to cry. "Daddy," Elena whispered, caressing his cheek. She raised his hand and kissed it. Her father opened an eye and a long wailing "Ooooohaaaaa" came out of his parched mouth but then abruptly stopped, as if his voice had run out. He turned the same eye toward Eva and flinched. "N-n-n-no" he stuttered, covering his face with his hand. "But Daddy, Eva came to see you. Eva!" Elena said, turning to the child. "Here's Dedo. Blow Dedo a kiss!" she said with a forced smile, barely managing to keep her voice from breaking. Eva began to whine and push her fists against Elena, trying to wiggle out of her lap. Elena's father had kept his face covered, but she could just glimpse his contorted mouth under his palm. "Just a second, honey, just a second," Elena repeated in an effort to quiet the child as she took out her phone and found a cartoon to distract her. She let Eva take the phone as she edged closer to her father. "Daddy, Daddy," she whispered, seeing a tear roll down his cheek. "Don't you worry Daddy, everything will be okay," she said, softly. "I'm going to talk to the doctors and we'll get you out of here and take you home, and I'll be there with you until you get better, you hear me Daddy?" Her father emitted a deep nasal sound like a low wail. There was a sharp bang. Eva had dropped the phone and Elena saw that the screen had cracked. The child let out a shriek so loud that everyone in the room turned toward Elena. "Mother," said a nurse appearing out of nowhere, "calm the child down and then come back," leading Elena out by the elbow. "Daddy, I'll be back," Elena said from the doorway. "I just have to calm Eva down." And again her father moaned, "Ooooohaaaaa."

In the hallway outside, Eva would not stop shrieking. "What's going on here?" a doctor suddenly emerging from a door demanded. "Either calm her down or take her somewhere else! This is no place for kids," he said as he shoved her toward the exit.

"But I just wanted to ask about my father," Elena blurted, but the doctor spoke over her. "How do you expect me to talk to you like this! God, the nerve of you people!" he shouted, slamming the door in her face. She found herself back on the stairs. She felt so drained that she collapsed in one of the half-broken chairs. Eva was screaming and writhing in her arms. Elena tried to put her down, but the girl locked her arms about her mother's knees. Elena picked her up, pressed her against her chest and lifted out a breast. Eva greedily seized the nipple in her mouth and the crying stopped. A woman descending stairs hissed, "How disgraceful!"

Eva was now calm. She could be angelic when she was not crying, like a perfect miniature of Richard: a baroque cherub with honey-sweet dimples and rolls of baby fat you just wanted to press against your face. When Eva was suckling at her breast or broke into laughter, it felt like nectar was running through her body, entirely erasing the memory of how tired or upset she had been. But if the child was screaming, or demanding her "tsi-tse," the nectar was forgotten, and Elena's whole being felt like an old rubber band about to snap.

She staggered to her feet, balancing Eva on her hip. Her arms ached from carrying the child, who had always adamantly refused to sit in a stroller and didn't like to walk. Elena steered toward the taxi station, down the same pot-holed and misery-ridden lane on which she had come to the hospital entrance. One-two-three-four, one-two-three-four, she repeated, increasing her pace in a fruitless effort to stamp out her memory of the state hospital. *Don't run from pleasure but allow yourself to experience it precisely when you suffer most. And never harbor a moment's guilt because what you are searching for is joy.*

"The National Library, please," she told the taxi driver as she scrambled into the back of his cab.

"Where's that? Bunjakovec?" he asked.

"No," Elena said, "Mavrovka."

"Oh, yes, of course, I knew that," the taxi driver replied, as he turned the engine over.

It was three-thirty by the time they arrived. The entire way Eva la-la-ed a nursery rhyme, and when they got out, she romped around the platform in front of the library, playing with a ball Elena carried in her bag along with everything else she needed for the child. Ten minutes, she said to herself, ten minutes so that Eva can have a good run and we get there before he leaves work. And then we can go somewhere or at least arrange a time to get together. She sat on a bench with her eyes half-closed, listening to the intermingling of Eva's piping voice and the hubbub of traffic coming from the intersection behind her. A soft, spring breeze bringing waves of cool and warm air caressed her cheeks like unplaited lace. The breeze reminded her of childhood, of unseen possibilities, of the intense impatience of wanting to grow up. She looked at the cracked screen of her cell phone: it was three-forty. She decided it was time to go in. She took Eva by her little hand and headed toward the heavy glass entrance door. Inside, there was a reception booth to the right, where you had to bend down if you wanted to see the receptionist's hands, much less her face. Elena asked if she could "please see Mr. Jovan Anastasov" because he was expecting her.

"Jovan . . . from Archives?" the receptionist said.

"I don't really know?" Elena replied, realizing she hadn't the slightest idea what Jovan's job was. The woman turned and whispered to someone else Elena could not see "Hey, you know who Jovan Anastasov is?" There was some muttering and then an "Okay, I'll ask . . . Hello, hello? Is Anastasov Jovan in this department? Okay then, tell him there's someone here to see him, some . . . woman." The receptionist hung up and stretched her neck down to look up at Elena.

"He'll be right down," she said, "but you should know that children are not allowed in the library."

"Says who?" Elena said, surprised by her own tone.

"What do you mean, says who?" the baffled lady asked, repeating Elena's phrase.

"Well, I mean just that. According to who? How would I know children aren't allowed?"

"I don't know, ma'am, but you should! This is a library!"

"So? Don't you have children's books?"

"We do, but . . ."

"Look—there's no one else to watch her but me. You got kids?"

"I do, but . . ." this time the receptionist was cut off by a knock on a door inside the booth. Elena's heart leapt into her mouth and her face flushed. It must be him, she thought. And she heard a voice persuading the woman to let Eva in, asking her to make an exception because he would be punching out soon anyway.

Elena heard a buzz and the automatic door swung slightly open. Elena pushed it in and saw Jovan standing behind the door, as if he were hiding from her. "Here I am!" he blurted awkwardly and smiled: "I came down to see you!"

As he approached Elena, it was evident he was bewildered as to how to greet her. "Heyyy," he said, belatedly, patting her shoulder. But then he approached her and gave her three air-kisses on the cheek. "And who is this? The daughter?" Jovan bent over Eva. "Hell-llo! What's your name, little girl?" he said, poking her in the belly with his index finger. Eva's brows knitted, and she hid behind her mother.

"I guess she's embarrassed," he said.

"Yes, but she'll come round," Elena said, unable to take her eyes off him. He was the same height as she was. Why had she been certain he was so much taller, that when he sheltered her under his jacket and they ran in the rain, that his head towered a foot above hers? Nor were his shoulders as wide as she had imagined them to be. In fact, he was quite slouched, like a bird, like a buzzard. He was as thin as a rail, too, and his clothes were frumpy and had the color of the library: dull cement. When he had drawn near her, she noticed he smelled greasy. He was half-bald, his crown covered by a wisp of hair like a baby elephant's. Moreover, he wore horn-rimmed glasses that were much too large for his face. They stood staring at each other until Elena became conscious that she herself was not as young and as pretty as she had been that day it had rained, that her eyes were probably quite puffy from the jetlag, that the sharp folds stretching from her nostrils to the corners of her mouth had become deeper and more prominent.

"Sorry," she said tentatively, "I guess I came unannounced. But you said to come whenever I wanted to, and I was in the neighborhood . . ." she added, wincing at the thought that she had just uttered the most unoriginal American excuse.

"No, no, it's really not a problem . . ." Jovan stammered, fixing his gaze upon the floor. He had clasped his hands behind his back, like an old man on his daily stroll.

"Are you still busy?" she asked. "You want me to come

another day?"

"No, no, no . . . it's really not a problem," he replied. "What would you like to do?"

"Well, I don't know . . . you said you'd show me the library?"

"Ma-ma!!" Eva squalled.

Jovan's brows knitted. "*Shhh!*" he whispered loudly, raising a finger to his lips. "There are reading rooms upstairs!"

"Oh, I'm so sorry," Elena said. "Should we go somewhere else? Maybe you can show me your office or something?"

"No, my coworkers are working there. It's in the basement and it's really dusty down there. Not suitable for children. I'd take you to our storage room where there are a lot of inter-esting books, but that's dusty too," said Jovan, then suddenly shushed Eva with another loud "*shhh!*" when she began bab-bling in her boredom, her strident voice filling the dark library entrance hall.

So, it's not as I imagined, Elena thought.

"Don't you have a children's corner?" she asked.

"Ha!" Jovan laughed. "This is the *National* Library!" he said indignantly.

"What I meant to say was," Elena lied, "don't you have children's books?"

"Well, yes, in storage!" Jovan replied, as if the answer were obvious. "Come on, let's go to the cafeteria. No one's studying there. I punch out in 15 minutes, anyway." He didn't bother mentioning what they might do afterward.

He turned and walked briskly away. Elena had to race to keep up with him, taking Eva in her arms. His pace was so swift that she had the feeling he was annoyed with being seen with her. When they got to the cafeteria, he almost forgot to hold the door for her and the child. He took a seat at the far-thest table, by a spacious window through which Elena could see that the wind had risen and the sky was a deep dark blue.

"It's going to rain," he said. He called out to the waitress at the counter: "Hey, can I have a macchiato? Oh, and, yes, you, Elena—I mean both of you. What would you like?"

"I'll have a macchiato, too," she said. "She still can't really drink anything. I mean, she likes milk. I mean, you know."

"Ah, yes," Jovan said, blankly staring at the back of Eva's head. The child was sprawled across Elena's knees. Elena had given her the phone, which was playing a cartoon.

"I'm sorry, could you please turn it down?" Jovan asked. "It's clashing with the music." A radio was playing Macedonian pop in the background. Elena tried to take the phone from Eva, but the child shrieked, and once again Jovan pressed his finger to his lips with an insistent "*Shhh!*"

"I'm sorry," Elena said. "She's not usually this cranky."

Jovan said nothing.

"We were at the hospital," she added.

"Oh, yeah, right. So, how's your father?"

"Not well, not well at all," Elena replied, as her eyes welled with tears. She wondered if this was a good time to renew the intimacy they had shared online the last few weeks. If there is intimacy, she thought, maybe we can really talk.

"I'm so sorry," Jovan said, but his face remained expressionless. The waitress placed their coffees in front of them. She watched as he nervously poured two packets of sugar in his cup and began stirring with a plastic spoon.

"Sorry to say this, but . . . It's horrible in there."

"In where?" Jovan said, watching the coffee swirl in the cup.

"Well, the State Hospital. And everything there."

"Well, that's Macedonia for you!" Jovan said, suddenly perking up. "You know," he said in a declamatory tone, "It's a reflection of the absolute deterioration of the system on the one hand, but on the other, of human moral values. You know, it's not only about the corruption of the system, the corruption on a physical level, which for a hospital, you know, is absolutely crucial. But here, here, we are talking about, you know, corruption, you know, on a *higher* level, you know, a level—how should I put it?—both psychological and cultural, you know. Corruption of the soul and all moral values," he concluded, crossing his legs and leaning back in his chair.

Elena nodded all the while. This was more like him, she thought. He worked in the library, after all. He was supposed to be well-read; he was supposed to talk this way.

"The interpersonal relationships there!" Jovan said, his voice rising. Eva turned around, knitted her brows, and slapped his knee. Jovan was taken aback.

"Eva!" Elena said in surprise, and added reproachfully "what are you doing?"

"That's how it is with little children!" Jovan remarked and continued his speech. "As I was saying, you know, just imagine the level of personal psychological deprivation!" Eva slapped him again in her irritation.

"Eva, darling, please stop," Elena pleaded. "This is Uncle Jovan. Say hello. *He-llo!*" But Eva only slapped him yet again.

"Little girl, how come you have no manners?" Jovan said, bending toward Eva. "When two adults are having a conversation, you need to keep quiet," he added, as if he were talking to a teenager.

Eva dropped her mother's phone and began angrily pushing the man, as if she wanted to make him go away. "Please honey, don't!" Elena pleaded, drawing her up into her arms, but Eva would not stop screaming and writhing. Jovan bent down to pick up the phone and, as he did, it rang. He looked at the broken screen. "It's Dragan," he said, handing it to her.

"Hey," Elena said.

"You there?" came Dragan's voice.

"No, I just left."

"When did you leave?"

"Just now," Elena said, shouting over Eva, who was still screaming at the top of her voice. Jovan had risen to his feet and was shifting from foot to foot. Everyone else in the cafeteria was staring at them.

"Well, I'm not sure how you could've been there just now, when Daddy died just now," Dragan said. "What did the doctors tell you?"

"What? What did you say?" Elena asked, clapping her hand over Eva's mouth. Jovan's eyes widened and Eva screamed even louder than before. "They—they said nothing."

"Get back home," Dragan said. "Keti's on her way." He hung up.

"Elena, perhaps we should leave the cafeteria," Jovan said. "I think we're bothering people. I can punch out early."

Jovan laid fifty denars on the table to pay for his coffee and stood frowning at the struggling child as Elena rummaged through her purse for her wallet "Shhh! Bad girl!" he hissed. Elena tossed a hundred denar bill onto the sticky cafeteria table and hurried toward the door. "Wait!" he called after her, "your change!"

But Elena was hell-bent toward the exit, Jovan racing behind her. Eva's screams echoed through the corridors. Two bewildered heads appeared above the banister on the second floor. "Wait," Jovan said, tapping on the reception window, "they have to let you out." The automatic door buzzed, Elena pushed it open and stepped outside. Jovan followed.

"I'm sorry," she said, turning to him. "I don't know what's wrong with her. I have to go."

"Which direction are you headed?" he asked, with a look as if he regretted the question.

"Karposh."

"Ah well," he sighed. "I'm off to Lisiche. Totally different directions. Wait, let me call you a cab," he said, taking out his phone.

Elena's ears filled with the sound of her trying not to cry, like the slow, heavy opening of a large wooden door. She gently bounced the child in her arms, humming a soothing melody, when her voice began to break.

"The cab will be here any minute," Jovan said, "It'll pull up right over there," he said, pointing. "I'll walk you," he offered, shuffling along the sidewalk with bird-like steps.

He stopped at the curb. Eva had calmed down a bit, but when she saw Jovan was still with them, she began screaming again.

"She must not like me," he observed.

"No, no, no," Elena replied. "She's just tired from all the traveling." She wanted to say: "Hey, my father died! Hey! My father died, and here I am with you. My father died, you hear me?" But she didn't say a word.

She felt something wet drop on her forehead. And then on her arm.

"It's raining," Jovan said.

"Yes," Elena replied. "It's raining."

It began to pour.

"Yikes," Jovan said, looking helplessly at the endless red traffic light and the long line of waiting cars. Just as helplessly, he glanced at the meager awning above the library entrance and decided it was too far off. Meanwhile, the rain fell harder and harder.

"You know that poem by Williams, the one about the rain?" Elena asked, her brows furrowing as she tried to hold back her tears.

"No, I don't," he said, as the rain continued to drench

them. Elena slipped her jacket off and put it over Eva. The child calmed down. A quiet seemed to spread over everything, muffling the noise of the jarring traffic. All she could hear was the hushing of the rain.

"I'd drive you, but the cab will be here any second now," he said. "Want to go under the awning?" Jovan asked, hopping back and forth from one foot to the other as if he had an urgent need to pee. Torrents of water slid down the bare skin of his bald crown.

"No," Elena said. The raindrops hid her copious tears. She let them go.

"But it's raining cats and dogs," Jovan said.

"And not for the first time," Elena replied, "nor for the last." But her statement meant nothing to him. His eyes were glued to the traffic light, as if he hadn't even heard her.

"Here's your cab! Thank God!" Jovan almost shouted with joy, as the line of cars finally began to move down the road. "I'll email you!" he said, scurrying backward toward to library. "Ciao!," he shouted, "Don't catch cold!"

"You believe this?" the cab driver muttered after Elena and Eva had settled in the back seat. "It's raining buckets! So, where to?"

"Karposh 2" Elena said, looking down at Eva, nestled in her lap. They were both soaked to the skin.

"Tsi-tse," Eva said. "Tsi-tse," she repeated, pointing at the large dark nipple outlined under Elena's drenched white blouse.

"Here, take it," Elena said, feeling the child bite, then pull. For a brief moment, everything was quiet.

I'M NOT GOING ANYWHERE

For a while now the smell of fried onions had filled Riste's room. Opening the window was out of the question. It was cold outside and the air reeked of smog. He was chilled enough as it was, perched on the edge of the bed in the room he had grown up in, the cold creeping through the cracks between the walls and the drafty window frames. All night the wind had whistled menacingly. It had ceased, but his fingers still felt frozen.

"Risteeee!" his mother called from the kitchen. And then again, "Risteeee! It's ready!"

He stood up and stretched, rubbing his hands together.

"Risteeee!" came the persistent call.

"I'm coming!" he barked back. Even if he had said "I'm not a rocket, goddammit!" she would have given him a blank, cow-eyed stare with a half-open mouth that always seemed to say, *What have I done? Why are you scolding me?*

She was standing at the kitchen sink, taking bowls down from the cupboard. The tablecloth had not even been laid.

"What did you call me for when it isn't even ready?" he demanded, plopping down in his chair. His eyes fell upon the faded sticker of a superhero squirrel from a jar of *Agrokrem*, which he had stuck upon the edge of the table when he was a kid, and he recalled the chocolate spread he used to have for

supper every evening on a slice of bread with a glass of warm
milk, "to make you grow up big and tall that much faster," as
his mother used to chant.

"What isn't ready?" she asked.

"Lunch, dammit!" he snapped.

"It *is* ready, honey!" she said, gently setting the bowls down
on the sideboard.

For some reason the faded sticker began to bother him.
Its edges were torn where someone had tried to scrape it off.

"Don't you have a tablecloth?"

"Of course I do, darling!" she said, with the same placid
composure, leaving the bowls where they lay to open a lower
cabinet drawer. Riste watched her as she bent down with dif-
ficulty, her large behind bulging, heart-shaped, a veritable
shelf of meat. As she hobbled back to the table, the beefy slabs
wobbled with each step, whereupon she brushed the table-
top with the side of her hand as if clearing away some imag-
inary crumbs, and then laid down the tablecloth. It looked
familiar, and he realized it was one of the tablecloths he had
grown up with, the white one with blue squares, now severely
stained and spattered with scorch marks, riddled with holes.
He eyed the cloth with hatred as his mother scooped goulash
and mashed potatoes into their bowls, the same detestable
bowls he had eaten from as a child, chipped, tarnished, and
crisscrossed with gray hairline cracks. She put the bowls in
their customary places, one in front of him, the other at the
opposite end of the table, near the kitchen, where she always
sat. As always, she had given him a much larger portion than
she had given herself. But this thought was interrupted by her
blurting, "Oh, the bread! I forgot the bread!" She rose to her
feet laboriously. Let her go and get it, Riste said to himself,
though it would have been good for him to move a bit. He
knew exactly what she would return with, those big fat slices

of bland white bread. The idea of whole wheat bread, the very idea of rye or cornbread flour, never entered her mind. She only ever bought this dull, white mush.

Whenever he returned to Macedonia, Riste could not help noticing how things were always getting worse, like this mealy bread, for instance, that his mother laid down on a cutting board on the table as she settled noisily into her chair. Riste grabbed a thick slice and bit off a chunk, not because he was hungry, but to feed his irritation.

"What the hell is this?" he snarled. His mother forked a chunk of meat and bit off a bite that was so hot she let half of it fall from her mouth into the bowl with a splash. The edge of the table cut into the folds of her belly.

"What's that, dear?" she asked, blowing air noisily through her mouth to cool off the bite she had taken.

"This bread! It's like everything else in this country. It just gets worse and worse! Just like the people. Poor, tough, and impossible to chew!" he pronounced, proud of himself for drawing such a clever parallel. He looked across the table at his mother, but she stared impassively back and continued chewing. He drilled her with his eyes until at last, with a weary shrug, she said, "Well, that's life, sweetheart." It was her timeworn response to most everything.

It irked him that he was expected to finish this bowl, the prospect of which had weighed on him since that morning when his mother had informed him she was making goulash for lunch. Not that it really mattered what she cooked; everything she made was perfectly detestable. She could make fries, for sure, which was one obvious reason why she had grown so heavy. Decades of fried sliced potatoes permeated the flat. The smell of fries and burnt oil clung to the carpets and to the walls, which hadn't seen a fresh coat of paint in years. And true, she had a way with roast chicken, but everything else she cooked fell flat. There was never enough salt, there were far too many onions and too much fat, and every dish was either too watery or dry as a bone. The vegetables and pasta were so overcooked that they fell apart on your plate. And because her eyes were always stuck on the TV, everything she baked wound up burnt. On top of which, in an effort to be thrifty, she always loaded the stuffed peppers with too much rice, the meatballs with breadcrumbs, and her soup with far too many carrots.

With a painful flash he recalled that day they had all walked out. She had announced that morning she would be making meatball soup for lunch. And when it was ready, they took their appointed places: his brother to his left, his father on the right, and his mother, as always, at the end of the table, near the kitchen, opposing him. She placed the pot on the table, lifted the lid, picked up the rusty tin ladle and began to serve the soup, which was surprisingly fragrant, into their bowls (the very bowls he and his mother were eating from now), first serving his father, then Riste, then his younger brother, and last and least herself. Each bowl had only two miniscule meatballs, except her own, which had none. A few small pieces of potato, a handful of overcooked noodles, and a plethora of diced carrots swam in a pool of watery broth. Riste grabbed the ladle and stirred the pot to see whether there were any meatballs left. There were a few, which were even smaller than the ones in his bowl.

"You call this meatball soup? It's carrot water!" he shouted. His father and brother remained silent. Each had taken up a spoon, but had not yet ventured to try it.

"Can't you at least taste it first, sweetheart?" his mother said. "I'm sure you'll like it. It's very wholesome," and as if to prove the point, she swallowed a spoonful and smiled.

His father took a reluctant sip, then threw down his spoon,

and rising to his feet, declared, "This just won't do!" Angrily pulling out his wallet, he said, "We're going out for some kebabs!"

Riste and his brother followed their father to the door while their mother sat there, continuing to eat in silence. No one said a word to her as they put on their shoes in the hall, but they could hear the sound of her slurping and the clink of the spoon on the bowl.

On occasion, perhaps once every month or two, their father would bring home pork chops and fry them himself. He would tie on his apron with a flourish and, making a big to-do of tenderizing the meat as if he were cooking up a storm, sing to himself as he seasoned each side of every pork chop. His mother would fry up a heap of French fries as a side dish, which swiftly disappeared. When his father finally served the chops, Riste and his brother would fall upon them with gusto, smacking their lips over every bite, and, when there wasn't a morsel left, they would loudly suck on the bones.

"Daddy's even better than that guy on TV!" Riste would exclaim. "Better than Karapandža!" And his brother would chime in, "Daddy makes the best chops ever!" and their father would swell up like a pigeon. "Well, of course, you know," he said, pausing for emphasis, "the secret is to get the best chops." Then, lowering his voice as if he were afraid the neighbors were listening, he confided, "The butcher always gives me the choice cuts from the stash he sets aside for himself."

But Riste did not want to dwell upon that now and, without thinking, spooned some goulash into his mouth and immediately spat it back into the bowl.

"What is it, son? Did you burn your tongue?" his mother said, chewing with her mouth open, her double chin wobbling as she spoke. The steam from the bowl had fogged her glasses, no doubt the same square, pale orange–rimmed pair she had worn twenty-five years before. The lenses magnified her eyes and now nearly lashless eyelids. Her hair had thinned and the roots were white for an inch—it had been so long since she had dyed her hair, the same pale orange as her glasses. When had she become like this? Riste asked himself, glaring at her large and frumpy figure draped in a shabby floral dress which gave her the appearance of one of those crones who came down from the mountains to sell herbs on the street, hunched on plastic crates, clinging to their walking sticks. He often thought that was why his father had cheated on her, because she was so scruffy, submissive, and docile, and why, moreover, he cheated with women far below his station as a state-employed university graduate married to a woman who had, in her day, been a reputable school counselor.

His mother was nothing like his wife, Maja. Maja was a sex bomb—petite, with a pert butt, perky breasts, a flat stomach, and arms and legs as firm as an athlete's ("You're the Macedonian Kylie Minogue!" Riste used to tell her, before they moved abroad). She had stayed slim even after she had their daughter. She was like one of those reality-TV stars who manages to restore their figure within a few months of giving birth. Which was not to say Maja didn't work hard to maintain that figure. Every morning she did God-knows-how-many crunches and push-ups before taking the train to Saint Kilda Beach to jog in one of the many spandex outfits she had bought for next to nothing, like everything else in her wardrobe. When they were still living in Macedonia, she had already shown a knack for making herself look affluent. And then later, after they had moved to Melbourne, bought a house, and were forced to economize to meet their mortgage payments, she still found ways to look like a million bucks. That was the reason she had managed to find a better job than Riste so soon after their move Down Under. He wound up working as a croupier, despite having a degree, for he had no work experience in his field, and in fact, no work experience at all. By then, Maja had not only found a great job, but had managed to get herself a promotion, the first of many to follow, in large part, Riste believed, because she looked extravagantly delicious, like a strawberry parfait.

Meanwhile, Riste's career prospects did not improve. He earned decent money in the casino but there was little possibility of promotion or even a raise. In fact, the way things were going, the divide between their respective incomes would just grow wider. He often worked double shifts late into the night. He began checking her phone while she was asleep. He knew all her passwords and frequently combed through the search history on her laptop, though he never discovered a thing. Until one day, that is, he saw a flash drive on the floor behind her desk, on which he found a hidden folder containing text messages saved as screenshots from her phone, together with e-mails between her and Matthew Arquette, one of the owners of the company she worked for. Riste knew the words by heart:

I want you to tell me everything about your day and I want to tell you everything about mine. I want to listen to you, I want to smell, touch, and taste every little bit of this wonderful YOU, every moment, every second of what's left of our lives.

I can't believe that only ten months ago we couldn't imagine that we were so perfect for each other. You are I, and I am you. We are one, a perfection, two hemispheres that make a one and only world, without sharp north, without declining west. Is there anything more real than this? In my entire life I've never felt anything more real than what I have now with you.

I love every expression of your face, every look of your eyes, the way your cheeks blush when I talk dirty, the way you lick your lips when we dine together, the way you slurp your coffee, that naughty look you have when no one's looking, the way your hand brushes aside that lock of hair that keeps falling over your eyes, the wrinkle that forms between your eyes when you talk about people who annoy you, the soft smile when you talk about your lovely daughter . . .

I love you. I know that I do. Your lovely face is the last thing I think about before I fall asleep. And the first thing I think about when I open my eyes. The absence of your lovely face, far from the reach of my fingers, physically pains me. But let us be patient. Perfection is precious, and we have at least thirty more years ahead of us.

The feel of my cock in your hands when you kiss me, the feel of your mouth at the base of my cock, the feel of my cock at the back of your throat, the way you get excited when I'm forceful or give you a command, the thought of fucking you on the porch of our little cottage in the mountains where we'll escape once we are one, and the thought of watching your sexy little ass jiggling as I'm holding it in my hands fucking you from behind. There's nothing more real than this. I want to be a part of everything that's a part of you.

"Riste, darling! Why aren't you eating?" asked his mother, interrupting his train of thought.

"I'm, um, waiting for it to cool down," he stammered. "Is there anything to drink around here?"

All of a sudden he felt a terrific urge for alcohol. *Is there anything more real than this?* The line clanged in his head like a bell.

"I bought some beer for you," his mother said.

There were soup stains at the corners of her mouth. She wouldn't recognize a napkin if she saw one, Riste thought, getting up to get the beer.

On the door of the antiquated fridge was a photo of his daughter, Melanie, held in place by a koala magnet. Matthew—Matthew Arquette—had not mentioned Melanie by name when he was sexting Riste's wife, but he had referred to her several times. *I want to be part of everything that is part of you*—as if Riste weren't a part of Maja! As if he weren't a part of Melanie! For months he had felt his daughter slipping away from him and suspected at times that she only used him now to pay for her expensive phones, nightclubs, and life by the beach. And now she was the new stepdaughter of a rich executive, one with children of his own. Finally she had the brothers and sisters her mother had refused to bear for fear of ruining the body she had used to snare this rich CEO. Melanie had not even come to see him off at the airport when he left the country for Macedonia. She had simply texted him: "I hope you find a job in Macoland soon and I hope you'll be happy." The little whore! he thought. Just like her mother. He snatched the beer from the refrigerator. It was a cheap local beer, the kind favored by construction workers and sold in hideous two-liter bottles.

He returned to the table, poured himself a glass, and knocked back half of it. Sighing, he used his fork to spear the same piece of meat he had spat out before, blew on it, then smeared it with mashed potatoes and shoved it in his mouth. Not only was it both bitter and bland, but the mashed potatoes were sticky and lumpy, and the meat itself was little more than gristle. He could barely get it down, and then rinsed his mouth with the rest of the beer in his glass.

"How long did you cook this? Because, I mean, you do

know, don't you, that it needs to cook for several hours?" he asked his mother, who remained absorbed in the act of chewing. The muffled clicking of her jaws drove him to distraction.

"Yes, dear," she eventually said, "I do know how to make goulash. I cooked the meat for hours on low just like you're supposed to."

"Well maybe just that piece was bad," Riste muttered to himself and put another chunk of meat into his mouth. He felt the sharp edge of a gristly lump grind against his bad molar, painfully jolting the nerve. The tasteless red slush in his bowl made him think of cat vomit, and he felt sick to his stomach.

"What the hell kind of meat is this?" he snarled, flicking his fork into the bowl.

"Veal, son. It's veal."

"Veal, my ass! I bet it's beef from some leathery old nag the butcher picked up in a knacker's yard."

His mother returned his look with the expressionless gaze of the dumbest kid in a first-grade class.

"You seriously believe this is veal?" he said, enraged by her silence.

"Well, I don't know for sure, son, but I know I *asked* for veal," she replied with the same bovine expression.

"Who'd you ask?"

"The butcher, of course! Who else would I ask?" she said, as if it were obvious.

"Well, let me tell you something. They screwed you over, that's what they did!" he said, spilling foam on the tablecloth as he poured himself another glass of beer. As he lapped up the foam brimming from the glass, he felt his dignity dwindle. But he rallied and said, "I bet they can see you coming for miles! 'Here's a ripe one for the plucking!'" he added, taking a swig of the bitter beer.

His mother continued to stare at him with the stubborn impassiveness of an impenetrable wall.

"It's hardly surprising when they see you looking like some old bag lady from the village! And now you've got that limp to complete the picture! 'Here's the perfect patsy,' they probably said to themselves. 'Now we can get rid of that rotten batch of meat we've got. She probably won't even notice how bad it is.'"

His mother was silent, but as she resumed chewing, her jaw made the clicking noise that infuriated him.

"Who the hell sold you this meat anyhow?" he yelled. "Where'd you get it?"

"I bought it at that big supermarket," she replied.

"What supermarket? Doesn't your hip hurt too much to walk? There's a market with a butcher's around the corner for Chrissake!"

He stopped in his tracks, realizing what he had said.

"No, there isn't, son," she lied, looking down at her bowl. "You've been gone a long time," she added, trying to steer him from a topic that was becoming dangerously unpleasant. "A lot of old shops have shut down, you know."

He had touched on the subject they never brought up.

It was Riste who had seen his father with the butcher's wife. It was a spring evening when he had stumbled on his father and a woman sitting in his father's Zastava 101 parked in one of the small side streets behind their apartment block. His father was kneading the big white breasts of the butcher's wife as his tongue was rummaging in her mouth. The following morning, before leaving for school, Riste had told his mother what he had seen, but all she had said was "OK," and had continued getting ready for work. They hadn't mentioned the subject since, and Riste was no longer sure if he hadn't imagined the whole episode. Late-night quarrels had followed, loud whispers accompanied by subdued sobs and sudden knocks against furniture. Those arguments, vaguely heard through his bedroom wall, conjured up the following scene: his mother, who was then still shapely and voluptuous, with a luxurious head of brown hair tied back in a bun, steadily striding in her low-heel black shoes, her patent leather bag slung over a shoulder. She steps inside the shop, her grace at odds with the shabby interior. The image is so vivid to him that Riste feels as if he were standing right there in front of the shop window, watching the drama silently unfold. His mother says something to the butcher, whose face flushes. The butcher's wife comes out from the walk-in freezer in a bloodstained apron. Short, with unkempt hair, the woman stares at Riste's mother in what seems to be bewilderment. His mother leaves the shop.

His mind cuts to the day he visited Matthew Arquette's wife. He climbs their front steps. He rings the doorbell. He stands for a while, but no one appears. He hesitates to ring again because he does not want to seem rude. At last, the front door opens and a well-dressed woman can vaguely be seen through the screen door. The shadowy form listens in silence as Riste tells the tale of Matthew and Maja's affair. He then kneels down to leave a large manila envelope on the doormat containing the sexts he had found on the flash drive. He turns away and walks unsteadily back to the car. He points the remote, and the door lock beeps. Mrs. Arquette opens the screen door and, stooping, picks up the envelope.

"Aren't you ashamed of yourself?" Maja confronted him after. "You're forty-six and you're doing this?"

Riste's father was forty-six when he died on the living room sofa, some two weeks after the affair with the butcher's wife was discovered.

Riste shuddered.

"For heaven's sake, dear!" his mother said. "It might be a *bit* chewy but it's not all *that* bad."

"Not all *that* bad?" he said, his voice rising as he added, "Can you hear yourself? Can't you see they cheated you? Don't you get it?" He was yelling now.

His mother said nothing.

"They sold you meat from some old nag that probably died of old age! Can't you see that?"

She looked back down into her bowl.

"They disrespected you. You get that?" he shouted.

She continued to fix her eyes on the bowl, but then the fork in her hand began to shake.

"Look, no one's gonna treat *my* mother like that," he declared, rising to his feet and storming into the kitchen.

"Where are you going?" his mother asked, straining to follow him with her eyes. He rushed back with a plastic bag, grabbed her bowl of goulash and dumped its contents into the bag, and then did the same with his own.

"I'm going to that supermarket and I'm going to fuck them up," he said. "If I have to I'm gonna throw this shit in their faces. Then they'll know who they're dealing with."

"But, honey . . ."

"No 'buts'!" he said, cutting her off. "Not one single 'but.' You understand? They'll never dare sell you meat like that after I've told them what's what. Or else I'll see they get their asses kicked out of there!" he yelled, jabbing the table with his index finger. "The next time you buy meat from there it'll be so tender you'll want to eat it raw! You hear what I'm saying?" he yelled from the hall as he wrenched his shoes on and thrust his arms into the sleeves of his winter coat. As he lifted the bag of goulash off the floor, he saw that it had left a greasy smear on the scratched parquet. He left, slamming the front door behind him.

He called the elevator. Nothing happened. He tapped the loose black button with mounting irritation, swearing under his breath. Finally, from somewhere high above, the elevator jerked into motion. He stood there, not knowing what to do with his rage. I should have taken the stairs, he said to himself, but five floors had seemed too great an effort. When at last the elevator appeared, he opened the door to find the old woman who lived two floors above him.

"Riste? Is that you?" she asked.

"Yes, it's me, Tetka Cvete."

"Oh my, I haven't seen you in ages," she said, lifting her head to get a better look at him, and, smiling, she stroked him on the cheek as if he were a child.

The smell of goulash rising from the bag at his side began to fill the air. "Yes, it's been a long time," he replied, deeply regretting that he had not taken the stairs. But he had to be polite and kind to Tetka Cvete, however furious and determined he was feeling.

"Didn't you move to Australia?" she asked.

"Yes. Yes, I did," he replied impatiently.

"And now you've come to visit your mother?"

"Well, yes," he lied. He had no intention of explaining why he had returned.

She would find out soon enough anyway.

"What about your wife and daughter? Are they here too?"

"No, they aren't," he replied.

The elevator began to slow as it approached the ground floor.

"Oh, well," she said. "They'll come next time no doubt. How old is your daughter now?"

"Sixteen."

"My, how time flies! We've grown old, Riste!" she said as the elevator shuddered to a stop.

He held the door open for her. She had trouble walking and tottered forward in little steps in splayed black shoes. Riste knew he should hold the lobby door for her as well, but that would probably have led to his having to escort her to her next destination. He decided to escape instead.

"I'm really sorry, Tetka Cvete, but I'm in a terrible hurry," he said, and ran off as if he were genuinely pressed for time.

The whole episode left him feeling as if he had lost some of the rightful indignation and pent-up fury he needed for the performance he was preparing to deliver to the butcher at the supermarket.

He practiced what he planned to say: *Good afternoon. My mother came here yesterday to purchase some veal for a goulash, and instead you sold her some rank old beef that was so tough you could barely chew it. So I would like to ask you: are you not ashamed of yourselves? Is it because she's old that you treated her like this? Simply because she's advanced in years? Have you no heart?*

But then he realized this would be too lenient.

Hey! Yesterday somebody here fobbed off a pound of rotten meat to my mother. You wanna try it? Here, fucker, have some! And he saw himself hurling the bag of goulash onto the glass display case as his imagined adversary—no doubt a young, arrogant butcher—looked on in horror.

Or better yet: *I demand to speak to your manager, now!* Which is something you could say in Australia, so why not here? These savages need to learn a thing or two about work ethic, he grumbled, picking up his pace.

Lost in arguments with the imagined butcher, it took Riste a moment to discover he had been walking in the wrong direction. He also realized he was not quite sure where this big supermarket was. He had had a general idea in which direction it lay when he had left his mother's apartment, but now he was completely disoriented. But then he vaguely recollected it was somewhere near the new multistory parking lot.

He reversed direction and followed a narrow alley that ran behind his mother's apartment block. He could see his figure reflected in the empty windows of the closed-down shops, a short, balding man in a hurry, hatless despite the biting cold. His ears and nose must be livid by now, he guessed, though it wasn't apparent in the reflections. His coat was worn, his sleeves far too long for him. He had only bought the coat because he hoped it would conceal the potbelly that he had been growing over the last few years. He still believed he would get rid of this belly if he could just eat less, or that he would at least get used to it. But he could neither eat less, nor accept the bulge above his belt. When he stood up straight, he could not even see his penis.

"Well, it's only normal for a man your age," Maja would say.

Matthew Arquette didn't have a potbelly, and he was fifty-two, six years older than Riste.

That much was all too clear the time Riste had tried to ambush them outside the Heart of the Deep restaurant in downtown Melbourne. He had waited in his car outside until the lovers came out. He then pulled up to the curb, slammed on the brakes, and flung the car door open to confront his nemesis. It was then he realized Arquette was not only a whole head taller than he was, but built like a halfback. He didn't look at all like the profile photo on the company website. Is this the asshole? Just look at him! he had said to himself when he first saw the picture of a pale, beardless man with golden locks. But the man who stopped in front of him was tall and muscular and was wearing threatening sunglasses and a black baseball cap. He simply said, "Get the hell out of our way," treading on one of Riste's loafers.

Riste was now standing at a crosswalk with a set of newly installed pedestrian lights. "Well, at least they've learned to do *something* right!" he blurted, waiting for the light to change beside a tall girl wearing a pollution mask. The girl glanced down at him, contemptuously, he thought, then lowered her gaze to the bag he was carrying. He looked down himself and was astonished to see pale brown goulash dripping on the sidewalk. The whole time he had been walking, he had left a trail of diarrhea-like sludge in his wake. Demoralized, he scuttled across the boulevard, ignoring the fact that the light had not yet turned green.

He no longer felt like hurrying. His fury had waned, transforming into a new and unfamiliar feeling.

Crossing the boulevard, he entered the neighborhood where the market began. Everything looked deserted, empty, and gray. No one was around. A big stray dog appeared out of nowhere, no doubt drawn by the smell of goulash, and followed Riste down the street. A few feet farther on, Riste stopped in his tracks, fearing again that he had taken a wrong turn. The dog stopped, too, wagging its tail and licking its chops in anticipation. A young man swept by.

"Excuse me!" Riste called after him. The young man turned. "Isn't there a super- market around here?" Riste said, but then realized how stupid and lost he sounded.

"Which supermarket?" the young man asked impatiently, as anxious to move on as Riste had been to escape from Tetka Cvete.

"I don't really know," Riste stuttered. "I'm not from around here," he added, and felt even more lost. He wanted to explain that he wasn't some hillbilly from a mountain village. That he wasn't even from a small town. That he was from Skopje and had been born and bred in Skopje, and had moved to Melbourne, a great metropolis, and had lived like a king there for years. He damn well knew what a supermarket was.

"There's a Ramstore down the road to the right of the multistory parking garage," the young man said, turning to leave.
"And if you continue down this road here there's a Tinex," he
added and disappeared into the smog.

Riste just stood there with that same helpless stare as his
mother. The dog plopped down at his feet, sweeping the dirty
concrete with its tail and cocking its head endearingly. Riste
turned around, wondering what to do, and then saw the
butcher shop beside the old stationery store, with its dusty
display of cheap notebooks, colored pencils, and pencil sharp-
eners, and realized he was in his own neighborhood. It was
like waking from a dream, recognizing all these buildings.

"Here," he beckoned to the dog. "C'mere," he added as
he dumped the goulash on a patch of grass and turned to the
butcher shop.

He stopped in front of the shop window and peered inside.
The place looked exactly as it had thirty years before, shabby
and cramped, with a curtain of wooden beads hanging across
the entrance to keep out the flies. A clock with faded digits
was hung on the wall and an equally faded postcard depicting
some little town on the Adriatic was pinned beside it. Through
the grubby windowpane he could not tell for sure whether
the woman sitting on the stool behind the meat display case
was the same woman who had been sleeping with his father
all those years ago. A pair of thick spectacles were poised on
the tip of her nose, and she held a pen in one plump hand
and a magazine in the other. She looked like she was doing a
crossword puzzle. Her hair was almost identical to his mother's,
though the dye was a darker shade of orange. She was wearing
a thick, brown, hand-knitted cardigan sweater under a bloodstained apron. Her head nestled comfortably in the folds of her
soft double chin, and her lips were curled into a vague smile.

He didn't know why he wanted to go inside, but pushed open the door anyway, making the wooden beads clatter against the glass.

"Hello, love! What will it be today?" said his father's old lover, lumbering from the stool and removing the glasses from her nose.

She smiled up at him. She had lost her upper left canine, but he knew it was her. He recognized the eyes, watery green and flecked with brown.

"Veal," he said, "Have you got any veal?" The words tumbled from his lips.

"How much do you want?"

"Half a kilo."

"Any particular cut you have in mind?" she asked, stuffing a plump hand into a plastic glove. "Oh, but wait!" she said. "Have I got a slice for you, my love!" He noticed how the woman's wedding ring cut deep into her finger.

"This veal is so tender you'll want to eat it raw!" she said.

Riste stood in silence, the silence of his mother, it occurred to him. Say something! he told himself, but he couldn't utter a word. His tongue lay limp in his mouth.

"Is your wife cooking something nice?" his father's lover asked, spreading a sheet of butcher paper on the scale.

"I don't have a wife," he blurted as if in a dream. "It's for my mother. I love her very much."

"And so you should, my love. You can always replace a wife, but you only get one mother," she said, flopping the slice of veal on the butcher paper and watching the scale's quivering needle until it came to rest. "Five hundred and sixty grams. You good with that?" she asked, looking up at him with her speckled eyes. Riste nodded.

"God never blessed me with any kids of my own, but I've been feeding everybody else's all my life," she said with a broad smile. "You're all my children," she added, handing him the meat in a plastic bag. "That'll be three hundred and fifty denars, my dear."

He took the bag and rummaged in the left pocket of his coat, and then the right. He patted the back pockets of his trousers. "Oh, I think I left my wallet at home," he said, his panic rising. "How could I have done that? How could I forget my wallet?" he went on. "I always have it with me. I always carry cash," he muttered, frantically searching through his front pockets, his shirt pockets, the inside pocket of his coat.

"It's all right, son. You can pay me later," his father's lover said, "It's not like we're gonna run off somewhere."

She smiled at Riste again. A strange new feeling welled up in him and he stood there, rooted to the ground.

"I'm right here," he said. "I'm not going anywhere."

"Well, good for you, love."

"Well, good-bye then," he said. "I'll be back."

"Bye!" she said and plumped back on her stool.

Clutching the bag of meat in his hand, Riste left the shop and took a few steps before something made him turn back to look once more at his father's old lover. She had returned to her crossword puzzle. At that moment the butcher himself appeared, now an old man with a graying moustache and thinning silver hair. He laid a hand upon his wife's back and said something to her. She looked up at him and smiled, saying something in reply. He smiled back, kissed her on the crown of her head, and disappeared. Riste just stood there, unable to move. The meat he was holding was cold, but his arms and legs grew warm, as happens at times when you are falling into a deep sleep.

MEDUSA

Sofia has a few things going for her. She's a great host, for example. And she's also an amazing geologist, but everyone knows that.

That's about it.

She and her husband Ivan live in Meadow View, the suburb with all the rich people. Ivan used to be in academia, but never really tried to outshine his wife's success. He has a PhD in archaeology.

"We're both into the Earth!" Sofia had chirped when we first met. "He's a Capricorn and I'm a Virgo. Ha ha ha!"

I wasn't sure what she was trying to tell me.

"Earth signs, you know," she explained.

Ivan is one of the co-owners of a company for dental implants run by his family—hence the palatial home in Meadow View. Sofia and Ivan have two children, as do we, except ours are younger and are girls.

That evening our daughters were watching as Simon— that's my husband—and I were getting ready for Ivan and Sofia's "Boogie Nights" theme party in Meadow View. I'd gone so far as to order a pair of vintage roller skates, but I didn't dare wear them in front of the girls. They were already screaming anyhow, refusing to give us back our wigs. Mine was a blonde bushy afro, and Simon's an Austin Powers knock-off. In his white bodysuit unbuttoned to the navel he was supposed to look like a pimp, but he wasn't terribly convincing. Looking at ourselves in the mirror we both felt a bit disappointed but refused to admit it.

"We look groovy!" we lied to each other.

"We're so rad!" we egged each other on.

"You're my Professor Pimp!" I teased him, though in truth the way his spidery black chest hair stood out against his pale skin struck me as somehow distasteful.

Another problem was that my own costume—a short floral dress with bell-sleeves—had turned out much too revealing. I consoled myself that my legs would look longer and not as lumpy once I put on the roller skates.

Knowing we'd be drinking, we called a cab. Our daughters' screaming finally faded out of earshot as we shut the doors of the taxi.

"154 Meadow View, please," I told the cabbie, conscious of the cachet of that address. Just saying it made me feel more important and dignified than usual, though I would have been ashamed to admit it in public. I understood why Sofia and Ivan lived there: to appear to be well-healed and famous. They didn't have the millions they'd have needed to afford a house in the heart of this neighborhood, so they'd settled on the very edge, over a gully and with an expansive view of the busy road with its constant drone and exhaust fumes, directly below.

Their home was undoubtedly a mansion all the same. Maybe that's why their two sons never made an appearance at their parents' parties. Probably they were locked up in one of the many chambers of the family palace—perhaps in one of the several living rooms or down in the basement that had been converted into a cinema. Or maybe they just never made an appearance because they were teenagers. But there were times when one of them would creep soundlessly into the kitchen like a ghost and snatch something out of the fridge.

"Is that Mark?" Sofia would call out. The boys have English names, by the way. "No, I think it's George. George! Georgie! Georgay!" she'd bawl if she was already tipsy. But neither Mark nor Georgie ever even said hello.

Ivan's origins are from Rijeka, though he might be Serbian. Most probably he's mixed just like everyone else. He says he's "Yugoslav" and insists on speaking "our language" with us, even though Simon and I don't consider this language to be really ours. Sofia's origins, meanwhile, are more mysterious. She says she was born in Belgrade but she's definitely not from there. I know this because she can't speak "our language," and keeps switching to English, though she probably catches on when we're talking with Ivan, and I can tell she can understand what we're saying when Simon and I are having a conversation. Her favorite dish is a fried, oily, onion-laden minced-meat dish we call *kjofte* and she calls a meatball. She sometimes boasts of having an exotic past and of having resided in several Balkan cities. She might be a refugee—who knows.

One of her common complaints was: "I'm sick and tired of being asked where I'm from!" adding, "It's downright racist!"

"We're all from somewhere!" I heard her say once. Everyone around her nodded with compassion. "What's it to you where my accent's from anyhow?"

"But sometimes it's just a way for people get to know each other," I replied. "They learn things about each other's history, culture, stuff like that. Hardly a bad way to start a conversation, don't you think?"

This was something I confronted her about back then, though after several years living in England I must confess I've started leaning toward her opinion.

She'd looked straight through me, though, not even bothering to respond. The truth is, she'd only started giving me the time of day after it dawned on her I was Simon's wife. Also, ever since she found out I was a published author ("Literary theory! Sounds fancy!" she tittered) she hasn't turned her back on me quite so much.

We were going to be late for the party. I figured I was stalling because I secretly didn't want to go, and I was hoping maybe Simon didn't, either. But even after so many years spent living in England, it was on rare occasions that we were invited to socialize.

The last two theme parties Sofia and Ivan had hosted after moving to their castle had turned into fiascos.

The first was a "Famous Couples" party where we couldn't decide whether to go as Sonny and Cher or Bjorn and Agnetha, but finally went as the latter. The other two couples invited—I thought there'd be more of us—also showed up as Bjorn and Agnetha. So, there we were in the living room, listening to ABBA, chit-chatting in our ridiculous outfits, nibbling on tortilla chips and a selection of store-bought dips. Sofia had prepared her signature delicacy: the meatball. We toasted with the sangrias and margaritas that Ivan, a self-declared "cocktail master," would always make and then wait dog-like for a compliment every time we took a sip.

After getting himself thoroughly plastered, Ivan announced it was time for karaoke.

None of us were keen to sing, although Simon was tempted after Sofia insisted that my husband needed to "chillax" and that, besides, she wanted to see his "artistic side."

"What do you think? Should I sing?" he asked me, his eyes torn between panic and excitement.

"Do what you like," I replied, which clearly meant "no."

In the end Simon decided not to sing, so at least I won that battle. On the downside, though, Ivan immediately grabbed the microphone and wouldn't let go of it for half an hour, singing Sonny and Cher, Tina Turner, and ABBA tracks all the time, including two renditions each of "Mamma Mia" and "Take a Chance on Me." Sofia accompanied her husband for "Take a Chance on Me"—standing beside him on the "podium" in front of their enormous TV screen and jiggling her butt in an attempt to imitate the choreography from the video.

"We're so crazy!" she howled, panting as she took a seat after the track had finished and Ivan had gone to take a leak. "I'm just so nuts!" she kept on repeating, fanning her sweaty face with a napkin.

"We really *are* crazy!" we agreed, taking long sips of our margaritas, our foreheads gleaming under our cheap wigs.

Then there was their "Tropical Paradise" bash, which included the same two couples who had suffered through the "Famous Couples" party with us. The e-invite for the event, which was held in early July, was awash with images suggesting how we were supposed to dress: Bermuda shorts, Hawaiian shirts, and dresses with loud floral patterns.

On our arrival, Ivan and Sofia beckoned us into the garden and had us pass beneath an archway of flowers.

"Aloha!" Sofia repeated as she hung leis strung with plastic lilies around our necks. Then she placed a turquoise garland on my head that felt prickly on my scalp. All the women— there were six or seven couples present this time—were identically adorned. White paper lamps with flickering candles lay strewn across the lawn, with some dangling from branches. Soft music reminiscent of beaches and waves hummed and babbled in the background. If it hadn't been so cold and damp the atmosphere might almost have been pleasant, though there was that constant drone from the road to contend with, too. Again we were regaled with Ivan's famed margaritas and sangrias. We should have guessed that the same scenario would play out as soon as he'd got himself hammered. And sure enough, the music suddenly came to a stop, followed by loud crackles and spluttering sounds from the speakers as Ivan's voice blared, "One-two-one-two," testing the mic before announcing that the best part of the evening had finally arrived: the part where we were all going to sing karaoke.

"I'm going to sing something to get you all in the mood!" he boomed, turning on a once-famous YouTube track called "Over the Rainbow" sung, I think, by some fat guy from Hawaii who was now dead. To be fair, Ivan is not entirely unmusical in the sense of being tone-deaf or wildly off tune. He knows how to begin and end a musical phrase, by which I'm not saying you would revel in his performances—his bland and unsteady voice distorting the notes in cheap imitation—or that you could share in the all-too-obvious pleasure he got from parading his unwarranted confidence and boorish joie de vivre.

Sofia had herded us all toward the "stage," a clearing on the lawn marked out with paper lamps and bid us to stand there listening as Ivan sang his throat out. His second song was "Kokomo," which is when we slipped into a hesitant dance, with some of us taking our shoes off to do the twist on the wet grass as he moved on to "Surfin' USA." Though I was also getting down and trying hard to enjoy myself, I was soon overcome by a sudden sense of weariness and headed off for the table with the drinks and snacks. I dipped a chip into the guacamole. I gobbled it up and helped myself to another one. I gazed into the green goo as Ivan went on howling to the audience's woo-hoo's. The color and texture of the dip felt somehow soothing, while the crunching of the tortilla chips that reverberated in my skull calmed me down. I then observed an invisible object fall into the dip, pitting its surface. Rain, I realized, as another drop landed on my cheek.

Suddenly, like a hail of bullets the rain began pummeling the table. One by one the paper lamps went out, but the guests danced on, rallied by Sofia who kicked off her shoes and started spinning around on the wet grass, her face turned up to the sky.

"Freedom!" someone yelled into the silence that fell as Ivan began lugging the sound system out of the rain. A YouTube commercial briefly blasted on, followed by the George Michael song. My husband was among those dancing barefoot in the cold rain. "There's something deep inside me, there's someone else I've got to be!" he wailed, squatting slightly with his eyes closed in a dazed state of ecstasy I had never witnessed before. To my astonishment he whipped off his floral garland and started whirling it above his head. "Freedom! Freedom!" everyone sang in a trance-like state. A large drop of rain had gathered at the end of my nose, and when it dropped, I went into one of the empty living rooms and plopped down on a couch. The rain was now battering the windows, drowning the voices outside. But I didn't get to enjoy my solitude for long. In a minute or two the clatter of voices rose again, now entering the house. Soaking wet and clutching their drinks, the party-goers poured into the living room. Simon was among them, his floral shirt clinging to his body, outlining his man boobs.

"You're shaking!" he said, stroking my cheek with puppy eyes. "Let's go, sweetie."

We eventually managed to leave, though only after profuse apologies and protracted quibbling with Sofia and Ivan who were trying to persuade me to change into Sofia's dry clothes and take a nap in one of their guest rooms, under the assumption that the cold and the alcohol had gotten the better of me.

In the taxi we were silent. I gripped his hand and wouldn't let go.

Which is why I wasn't exactly enthusiastic as we headed

out to the "Boogie Nights" party they held at the end of that summer. We kept our wigs on in the cab, though we didn't really need to, and our palms grew sweatier and sweatier as we held hands. I so wanted to tell Simon that I really didn't feel like going, but I didn't say a thing. After all, it's not like we have that many friends in this city. It was, in fact, an attempt to make friends that first led to inviting Ivan and Sofia over for "coffee and dessert" a year or two back. I had made pancakes, of which Sofia consumed no less than five. All evening long she and Simon had jabbered on about their work. He professed great admiration for her research and her travels, and she, in turn, made no effort to hide her admiration from him. They had forged some kind of semi-amorous professional bond, leaving me as a spare wheel, just like poor Ivan, who was never very good at small talk.

When we arrived at the mansion the place was infused with the smell of Sofia's meatballs and the party was in full swing. The moment we laid eyes on Sofia we could tell she was already drunk, which is why she took the liberty of feigning anger and chiding Simon for being late—her way of claiming a special intimacy with my husband and advertising it to the world.

"Shame on you!" she scolded Simon at the door, playfully grabbing him by the elbow. "The party started an hour ago!"

She was wearing silver lipstick, silver knee-high boots, and a silver dress, probably in imitation of Elizabeth Hurley in Austin Powers, minus the gun. She'd gone to the hairdresser and had her hair professionally coiffed. I admit she looked quite good, as far as that went.

"Yes, we know, we know," I said, trying to insert myself between them, "we're so sorry!" But Sofia just looked straight through me as if I wasn't there.

"Wow, you've really made an effort, haven't you?" she cooed, stepping back to ogle my husband. "Let me have a good look at you!" she said, bunching her fingers together and lifting them to her silver lips, with a loud "Mwah!" She then ran a quick glance over my own outfit and acknowledged it with a thumbs up.

We headed toward the central living room on the ground floor of the mansion, in the direction of the sounds of 70s disco. About ten other guests were scattered around the room, talking in small groups and sipping the inevitable sangrias and margaritas. I recognized a few from the "Famous Couples" and "Tropical Paradise" parties.

A man with a thick black handlebar moustache and police shades with yellow mirror lenses suddenly appeared before us. He was dressed in a tight-fitting one-piece suit in a jarring shade of violet and was holding out two margaritas.

"Hello," I said.

"What! So now you don't even recognize me?" Ivan said in Serbian, spinning around and wiggling his butt obscenely. "*Dobro doshli!*" he said, welcoming us in "our language" and shoving the margaritas in our hands. Sofia beckoned over some guests who were standing at the other end of the room and weren't wearing costumes.

"Let me introduce you," Sofia said as soon as they approached. "This is Professor Rockland, an expert on the Neolithic Era. You must have heard of him."

We shook hands. I had no idea who he was, but my husband pretended he did.

"And this is the renowned historian Claire Jenkins," Sofia continued her introductions. "You surely know her, too."

"By all means. Pleased to meet you!" Simon said, nodding and grinning profusely, obviously forgetting his bare chest and white bodysuit.

"And this," Sofia continued, pushing Simon forward with a loving nudge on his back, "is Professor Simon Popov, one of Europe's leading entomologists."

Rockland and Jenkins nodded appreciatively.

"Oh and this here is Biljana," Sofia added, gesturing at me, "Simon's wife. She makes the most extraordinary pancakes!"

The heavy silence that fell in the wake of this introduction was mercifully short-lived, thanks to Simon, who intervened in a chivalrous but deferential manner.

"Oh, Sofia!" he laughed, "Still envious of her cooking?"

"Oops that reminds me!" Sofia started, having clearly forgotten what she had said. "My dish is on the stove! I'll leave you all to get to know each other," she said, walking off toward the kitchen with the overly cautious gait of a person who is drunk but pretending to be sober.

"I'll come with you," I offered, though I wasn't exactly sure why I did at first.

But I soon realized that I wanted to be with her so I could *do* something to her. I wanted to be there when she took those ugly burnt blobs of mincemeat out of the greasy frying pan. I wanted to do something just a tiny bit hurtful if I could, or at least hope she would get oil on her dress or stink up her hair.

As I followed Sofia I overheard Simon trying to do me justice in front of the renowned scholars. "My wife is actually a published author. Literary theory, T.S Eliot and stuff . . ."

Catching up with Sofia at the kitchen door I heard her let slip a typical Macedonian exclamation: "*Lele!*" She was looking at the stove. "Shut the door!" she ordered me, switching quickly to English.

Although the balcony door was open and the ventilation fan over the stove was roaring on full steam, the huge kitchen still reeked of fried onions and hot sunflower oil.

"They're a little burnt, but it's not too bad," Sofia murmured to herself, tipping the meatballs into a large glass bowl that instantly steamed up.

"Mmm! Smells like home!" I said in Macedonian.

Now that she's drunk and feeling sentimental, I thought,

I might finally get the truth out of her, especially if I played the female solidarity card.

"Eh?" she said.

"You understand me?" I continued, again in Macedonian

"Of course! I understand *all* Balkan languages," she replied at once, obviously lying, "though I haven't spoken any for so long now that I really don't want to. English is my language now."

"But you had another language before," I insisted, approaching the meatballs. "*Imash viljushka?*" I asked her, testing if she knew the Macedonian for fork.

Sofia tilted her head in a way that could have meant either yes or no or both and then opened one of the cutlery drawers. To my great disappointment, however, Julia burst into the kitchen at just that moment. I say burst in because she careered through the door on roller skates, which made me feel worse for not having put on my own.

"Shut the door!" Sofia yelled, gesticulating wildly as Julia glided past us, circling the kitchen counter before making her way back to close the door. She slammed it shut with an elegant swipe of her arm and then swung round to halt theatrically in front of us with her chin jutting in the air.

"I'm famished!" she said in her sexy accent, "And this place smells like food!"

Julia is a doctor from I can't remember which Latin American country. For years now she's lived in England with her British husband who works for Ivan's dental implant company. She's one of those people whose origins I never inquired into, as she's never once mentioned where she's from or talked about what she did before she made it to England.

She was wearing a short, brick-red colored dress with a plunging neckline that revealed her pushed-up breasts. Julia is naturally tall, but in the roller skates she positively towered over us, making me feel fat and dumpy like one of Sofia's meatballs.

"I was just about to start serving them," Sofia said gleefully. "They were supposed to be ready before you arrived, but stupid me! I forgot to defrost the mincemeat. And then on top of everything else I had to drive Georgie to his tennis lesson."

"Frozen meat?" I said, grasping desperately at an opportunity to needle her.

"Yes, it makes things easier because the recipe for these meatballs is actually quite complicated," she explained, now laying out cubes of fluffy white bread to skewer with the burnt lumps of greasy meat. I inspected the meatballs. Their preparation could hardly have required any actual culinary skills. A bit of meat, a lot of bread, some eggs and a liberal sprinkling of *Vegeta* seasoning. I've always maintained that *Vegeta* was her secret ingredient, or some other cheap salty seasoning they sell in the worst Balkan supermarket chains. Whatever the case, it's disgusting.

"I just can't help myself!" Julia exclaimed, again inadvertently thwarting my plan to bring Sofia down a peg or two. She glided over to the meatballs, grabbed one of the hot blobs with her fingers and took a bite. "Ouch!" she screamed, and started hyperventilating to cool her mouth as wisps of steam curled up from the meatball she still held in her hand.

"Serves you right!" Sofia crowed, unable to contain her pleasure. Then suddenly her eyes darted over our shoulders. "It's Georgie!" she cried, "There he is! Look!"

From a door at the far end of the kitchen, from somewhere deep within the labyrinth of Sofia and Ivan's mansion, emerged the figure of Georgie, who had, until now, been hardly more than an apparition. From his expression you could tell he wasn't keen to approach us, but it was also clear that something was compelling him forward. He was the very picture of an ungainly adolescent, the living cliché of a chubby, daft, and spoilt teenager. His evident indolence was matched only by his insolence. To his mother's squeals of joy and her invitation to introduce himself he barely acknowledged us with a grunt before heading straight for the refrigerator.

"Are you hungry?" his mother asked with a desperate eagerness. "I made meatballs!"

Georgie ignored her. We watched him take out a plastic container of chocolate milk and begin to chug it. The cold light from the open fridge illuminated his protruding belly.

"Honey, be careful!" cried Sofia, "You'll ruin your shirt!" just as a trickle of chocolate milk dribbling down his chin, seeping into the fabric of his white top adorned with golden motifs.

"Oh, for god's sake!" Sofia cried, holding her head in her hands, her elbows on the counter. "Your goddamn shirt!"

Georgie turned for a second before plodding off with the bottle in his hand, which afforded me a glimpse of the front of his gaudy shirt on which, in large golden letters against a white background, the word VERSACE was surrounded by swirly golden patterns. As he turned his back to leave, I saw the other side: an enormous golden head of Medusa glaring at us.

The boy slunk off into the dark depths of the expansive kitchen, his bare white feet bulging out from his slippers, round and fleshy like an overgrown child's. The golden Medusa vanished around a corner in the distance along with Georgie.

Sofia was still clasping her head in her hands. "We got him that shirt in Milan," she moaned, "*Milan!* And you know they didn't even want to go with us! Neither Georgie nor his brother. Can you believe that? Turning down a shopping trip to Milan?"

Julia shook her head in sympathy.

"For the life of me, I can't get them to leave their rooms," Sofia continued complaining. "They've got PlayStations and iPads up there and some kind of really superfast computers . . . If a bomb fell outside, they wouldn't know, playing in their rooms day and night."

"That's what kids are like nowadays." Julia announced. "Technology's ruined them," she added, picking up a bit of the meatball that had cooled off.

"They also lack basic manners," I chipped in.

"Oh no, it's not that," Sofia quickly objected. "They go to the top private schools, you know. The problem is when you provide all this . . . this stuff," she said, throwing her hands up as if to indicate the enormous house and everything in it. "That's when they become unmanageable. That's the basic paradox of parenthood. You do everything you can for them, and it ends up destroying them. And it's always your fault, of course," Sofia said, putting on a face of a martyr. "As a matter of fact, it was Georgie who ruined my entire holiday."

At this point I noticed she had a slight tan. She had been on holiday, of course. Hence the silver boots and lipstick and dress. She was probably waiting for me to notice and to ask her where she had gotten that great tan, but I wasn't going to give her the satisfaction.

"We were in Capri, you know?" she offered me a look, acknowledging me. "Simon must've told you we bought an apartment there this summer?"

"No, he didn't mention anything," I lied.

"Oh, that's strange," she muttered. "But you've heard us talk about wanting to buy property there. You know us and our obsession with Italy! The cradle of modern civilization! The nectar of the Gods!" she exclaimed, trying to insert some poetry into her bragging. "We got ourselves a little apartment there so we can go on summer getaways with the kids," she went on, "You know, sailing, yachting—it would be nice to get a yacht someday but we're in no hurry . . . In short," she cut herself off, indicating this would be a lengthy anecdote, "Georgie is mad at me because of an incident in Capri."

Sofia stood up, as if she was going to give a performance, straightening her back and looking up at the ceiling with a look of distress. From the very beginning of her story, she hinted at how it would conclude. She said she'd tried to explain to Georgie that what had happened was his fault and his fault alone. She said she'd tried to make him understand he could learn a "life lesson" from the incident. "Life is not a bed of roses," she added, probably under the illusion that spouting clichés made her sound like a native speaker, despite the fact that her every attempt to mimic Received Pronunciation was marred by "v"s that should have been "w"s and the reverse, and that her plain vowels and explosive consonants were thoroughly Slavic. Georgie, she continued, had simply taken the "thorny path" in learning the truth about the cruelty of life, a truth Sofia had learnt to accept from a very early age—"unlike Ivan," she added, guzzling her margarita.

In the brief but heavy silence that followed, I prayed her confession would turn into one of those deliciously intimate moments when the wife attacks her husband and maybe even her son.

"Still," Sofia sighed. "He did end up in hospital."

"Who did?" I asked, perching myself on one of the high barstools. She had my full attention.

"The *hospital?* Who?" Julia asked, pulling a chair up herself. Seated, she was considerably less intimidating.

"Georgie," Sofia answered.

"Wait!" interrupted Julia, "Before you go on, I'm going to get more margaritas. Don't start without me!" she repeated and skated out of the kitchen.

"Should we get the meatballs ready?" I suggested, anxious to find a way to pass the time until Julia and the drinks arrived.

Sofia agreed, and I gulped down the last of my margarita. I was becoming dizzy with a feeling of mild enchantment and sweet uncertainty at the prospect of something exciting about to happen. Entirely forgetting that I had intended to offend her, I joined Sofia in skewering the fat greasy meatballs and clumps of bread.

"I've also got some *tarator*," she said, looking distracted. The word slipped out with a Slavic rolling "r."

But then Julia rolled back in with the three drinks pinned against her breasts. We applauded her dexterity and elegance. Then we clinked our glasses and turned to hear Sofia's story.

"It's not like we had the money to buy the apartment outright," she resumed. "There were so many things we had to sacrifice in the meantime. The most precious, though, was our free time," she explained.

"That's so true," Julia said. "There's nothing more precious than free time. Except, perhaps, silence?" she suggested with an upward gaze that looked as if she had been struck by a sense of wonder.

"That's right,' Sofia tentatively agreed. "But we were desperate to escape this miserable wet weather. It just clashes with our natural energy. We do have southern blood, after all."

"You can say that again," Julia chimed.

Someone turned the music up in the living room as the opening bars of "Staying Alive" came blaring in.

"We simply had to!" Sofia continued, ignoring the music. "We had to have a different environment to live in where our bodies would feel healthy and natural—somewhere where the water we *intentionally* put on our skin would *unintentionally* evaporate."

Sofia paused to see whether we had understood her. It was typical of her to toss in some enigmatic statement she thought sounded intelligent and poetic, and then sit back to enjoy our befuddlement.

"I mean I want to bathe in the sea and have the sun dry my skin," she explained with obvious pride and pleasure.

"Oh!" Julia said, nodding.

"So, we tightened our purse strings and got ourselves a cute little place in Capri," she said, suddenly studying her manicured nails.

I wished I had had the nerve to say how I felt about her "tightening her purse strings to get something cute and little in Capri," but I didn't. Sofia went on with her story.

"We mainly got the place so we could do water sports," she continued. "Mark and Georgie both take swimming lessons at school, you see, though they're more into tennis. But do you know what they're into playing most?" she asked, not expecting an answer, "Computer games! Ha ha ha!"

"Ha ha ha!" Julia laughed back, and so did I.

"And then, as I said, we're also saving up for a yacht, so we wanted to learn how to sail. Which is why we rented a yacht and a skipper. You know, a bareboat?" she said, but the word that meant nothing to me.

"I don't know if either of you have ever been on a yacht," Sofia looked me knowingly in the eye.

Julia replied, "Of course," but, again, I said nothing.

"Once you get a taste of it there's simply no going back!" Sofia enthused. "A house on the waves!" she added, in another effusive burst of poetry.

I remembered the time Simon and I had taken a speedboat from Split to Korchula. The sea had been rough and we'd almost puked our guts out. I thought, the last thing in the world I would ever want to live in is a "house on the waves."

"You two will have to join us! We're thinking of buying it next year, you know. Ivan's taking a skipper course and applying for his captain's license."

As she looked at me, I sensed Sofia had interpreted my silence to mean that I had never been on a yacht, which was, indeed, correct. I had only seen yachts polluting the little bays where we swam on our summer holidays in Greece.

"We were also thinking of buying a yacht," Julia said, "But then we remembered how Beyoncé and Jay Z had decided to rent. It's so much simpler that way."

"Oh, I *do* know what you mean," Sofia said, "but I live with a Moby Dick, you get my drift? He likes to think of himself as a sailor!" She cocked her chin in the direction of the living room where Ivan's voice was turning the refrain of "Staying Alive" into a whiney faltering falsetto.

I was about to comment on Sofia's reference to *Moby-Dick* when Julia cut me off. "And then what happened? Did you have an accident?"

"Yes, in a way," Sofia sighed.

"And?" I urged her on, hoping I would get a kick out of her misfortune.

"Everything was so wonderful—so idyllic!" she began. "Ivan was on the upper deck with the skipper. I was sunbathing on the main deck. Lunch was on its way . . . We'd hired a yacht with a chef, you know?" she said, addressing Julia, who raised her eyebrows as if to say this was only to be expected. "But who appreciates the value of these things? My kids? No way! Downstairs *all day long* playing on their tablets, phones or whatever else they have. But look—I'm sure you'll agree with me—it's the older sibling who's always more to blame. Am I wrong?"

I thought of my own younger sister. Once I climbed up a tree and she followed, always copying every step of mine. So

I pushed her off, as if by accident. She fell and broke her arm. Our parents blamed me anyway for not keeping an eye on her. Either way, it made no difference: it was always my fault.

"Not so sure I'd agree with you there," I said.

"Oh, no! You're absolutely right, Sofia," Julia spoke over me. "It's the older children who set the example," she added, pleased with her platitude.

"Well, of course! I mean if the older one's playing video games all day, then what's the younger one going to do? The same," Sofia went on. "Sometimes they play together, it's true. But Georgie shows *no* initiative whatsoever, no desire to do anything except play games and eat chocolate. So you can imagine my excitement and joy on seeing him actually come out of the cabin and ask if we could stop at a resort nearby to see a friend from school. Maybe you know it? The Imperial," she said, looking at Julia, "the private club, with a private beach?"

"Oh, I've been there," Julia cooed, "It's incredible!"

"So you know then." Sofia said, sipping from her drink. "That's where Elton was, Georgie's friend. Elton is Gordon Lawrence's son. You know him? The banker?"

"Yes, of course," said Julia, "his wife owns a gallery."

"Exactly. So, anyway, then Georgie started whining about going to see Elton . . . and really, he doesn't have many friends," Sofia continued. "You know what young kids are like today . . . Ivan and I were over the moon, but there was no way we could just sail into a private resort. We weren't even allowed to anchor the yacht in the bay, and if we went by foot we would've had to climb up a dirt track for several kilometers in the heat. No way! So we anchored as close as we could and thought 'Well, okay, we can just swim there!' I'm in terrific shape, obviously, and Georgie takes swimming lessons, so the coast didn't seem too far away for him."

In the living room Ivan was now amusing his guests with his rendition of "How Deep is Your Love."

"Oh, I'm missing all my favorite songs!" Sofia exclaimed. "But let me just wrap this story up," she said, taking another sip of her margarita. "We swam for about fifteen minutes. I was way ahead of Georgie by then because he'd dithered around for so long at the beginning, lagging behind and fidgeting with his phone pouch. He kept whining about being tired and it had really begun to get on my nerves. 'Tired? I'm the one who's swimming because of you!' I told him. So, I swam on ahead to motivate him. And then suddenly from way behind there was this terrible screaming and splashing . . . It makes my blood freeze just to think about it! 'But I have to keep calm,' I told myself, 'I have to stay rational.'" Sofia's eyes closed as she recalled the horror, pausing for effect.

"A shark?" Julia said, articulating the first thing that had come to our minds.

"Medusas!" Sofia said, "A whole flock of medusas!"

"Jellyfish," I said, pleased with myself for being able to correct her English. "What you mean is a swarm of jellyfish." But then I remembered to offer some sympathy. "Oh, how terrible!" I added.

"A whole flock! A whole flock of jellyfish crossed Georgie's path!" Sofia said, ignoring half of my correction. "They stung his entire body. He told me later how he'd suddenly felt something cold and soft touching his skin here and there, and then a terrible burning sensation all over. He was thrashing around and screaming in panic. By the time I reached him the medusas had gone. Nothing. As if he made them up!"

"You didn't have a single close encounter?" I asked, hoping she had gotten at least a few well-earned stings.

"Not one! Oh, but Georgie! Oh, how he screamed and moaned!" she covered her face with her hands.

"How terrible!" said Julia, sighing in sympathy.

I sighed along too, half-reluctantly.

"Yes, terrible." Sofia repeated. "But the most terrible part of all came as we were reaching the shore. Georgie was bawling like a baby, wailing like a siren!" she cried, as if the memory amused her. "And the closer we got to the shore, the louder he howled—even louder when he realized he had lost his phone pouch. And you know I *told* him not to play around with it. Anyway, we got to the beach, and he just stayed there plopped in the shallow water. The jellyfish had got him really bad, and there was no one to help us, of course, because we didn't have a phone. Such a mess . . ."

A clear image came to me of Sofia out of breath, slouched ankle-deep in the water, wagging a finger and screaming at her child: "I fucking told you not to play around with your phone pouch!" The beachgoers all staring at them. Georgie sitting slumped in the shallows, like a beached baby whale, crying inconsolably, his skin purplish and swollen from the jellyfish, his drooling mouth twisted into a crooked *O*. "I told you! I told you!" Sofia is yelling in Macedonian, Bulgarian, Bosnian or whatever.

"Couldn't you call security and ask for a doctor?" Julia asked, sounding reasonable.

"Security?" Sofia scoffed. "The guards from The Imperial ordered us to leave the resort immediately. Three big guys in black, all muscle. One of them wanted to drag me out of the water and physically remove us from the resort. Can you imagine me walking down that beach with this snotty screaming brat? Can you imagine the police escorting me to my husband? No way!" she said, rolling her eyes.

"Where were Elton's parents? . . . Gordon Lawrence and his wife?" Julia continued.

"I don't know," Sofia shrugged. "A lot of people had left the beach by then. I had no intention of asking for help once I realized what was going on. It's not like we're crazy. It's not like we're refugees!" she cried. "So I dove back into the water and

told Georgie to swim after me. There was no other option—
we just had to swim our way back. Of course, he bawled the
whole way back, but then again he was asking for it!" Sofia
finished her story with a triumphant grin.

"What happened next?" Julia asked.

"Nothing," Sofia replied. "We went to the hospital, and
they gave us some ointment. I'm telling you, the jellyfish got
him good. And then we punished him for putting us through
all that trouble and for losing his expensive phone."

"What was the punishment?" I asked.

"Well, he's going to have to wait two weeks before he can
have a new phone for a start," she said. "Plus, I'm never taking
him shopping ever again. Designer clothing? You saw him just
now. He doesn't appreciate the value of things."

Ivan's sharp falsetto wailed from the living room: "Girl,
I've known you very well, I've seen you growing every day,
I've never really looked before, but now you take my breath
away . . ."

"I'm missing out on all the best songs! Let's go!" Sofia
exclaimed, downing her drink and grabbing the tray with
the meatballs.

"Wait!" I called out. "Look!"

There, in the half-lit hallway leading to the kitchen sat
Georgie like an apparition, cross-legged and hunched over
something in his hands. The golden patterns on his shirt glis-
tened in the near darkness, his face obscured by shadows.

"She's lying," Georgie's voice echoed, deep and prophet-like.

"Excuse me?" Sofia said, laying the tray back down on the
counter, as if getting ready for a fight.

"It was Mother who wanted to swim to the shore," Georgie
said in the same oracular voice.

"What did you say?" Sofia's body assumed the position of
a fighter. "It was *me* who wanted *what*?" she raised her voice,

but then checked herself and turned to us with a forced smile. "That's simply not true," she said, addressing us.

"It *is* true," Georgie insisted, stepping out closer to us and into the light. Brown smudges stained the corners of his mouth. The object he held in his hand was a plastic cup of chocolate pudding of the cheapest, most artificial kind. The container was open, and he had no spoon.

"No, it is *not* true!" Sofia retorted, her own voice deeper now.

"It *is* true!" Georgie squeaked. "Just go on and ask her why she'd put on her *special* swimsuit," he blurted in a mocking tone, staring at me. Yes, it was definitely me he was addressing. Which finally made me feel bad for having such a low opinion about the child.

"Ha ha ha!" Sofia made the sounds. "What's that got to do with anything?"

"You're lying to them!" said Georgie. His lips were quivering and, in his desperation, to stop himself from crying his chin had puckered into a wrinkled angry blob. "You're lying that I cried," he protested, "and that's not how it was at the end, either," he whimpered, his voice breaking. I knew I should feel sorry for him. It wasn't his fault that he was Sofia's son. And Ivan's, too.

"You're crying again right now!" his mother snapped. All the time she kept glancing at me and Julia as if she were seeking our approval for her parenting skills.

"I'm *not* crying!" Georgie yelled in a throaty voice, his eyes red. "It was *me* who jumped into the water first. And I swam faster than you! Why don't you tell them that?"

"I have absolutely no idea what you're talking about," Sofia said, her face completely motionless.

"Elton's parents were right there," Georgie insisted, "and you were screaming at me in that stupid language of yours. Everyone was staring at us!" he shouted. "It was so embarrassing!"

Georgie kept looking at me as if he were pleading for justice. Maybe the poor creature recognized that he had an accomplice—someone to hate his mother with.

"Mother—mother was holding the policeman's hand!" he said, his voice cracking and his eyes wide, desperately seeking my approval.

"Policeman?" Sofia asked, her eyes full of disdain. "What are you talking about?" She turned to us. "You see now how he's making this up?"

Sofia was directing all her attention to me now, too. Not just her gaze but her whole body turned toward me. All of a sudden, I was important. They needed to prove something to me, while Julia just towered between us like an exotic plant.

"The man who tried to get us off the beach," Georgie explained. "The guard or whatever. You came to him and took him by the hand!" Georgie blurted, barely able to finish his sentence.

Sofia looked at me with eyes that said, "This kid has no idea what he's talking about."

"I'd rather *drown* than be seen with you!" Georgie shouted.

"So why did you come with me then, huh?" Sofia yelled back.

"I didn't!" Georgie protested, shouting even louder now. "I was trying to get away from you!"

Georgie let the box of pudding splatter on the floor. He turned and scuttled back into the shadows from which he had emerged, only to trip over the rug and lose one of his slippers. I watched as he clambered back up, grab the slipper and scamper down the hall like a baby elephant until he disappeared around a corner.

"More than a woman . . . More than a woman to me!" Ivan

wailed in the living room.

"Go ahead and run!" Sofia screamed after him. "Run away, you ungrateful little piece of shit! Just you watch me ground you for another two weeks!" she roared. "I'll make you live with your grandparents! That'll teach you what *real* life is!"

The sound of Georgie's flat feet on the floor and the cries of his despair were drowned out by the karaoke machine and the rhythmic clapping of the guests in the living room.

"You see what a spoilt little brat he is!" Sofia panted, looking at us with googly eyes.

Well, this is exactly what I came here to see, I thought to myself. But I waited to feel some kind of pleasure, and felt nothing.

"It's so hard to teach children respect nowadays," Julia babbled, trying to change the topic. "Technology has ruined them, you know."

"It's the genes as well," Sofia stated, her eyes closed as she focused on calming down her breathing. "There's no such thing as easy parenting. This is nothing to get too worked up over," she said, taking deep breaths through her nose and exhaling through her mouth.

"What was that thing with the bathing suit all about?" I asked.

Sofia perked up. "I don't know," she said. "Maybe Georgie's jealous—just like his father?" she said, smiling coyly and reaching into her right pocket to take out her phone. "I just have to show you this!" Sofia almost squealed with glee. "We have a recreation room downstairs with a jacuzzi and a sauna. I hired a personal trainer who comes round four times a week. Just look at me in these pictures!"

Sofia turned the phone screen toward us and our heads leaned together to look.

Ivan is sitting on a white leather sofa, dressed completely

in white. One hand cradles a glass of a brownish spirit while the other is caressing Sofia's tanned thighs as she stands beside him in a black one-piece bathing suit with golden stripes. She is wearing a pair of enormous rectangular sunglasses and her freshly washed hair is being gently swept by a Mediterranean breeze. Her swimsuit has two large oval gaps on each side of her waist, with golden discs glistening on her hips. A third gap at the center of her bust lewdly exposes her cleavage. Her tan shimmers like bronze—the color of Ivan's face and hair. She's pouting like a teenager, and has tucked her belly in for the shot.

"Wow! Is that Versace, too?" Julia gushed.

"You bet!" Sofia said, swiping through reams of other photos of herself in her golden swimwear, posing in every possible angle of the yacht.

"Wait!" I said, "Go back a sec!" I stopped her when she started racing through the photos.

"This one?" she asked. "This one was taken just before the accident. It's me and Georgie. I hate this picture of me."

The two of them, mother and son, are standing at the helm. Sofia has her arm around Georgie. She is smiling, but the angle of the light has flattened her nose and hair. And because she clearly wasn't posing, you could see what her body really looked like. It is neither remarkable nor unremarkable, embellished in the gaudy colors of the swimsuit tinted a Mediterranean blue that seemed slightly ominous. Georgie stood beside her, a sweaty, squinting child in blue shorts crumpled up between his chunky thighs, his fat little boobs drooping, his shoulders slouched and his belly sticking out. His mouth hangs slightly open, and his gaze is murky and muddled.

"Oh my God, listen!" Sofia cried out, yanking her phone from under our noses. The opening piano chords from "Imagine" echoed from the living room. "Come on, let's go sing!" she chirped, shoving her phone in her pocket, and picking up the tray of meatballs again.

"Sounds good to me—I could do with another drink!" Julia said, skating on ahead to hold the door open as Sofia as she made a dramatic entrance into the living room.

Ivan was just about to begin the opening line. Simon, my husband, stood behind one of the sofas, a glass of sangria in one hand and the other waving a lighter in the air. His eyes were closed.

Sofia placed the tray on a table, approached her husband and stood beside him. They sang into the same microphone, a silver and violet couple taking turns singing a verse. The audience took pictures and videos, woo-hooing now and then.

Simon's face glowed as he slowly swung his hips in his tight one-piece costume. I came up close to him and whispered in his ear that I was feeling sick. I asked him to leave right away without saying goodbye so we would be spared all the why-don't-you-stay-little-longers and how-come-you're-leaving-so-earlys and just call a cab when we got outside.

Out in the cold damp air, my husband held me close to his chest and stroked my hair. I lied and said that I had simply had too much to drink. Then I told him that I wasn't really sure I liked those people.

"But those are our friends," he said, gently pulling me closer. "Isn't it nice that we have friends?"

Stepping into the house, I felt a strong urge to hold my daughters. When we were little, my sister and I shared a room and at one time even shared a bed. Every night my mother would slip between the sheets and cuddle us, stroking our hair and cheeks with the tips of her silky fingers. Sometime my father squeezed in with us, too.

I tiptoed into my younger daughter's bed first and held

her. Then I snuck into my eldest's room and lay there with her, feeling her soft steady breath on my neck. In the warm darkness, I decided it was time to call my sister. I dialed her number and let the phone ring for the longest time, but she didn't answer. It was late, so I guess she must have been asleep.

CHEROKEE RED

As they got off the airplane, a hot wave of air hit Matej and his mother Beti in the face like a blast from a blow-dryer. "Oh my, we're in the desert now," she said. Matej couldn't believe such heat existed, especially after they stepped into the cold, carpeted terminal, where the boy saw that many people were sitting on the floor. As he and his mother waited for the black rubber drapes to spit their heavy suitcases out onto the moving track, he too sat down on the floor. "Get up off there, it's dirty!" his mother snapped, turning for a second from her phone. He reluctantly got up and stood slouching until the large metal machine jolted into motion with a buzz. When their bags appeared, he helped her wrestle them onto their cart, the whole time asking, "Where's dad?" Beti would absent-mindedly reply, "He's probably here somewhere", or "He'll be here any minute", or "He's picking us up."

It had been more than a year since Vlado—"Here they call me Vlad," his father had told Matej over Skype—moved to Phoenix, Arizona. Matej was proud his father lived in America and had bragged about moving to the great envy of his class-mates. At school he would wear T-shirts and hoodies blazoned with the American flag and "Phoenix Suns" that his dad had sent him along with candy you couldn't get in Macedonia. When his parents and relatives had first talked about their moving to America, Matej had been struck by the repeated use of the phrase "take in," which he came to understand meant that his father had to go first and get settled before he could bring the rest of them over. "Get out as fast as you can," all their relatives would say, as if the country were on the brink of disaster, but only his grandparents and an aunt came to the airport to see them off. They sat there crying, and when it was time to board, they wiped their tears and stroked his cheek with their wet hands. They took him tightly in their arms, scratching his face with their zippers and buttons.

Matej heard a flurry of muffled footfalls and felt someone lift him off the ground and squeeze him tight. If it weren't for the voice, he wouldn't have known it was his father. He didn't smell like his usual self, but like fried food. His mother fidgeted excitedly as she waited for Vlado to put Matej down. His parents embraced in a way he had never seen them embrace before. They were pressed tightly against each other and their kiss was long, wet, and silent. The image of a slug popped into Matej's head and he turned away.

The same hot blow-dryer air hit them when they stepped out of the terminal building into the night. "I told you it was hot!" Vlado said, leading the way through the multi-story parking garage, "but you'll get used to it." Matej gawked at the lines of clean shiny cars that were so much bigger than the ones back home. Vlado stopped behind a beat-up old automobile painted gold. "This is us," he said, manually opening the driver's door with a key. He reached across to pop the passenger door open, did the same to the back door on the passenger's side, then vigorously rolled down all the windows. "Ford," Matej said to himself as he read the logo above the trunk. His father came around to load the suitcases. "It's a little screwed up," he said as he struggled to get the trunk open.

"The air-conditioning isn't working," Vlado said as they

emerged from the parking garage. "It's too expensive to get it fixed, and money's going to be tight until you get a job," he said, turning to Beti. Matej leaned his cheek against the window frame and let the warm air pummel his face and roar in his ears. His parents' conversation waned to a murmur. "Look! A cactus!" he cried out as they drove by a tall, two-armed saguaro, but Vlado and Beti apparently didn't hear him. Matej saw many more saguaros pass by. In the dark, from this distance, they looked like shadowy people frozen with fright. Matej recalled the streaming rivers of glowing lights he had seen from the airplane window as they were landing and of which he was now a part: a bloodstream of cars running over the black earth. Little white phosphorescent dashes separated the highway lanes, and each time Vlado passed a car ahead, the tires went *tup-tup, tup-tup*. Now and again they saw a brightly-lit billboard, or a block of buildings filled with fast food restaurants illuminated by towering neon signs. "Now we're entering the city, and then we'll get to our neighbor-hood," Vlado said, waking Matej from the sleep he was drift-ing into. The streets were wide and empty. There were no people. Everyone was locked inside their car, mostly alone, one hand on the wheel, their eyes fixed dully ahead. "They have great Chinese food here," Vlado said as they drove by a block of identical-looking buildings, "and cheese just like ours," he added as they passed what he said was called a "strip mall." "And this is where I get my hair cut," he said, as they rolled by an empty carwash. "We're almost home."

There was a pool—that's what Vlado had told him over the phone. "But then, everyone has a pool here," he added, and then corrected himself, saying "well, most everyone, anyway." Matej begged his father to show him pictures of the pool, but Vlado would always say he was too tired to leave the apart-ment or that it was too hot outside. They drove through the darkened neighborhood, the only sound the clicking of the turn signal. All around them stood the shadows of low houses, palms, cacti, and the leafy crowns of trees. "We're here," Vlado said, as the car rumbled to a stop in a sprawling parking lot bordered by a wall the height of a grown man. A path ran from the parking lot toward several two-story building blocks whose ground floors were lower than the street and lit up by lighted windows or lamps above the entryways. Between the street and one of the apartment blocks a patch of blue rippled in the night. "The pool!" Matej cried. "Be patient," Beti said, "there's time for everything."

"It's closed after ten anyway," Vlado added. On the iron fence that enclosed the pool was a large sign written in red:

POOL HOURS: 8 AM - 10 PM
NO UNACCOMPANIED CHILDREN BELOW THE
AGE OF 12 ALLOWED
NO SMOKING
NO DRINKING
NO DIVING

"It's really nice at night," Vlado said, dragging the suitcases down stairs leading to what appeared to be a basement but which his father said Americans called a "garden apartment." "We'll take a long walk tomorrow," he said, unlocking the front door. Matej caught a whiff of carpet and air-conditioning, which reminded him of the airport. His father flicked a switch and a ceiling light came on, revealing a couch and armchair that didn't match, a coffee table with a TV even smaller than the one they had had at home, and two table lamps placed on the floor because there wasn't anything to put them on. To turn the lamps on, you had to wrench a black, ragged switch hidden under an old-fashioned lampshade. The bare walls were the color of egg yolk.

"A dining space," Beti exclaimed as she caressed the top of

a small, round table ringed with three tattered chairs. "Where do I turn on the light?" she said. Vlado showed her the tooth-shaped switch next to the buzzing refrigerator. "Hey," she said, turning to the stove, "look at those burners!" They were coiled. Beti turned one on. They watched as it slowly burned into a glowing orange.

"Hey, what are we doing?" Vlado said. "You haven't seen the bedroom, or your room, Matej," he said, ruffling the boy's hair. His room was the first door down the hallway. It too was bare save for a window covered with venetian blinds and what looked like a hospital bed with white sheets and covers and a bed-stand with a beat-up lamp like the ones in the living room. "Don't worry," Beti said, rubbing Matej's back when she saw his disappointment, "We'll decorate it. And look! There's a built-in closet for all your things." Vlado opened a sliding door to reveal a space in the wall behind it. "How practical! How spacious! Do we have one too?" Beti asked. Vlado nodded. "Look, it's like a little house," she said, hunching down inside. "You can hide from us in there," Vlado added.

Their bedroom was equally bare—only a king-sized bed and a pair of bedside tables. Beti was in awe of the walk-in closet and of the bed. "It's so high and wide!" she said, throwing herself on it. Vlado stood tall, grabbed a wooden bedpost at the foot of the bed and shook it. "It's sturdy, see, it won't creak," he said with a knowing smile. Beti blushed. Matej looked away.

There was only the bathroom left to see. Matej was amazed by how big the toilet bowl was and how much water it held. The showerhead was odd too—a sprinkler fixed high up on the wall. "Look at that weird faucet!" Beti exclaimed. "Wait, wait," Vlado said, reaching over her. Matej saw his father gliding his hand down his mother's behind. There was a sharp clink and water began gushing into the tub.

That night and many nights that followed, Matej dreamt he wasn't asleep. The streetlight in the alley behind his room streaked shadows across the wall. He could hear strangers walking by above his head, their footfalls and voices seeming dangerously close. No cars or rustling leaves broke the silence. His bed creaked every time he turned. Although his father had bragged about the sturdiness of their king-size bed, Matej could hear the squeaking of its springs and the *tup-tup* of the wooden headboard thumping against the hollow wall. Now and then his mother would softly moan and sigh as if something was deeply hurting, as if she were dying.

Matej suddenly found himself awake, surprised that he had slept. He could tell it was day from the light streaming through the blinds. He stepped barefoot into the new, empty hall, then slowly ventured into the living room, half-lit from the morning sun striking the flowery armchair by the window. His mother was down on her knees unpacking. "Hello, darling," she said as she got up to give him a hug. She smelled like home. The same fragrance rose from the suitcases. "Let me get you some chocolate milk," she said, "I brought your favorite mug." It was one his father had sent him, with a black scorpion on one side and "Arizona" in capital letters on the other.

Matej was disappointed they had to wait all day for his father to come home from work before they could go to the pool. His mother couldn't find the key to the iron fence with the red-letter warning sign. "It's 42 degrees outside," Beti said to Matej. "It would be crazy to check out the neighborhood now." She spoke as if she were convincing herself, since Matej hadn't insisted on going out. He only wanted to go to the pool. "We'll take a walk in the evening," she said more than once.

As Beti unpacked and made a feeble effort to decorate the apartment with the things she had brought from home, Matej watched TV. "We need a little table here," she murmured to herself. "And maybe a plant," but then she sighed, "yeah right, as if they'd survive without light." She started scribbling a list on a scrap of paper, repeating each word under her breath: "Hangers . . . *Domestos* . . . toilet paper . . . paprika . . ." Plopped on the carpet, Matej scrolled through the channels but couldn't find anything worth watching. They had no cable or satellite TV, so he watched commercials and news reports. All the news was local. Middle-aged women in blue blazers with blonde, helmet-like hairdos and older men with gelled down hair anxiously recounted murders, robberies, and break-ins that had taken place in the city. There was the occasional human-interest story: a neighbor who had returned a run-away cat, another who had found a talking parrot; a family that had donated money to help a sickly child. The weather reports frequently mentioned "Maricopa County," but Matej didn't know what that meant. Beti explained that a county was something like a municipality, but that didn't make sense to Matej. To him, a "municipality" was the big office building near where they had lived back home. The news also men-tioned something called a "drive-by shooting," which got Matej worrying about his father driving through the empty city with the windows down.

It was late afternoon when Vlado finally returned. He smelled of fried food and sweat, and his hair was tousled from the drive. "It's really hot outside," he said, gently pushing Beti and Matej off: "Let me hit the shower first." Matej heard the snapping of the faucet, the spurting of water. He hoped they would go to the pool after. But when Vlado came out of the bathroom he said, "What do you say we go to McDonalds?" Matej leapt with joy. "And then we'll go to the pool. Sorry about not leaving the key." Matej was ecstatic.

"This is the best day of my life," Matej said to his parents as they settled into their plastic seats. Vlado let them know that refills were free. Matej filled his huge paper cup three times with Coke. Vlado and Beti also made frequent trips to the soda machine, and, before leaving, filled their cups to the brim so they would have some for tomorrow. Beti stuffed handfuls of sugar, ketchup, and mayonnaise packets into her purse, together with clumps of straws and napkins. "Hey, don't go overboard," Vlado said. "But why not?" she replied, "if we're paying for it." A man in khaki shorts, a red baseball cap, and a blue shirt embossed with a "Doritos" logo sat watching the three of them bunched around the soda machine and condiments stand. When their eyes met, the man stopped sucking on his straw and smiled. "What a perv," Beti murmured.

"Look! Just look at that sunset," Vlado kept saying on the drive home, even though their eyes had been on it the whole time.

"Spectacular," Beti chimed.

"Look, Matej! Just look at that! Do you see?" Vlado repeated. The sunset was a raging fire all along the horizon.

Matej could not take his eyes off it. He felt as if the colors were reaching into his head and radiating to his fingertips. His eyes welled with tears as the sunset took his breath away. But he didn't utter a word because his father would think he was crying.

"That's America for you! That's Arizona! There's not another sky like this in the whole world. Look! *Majeek!*" he said in English. His father's constant blabbering annoyed the boy because he felt it was ruining the beauty. Nonetheless, he was very happy, and when it occurred to him that they would be going to the pool when they got home, he finally felt free to tell himself that everything would be okay, that everything would be much better than it used to be, that they would finally be able to get away from whatever his parents were trying to get away from.

"God, it still feels like a sauna," Beti sighed when they stepped out of the apartment into the ultramarine twilight in their matching orange bathing suits.

"The heat'll let up soon, and the water'll cool us off," Vlado said. "But don't go walking barefoot. You don't want to step on a scorpion," he warned.

Matej was thrilled, saying "You've seen them?"

"Pfff," Vlado said, separating the key to the pool gate from his keychain, "You wouldn't believe how many I've killed."

The turquoise of the pool mesmerized Matej, but then he saw that there were people in it. "Oh, we're not alone," Beti whispered in disappointment. "Fuck it," Vlado said, as he unlocked the gate to let them in. Two older men were sitting on a ledge at the deep end. They both wore baseball caps and held beer cans, which they rested on their bulging bellies.

"Hi there!" the heavier of the two said.

"How's it goin'?" said the other.

"Hello," Vlado said in English. Beti nodded, avoiding their eyes.

The pool was small. "Do you know these guys?" Beti asked in Macedonian as she stiffly settled on the little ledge at the far end of the pool.

"Yeah, they live across from us, in the next apartment block. I don't know if they live together or not, but they're here almost every night drinking beer. Although it's supposed to be banned, you know?"

"Daddy! Daddy!" Matej squealed, pointing behind Beti, his eyes wide. Beti shrieked, plunging into the water. A cockroach the size of a finger skittled across the concrete where she had been sitting.

"No worries son, it's just a cockroach," Vlado laughed.

"What kind of cockroach is that? It's huge!" Beti said, standing in the shallow pool, watching the insect disappear into a shrub.

"Wait till you see them fly," Vlado said with the air of someone imparting enlightenment.

"Wow!" Matej was in awe.

"La Cucaracha," the voice of the heavier man said, interrupting them. "Scary, huh? Gets me every time."

The three of them fell silent. Lowering her gaze, Beti crouched down in the water so the two men couldn't see her cleavage. Matej stared at them. Their nostrils and the stubble on their jowls were lit up by the pool-light, but their eyes were shadowed by their baseball caps. They were both smiling.

"Where you guys from?" the same fellow asked.

"Macedonia," Vlado answered.

"Wow, I don't even know where that is," the other one said, turning to his friend.

"Isn't it a little island in the Baltic Sea or something?" the first man said.

"No. Land of Alexander de Matsedonian," Vlado curtly said.

"Oh, right," the man replied. The other one nodded, as if he understood.

"I hope we're not going to have to talk to them now," Beti said in Macedonian. "They give me the creeps."

"Let's talk so that *they* can't," Vlado offered.

"I'm going to swim!" Matej yelled ecstatically and started splashing about. "Look at me!" he shouted and did a clumsy crawl, something his father had taught him at Lake Ohrid the summer before.

"Bravo, son, bravo!" Beti said, spurring him on through the splish-and-splash. The two men cupped their hands over their beer cans whenever Matej drew near.

"They're here almost every evening," Vlado said. "Like they own the pool or something."

"And they live together, you say?" Beti said softly, a knowing look on her face.

"Look at me!" Matej shouted and took a deep breath, pinched his nose and sank under the water.

"You don't have to whisper," Vlado said, "no one understands us here." He cleared his throat and loudly said, "You mean they're faggots?"

Matej's head popped out of the water, his mouth open, his eyes closed.

"Bravo, son. Let's see you do that again," Beti said. "And try holding your breath longer."

Matej could tell his parents wanted to say something to each other they didn't want him to hear. "I don't want to. I want to swim around some more," he said, gently stroking his arms to make as little noise as he could.

"Here come the other faggots!" Vlado guffawed. Two silhouettes in tight-fitting shirts and shorts adorned with fluorescent stripes were jogging toward them down the sidewalk by their apartment complex. "Hi!" they called out, waving. The two men in the water responded with a "How's it going?" and a "Hey!" The fat one tapped his baseball cap.

"How do you know they're faggots?" Beti asked.

"Trust me, I know. They live in the house just behind our apartment. I'll show you," Vlado said with an air of authority and self-importance, flashing a cocky smile at the two men.

"Yes, but how can you be *sure* they're faggots?"

"I've seen them," Vlado said. Matej had stopped swimming and was trying to save a drowning ant with a leaf.

"And what about these old guys?" Beti said, egging him on. "It's so weird no one understands a word I say!" she said, giggling with delight.

"Look at this fat slob," Vlado sneered, "look how ugly and greasy he is. The other one is disgusting too, but this guy is unbelievable."

"Come on, stop now," Beti said, slapping him playfully on the arm.

"You're stupid as fuck and even your mother doesn't love you," Vlado continued, his eyes fixed upon the man, who sat sipping his beer and looking out over the lawn beyond the fence.

Beti couldn't stop laughing. "Stop it now, you're killing me," she whispered.

Matej began to swim. The men watched as he approached them.

"You're fat and your wife's uglier than cock," Vlado said.

"Hey, wait a minute," Beti interrupted. "I thought you said they were faggots?"

The first few days were so similar that Matej couldn't tell one from the other. School hadn't started yet, and his father worked every day and most every night. Vlado put in a lot of overtime ("I'm the shift supervisor," he would brag) and so you never knew when he was coming home. Matej and Beti had to go to the pool alone. They would go before dark in hopes of avoiding the two men, but the men were always there or arrived shortly after them. They would just sit in the water with their little smiles pinned on their faces. "Let's get out. They can stew in this broth without us," Beti would say, and Matej would plead, "Oh, come on, just a little longer." He would stall until the couple in the tight-fitting shorts and shirts jogged by, hoping to see something that would confirm his father's *I've seen them.*

I've seen them: the phrase stirred up disturbing images. Matej recalled a video clip a kid in his class named Marko had sent him on Viber that was very different from the ones the other boys would share with him of naked girls rubbing themselves between splayed thighs or putting something pink inside them, sticking their tongues out and moaning as if they were in pain, much the way his mother moaned when the bed thumped against the wall. He recalled the clips Marko shared where a woman groaned in pain while her breasts flapped back and forth as a man drilled her like a sewing machine with an enormous pipe-like penis which, when the man was done, would dribble on the woman's lifted butt. In some the woman would get sprayed in the face and she would lick the spray with her lips. The kids called Marko a "perver" for posting those videos in the "boys group" on Viber, but there was one video Marko had only sent to Matej. There were two men in it, one of whom was choking on the other's huge penis, his face flushed, the veins popping out on his neck like the veins on the penis being thrust into his mouth. Matej stopped and deleted the video when he saw one of the men take the woman's position and let the other man plunge his penis in and out of him. Matej's mouth became dry-as-a-bone, and he felt a dreadful urge to pee.

The same thing happened to him each time he recalled his father saying *I've seen them.* Whenever he stood at the toilet peeing, he would look at his penis, like a finger, and he would recall the sight of the bulging knot in his father's tight speedos, or the fluorescent stripes on the two joggers' muscular behinds. After he shook out the last few drops, he would feel a burning in his groin, as if he still needed to pee. He would stand there for a long time, staring at the pool of yellowed water.

The phrase *I've seen them*, would run through his mind as he watched his mother leaf through *Home and Living* and *Fine Gardening*, making longer and longer lists of things they

needed for their home or cutting out coupons. Without wanting to, he would imagine her with her legs spread or propped
on all fours, moaning with pain as a pipe plunged in and out
of her. Then he would imagine a pipe lunging into one of the
joggers, the shorter one. Matej felt dirty inside. To cleanse his
mind and make the images go away, he would cuddle against
his mom on the beat-up couch and watch TV with her. He
would lay his head on her lap and let her caress his hair.
"Don't worry, your father said we'd get cable soon," she would
say as they watched the endless reports of people dying, of
women being raped, of families robbed and assaulted in their
homes. And there was always a shooting somewhere. Matej
would close his eyes, trying to focus on his mother's fingers
gently combing through his hair, on her fingernails running
along his scalp, or, if he was lucky, behind his ear, which
always gave him goosebumps and a tingling in his throat,
masking the burning sensation in his groin and his urge to
pee. The sound of his new homeland would rudely shake
him from this comfort: deafening police sirens, the sounds
of injury and death.

Whenever his father came home late from work, Matej
would recall his saying *I've seen them*, and wondered if he
would ever find out what it was his father had seen. "When'll
Dad be home"? he would ask, but his mother never really
knew. She told him there were days Vlado worked a second
job someplace. "Your father needs to work really hard until
I find a job. I want to do something related to design, or
maybe real estate," she would say, and Matej would have no
idea what she was talking about. He would sit in the flowery
armchair by the window looking up to the sidewalk leading
to their apartment. At night, cars pulling into the parking
lot sent bars of light streaming through the Venetian blinds.
The aluminum blades would always pop when Matej pried

them apart to see if the headlights were Vlado's. Whenever he heard steps, he would raise his eyes from the tablet and peer out, hoping to see his father's non-slip shoes going by. The ebb and flow of police sirens on the main road churned up alarming visions of his blood-drenched father slumped over the steering wheel, the passenger window riddled with bullet holes, the driver's window rolled down, as it always was, the crumpled golden car stranded in the parking lot of the Safeway where Vlado would buy roast chicken, potato salad, and four biscuits for $12.99.

The first day Vlado spent the evening at home, the three of them went out for a walk. "Let me show you where to throw out the trash, where you get the mail. You know, get a feel for the neighborhood," Vlado said, pulling on the sneakers he never wore to work.

"Here it's all blocks," he said, tying his laces. He had already told them this more than once. "They call them blocks. American streets are parallel to each other, and they all have signs. It's not like back home, never knowing where you are or where you're going," he went on.

"We know, you told us a hundred times," Beti sighed. "And it's not like we're blind and can't see for ourselves."

"If you know so much, why don't *you* show us around? You want to get raped by a Mexican in a dark alley?"

"Come on, now," Beti said.

"No, *you* come on. And just shut the fuck up for once, will you?" he snapped, looming over her, pushing his chest close to her face.

"Okay, okay," she said, laying her hand on his arm. "I'm sorry."

Vlado's fury had nowhere to go. His jaw was clenched and twisted to the left, as it always was when Matej angered him.

He and his mother knew what had to follow: gentle flattery until Vlado's wrath subsided.

"Here I am dead tired and still taking the time to show you around. I've been on my feet all day. And I'm doing all this for you. And for what? For you to talk back to me?"

Matej knew his mother would either say "I'm *not* talking back," whereupon his father would smash a glass or punch the furniture and swear; or his mother would apologize and Vlado would take them for their walk.

"Okay, I'm sorry, really. I'm really, really sorry," she said, laying her hand on his arm again.

"Come on, Matej, quit dragging your feet!" Vlado said from the open door. Matej felt weak in the knees.

"Oh, man is it hot! I'm so glad I didn't blow-dry my hair," his mother anxiously said. "In this heat it'll be dry in three minutes." She rattled on in what would have been silence but for the hissing of cicadas and the dry shuffle of their footsteps on the hot asphalt.

"The sky is so beautiful," she went on. "Look, Matej, ultramarine. That color is called ultramarine."

"And the color of the pool is turquoise," Matej replied.

"That's right," she said. They were approaching it. The silvery reflection of the surface rippled the concrete wall of their building. The men in baseball caps with beer cans wallowed in the water like hippos in a zoo.

"Look at those old faggots boiling their balls," Beti whispered to Vlado.

"They're not faggots," he murmured.

Matej felt an urge to pee.

"How's it goin'?" one of the men said, giving them a nod. The other one raised his beer and smiled.

"Good, thanks!" Vlado boomed in English.

"Hello!" Matej's little voice chimed, then added in

Macedonian, "Suck dick!"

Beti gasped, but the men replied, obliviously, "Hi there!"

Vlado could not hide the smile on his face. Once the men were out of sight, the three of them broke into laughter, but then Beti said in a fruitless effort to impose a little discipline, "Matej! How can you say such a thing! Where on earth did you learn to talk like that?"

"From Daddy," Matej replied.

"Stop scolding the kid," Vlado said. "The little one's got a sense of humor." Beti turned away to hide the smile on her face. "Just you be careful what you say in front of other people," Vlado added, ruffling the boy's hair.

"You know," Beti said, putting her stern face back on, "I don't really approve of such language."

"Oh, yeah, right! So I guess it was it was a little birdie who said something about boiling balls," Vlado teased. Beti bumped him affectionately, much to Matej's relief. It's over, he thought, at least for now.

"Okay, enough already, it's time to get serious," Vlado said. "Let me tell you where we're at, where we're going. You don't ever want to turn right on Alameda. Always go left. The Mexicans are on the right, the nice houses on the left." They turned that way when they came to the corner under a bright streetlamp—the only one for blocks.

The houses were barely illuminated by light from the windows and the lamps softly glowing in the yards. Like nightmarish creatures in a dream, the ill-lit houses, the trees and cacti looked to Matej as if they were about to come to life: the windows would blink, the cacti would take him in their arms, the branches of the trees would grab him with their claws, the scrawny desert shrubs would trip and scratch him. But not a thing stirred. The hot, dry air stood still. The only sound was their footfalls on the pavement, their hushed conversation and the rasping of the sprinklers watering the grass—psst-psst-psst. As he passed each sprinkler, Matej felt a brief breath of coolness, followed by a surge of heat that hit him like a hazing. He would veer toward the sprinklers wherever they had darkened the sidewalk, and when the water sprinkled his feet, it would rouse him from the feeling of being in a dream.

"Why in the world would you plant a tree like that in a middle of the desert?" Beti said every time they passed a trim lawn with a leafy elm or mulberry.

And Vlado would reply, "Because they damn well can"; or, "Because they've got the dough so they can do whatever the hell they please."

Most of the houses were low and long, sprawling along the street like slumbering creatures. Some had pointy roofs; others had flat; still others had his-and-her garages as big as houses.

"They call those *driveways* in English," Vlado said to Matej, pointing to where the asphalt curved up to a garage.

"How do you say that in Macedonian?" Beti asked. Vlado shrugged.

There was not a soul in sight. The garden furniture on the recessed porch entryways looked abandoned. Nothing moved behind the curtains or blinds.

"They don't have fences," Beti noticed for the first time.

"But they have guns," Vlado said.

"And they're always shooting at each other," Beti said. "That's all you ever see on TV," she added, stopping in front of a house with a large tree in the middle of the yard from which hung hummingbird feeders.

"Look at the size of that tree," she whispered. "And in the middle of the desert!"

A police siren wailed in the distance. Matej froze, imagining their running into a shootout between armed thugs and the police. But the wailing faded, and his parents strolled blithely on, as if they hadn't even noticed, then stopped in front of a low house with a gravel yard and desert plants.

"See how beautiful it is," Beti said, squeezing Vlado's hand. "This is called adobe style. A desert house. It looks like it belongs here. Because it comes from the Indians," she said, looking down at Matej. The three of them stood there, gazing at the house. Beti felt inspired: "You see it, it's built for this climate, with the colors of the desert. You see that darker color there?" she asked, hurrying to tell them as much as she could before they grew bored. "It's called Cherokee red. Frank Lloyd Wright's favorite color. He lived in the desert here."

"Who's he?" Matej asked.

"A super famous architect," she replied. "See that blooming shrub? You know what it's called, Matej?" Matej shook his head. "A bougainvillea. And those little green trees are called paloverdes. You'll see them around. They're adorable. And of course," she added, "this big guy is a saguaro. You know how long it takes a saguaro to grow a centimeter?" She asked, without giving Matej time to reply. "Five years!"

"Hey, you know whose house this is?" Vlado interrupted with an air of self-importance. He waited for Beti to shrug. "It's the faggots'!" he said, as if he were delivering the punch-line of a joke.

"Which faggots?" Beti asked. She looked confused. Matej felt the urge to pee.

"Those two joggers," Vlado said.

"Oh," she sighed absently.

"Well, it's no coincidence they have a dick in their front yard," Vlado added.

Beti lightly slapped him on the back. "You should be ashamed of yourself!" she mockingly scolded him.

"Come on! What did I say?" he said in mock-defense.

Matej started to giggle. Quietly at first, then more and

more loudly, until it turned into raucous laughter. Vlado was pleased. He strutted ahead, his hands in his pockets, his elbows wide.

"And a prickly dick, too. You know how we say back home: their dick is their yard," he added. Beti slapped him on the back again and gave him a playful shove.

"Oh, stop it, you!" she said, watching Vlado strut down the sidewalk with the casual charm of a gallant. Matej could not stop laughing, a loud, repetitive staccato: eight exhales followed by a long, raspy inhalation. He continued to laugh even after Beti and Vlado had turned to look at him.

"Hey, it's not *that* funny," Beti said, watching Matej clutching his stomach, his feet apart, his knees pinched together.

"I . . . can't . . . stop," he barely managed to say through his twisted lips. Tears broke from the corners of his tightly closed eyelids.

"That's okay. Laughing is good for you," Vlado said, though he had stopped smiling. "Just don't cry," he snapped. "It looks like you're crying," he turned toward Matej.

"I'm not crying," Matej said, wiping the tears from his eyes. He was still hunched over and his mouth was twisted into a grimace, but he hobbled after them.

"Come on, let's go home," Vlado suddenly said. "We'll turn here so you can see the back alley where we take out the trash. Matej, stop dragging your feet!" and added, with a gloomy air that was all too familiar to them, "I'm tired and hot." He led them down the unlit street and into a darker, more desolate alley. Even in the dark Matej could see the houses were no longer pretty, the yards were without sprinklers, groomed lawns, or luscious trees. The windows were unlit.

"It's kinda scary round here," Beti said.

"That's south Phoenix for you," Vlado replied. "We live right around the corner from it. See? That's our place over there. So you get how we got here, right?" he asked. They could see the building blocks ahead of them, the apartment complex for people who can only afford to rent. Matej gradually realized which apartment was theirs from the blue swatch of the shimmering pool. Every apartment looked exactly the same, every window, every door, every stairway that led to these temporary homes. A TV blared from one of them.

"Pay attention now," Vlado said in a serious tone as he turned down a side street. "There's another, smaller key on the keychain. That's the one that opens the door to the back alley where the trash is."

"Wow. You can't even see their garbage. Not like the pigs back home," Beti said, following Vlado as he disappeared behind the wooden door. Matej came after and found himself on a dark and narrow dirt path.

"Civilized people—that's what they are. Here's the trash," Vlado said, motioning toward three large tightly lidded garbage cans. Matej was amazed that they didn't stink like the ones in Skopje. "Just look at this place," Vlado went on. "The nice houses are on this side of the street, the Mexicans over there. And behind this wall here are the backyards of the nice houses. Look, we're right behind the faggots."

"The house behind us is where the faggots live?" Beti asked.

"Yeah. See the roof? Flat. What'd you call it, abode?"

"Adobe," Beti corrected him, lifting her to get a better look. "Hey, you're right," she said. By standing on tiptoe, Matej could just see the roof, the upper half of the curtainless windows, and the dark patches of Cherokee red adorning the walls.

"If we left our windows open I bet we could hear them going at it," Vlado said. Beti slapped him on the arm, saying, "Oh, come on now, Vlado, don't start that again."

As soon as they climbed down the stairs and entered their

apartment, Matej raced to the bathroom, where he pulled down his shorts and saw wet splotches on his underwear and a dark blotch on a pant leg. Long after he had finished urinating he continued to stand there, staring into the yellow pool in the toilet bowl. He felt like he still had to pee, but nothing would come out. He tiptoed to his room, afraid his parents would notice he had wet his pants. He stripped off his underwear and threw them in a corner of the dark walk-in closet, then slipped on a clean pair before crawling under the sheets. He tried to think of nice things that awaited him: the sprawling school with the newly carpeted classrooms, the luxury of having his own desk, and the colorful textbooks filled with happy pictures printed on smooth, shiny paper. He heard the doorknob rattle and could see the light shining through his tightly closed eyelids. "He's asleep," his mother whispered. A few minutes later he heard the rhythmic thumping of the bed against the hollow wall and his mother's stifled sighs, as police sirens wailed in the distance.

Yotso—that was Vlado's name for their family friend who had been living in the US for years. They went to his place for barbecue one evening. "I'm uncle Yordan," he said, introducing himself to Matej, "but here they call me Jordan."

"Hey, Joxie, what's up?" Vlado said, slapping him hard on the back. Yotso slapped him back and fisted him in the belly, and they burst into raucous laughs.

Yotso and Sandy's house was huge and on the other side of town. Scottsdale, that's what Vlado called the place it took them more than half an hour to get to, driving through the heat with their windows down. The house stood on a cul-de-sac as round as a balloon. There was not a scrap of litter or a single human being anywhere in sight. Huge garages bulged from every house. As Vlado pulled up in front of a garage,

Matej saw Yotso for the first time. He was standing on the
front porch, arms akimbo, feet apart. He wore a white apron
with a picture of a red pepper over which was written in
English: "MACEDONIA."

Sandy greeted them in a living room four times bigger
than their own, with ceilings that reached as high as a two-
story house. Sandy did not look nearly as old as Vlado had
described her on the drive over. He had said that Yotso had
finally managed to make it in America because he had "married into money"; that Yotso had originally lived in the same
apartment complex they were now living in until he struck
gold by marrying Sandy, a divorcee with two kids in college.
Vlado kept referring to her as "the old hag," but Matej didn't
think she looked like one at all. In fact, she looked about the
same age as Yordan but did have his big protruding beer belly.
Her hands were soft, as was her touch. Matej had a warm
feeling when she gently laid her hand on his shoulder and led
him to the backyard, where a pool with a diving board glowed
blue in the coming twilight.

Next to it, under an awning with a large fan, Yotso was
grilling meat. "What do Americans know about barbecue!
Look at this! *Leskovac* burgers!" he boasted. "You can find
everything here! And the meat is first-class, just like home," he
bellowed over the hissing of the sausages and burgers sizzling
on the grill. His face was flushed, his shirt under his armpits
stained with sweat. He wiped his brow with his apron, turned
to Vlado and said, "I know it's hot out here, but you're gonna
have to get used to it."

"I'm already used to it," Vlado replied, as he grabbed a
beer and slumped into a beige lawn chair, where he spread his
legs and slung his arms over the armrests. His head had sunk
between his raised shoulders and his crotch bulged indecently,
thought Matej as he jumped into the pool. The women were

nowhere to be seen. They had disappeared into the house, and were chatting quietly, almost as if they were sharing secrets. Now and again they would flutter past in their flowery dresses like light summer curtains stirred by a breeze.

"Let 'em have their conversations about design or whatever their thing is," Yotso said after Sandy and Beti came out to say that they wanted to see some houses for sale in the neighborhood before it got too dark.

"That's all the wife reads. Those magazines," Vlado said, then drained the rest of his beer. "She's busting my balls."

"Slow down on the beer, Vlado. I've got some first-class whiskey coming your way," Yotso said, fanning the hot sausages. "Sandy's on a roll. She sold a slew of houses 'cause a lot of old farts wanna move out here. The city's growing, there's a huge demand."

Vlado reached down and grabbed another beer from the cooler. Matej heard the pop and hiss of the bottle top as he jumped back into the pool. The water in his ears drowned the hissing of the grill, and the casual, yet forced baritones of the two men. Underwater he also escaped the smell of meat and sour sweat the fan blew now and then in his direction. He stayed under as long as he could, savoring the blue coolness that shielded him from the desert heat. When he came up for air he heard Yotso yell, "Hey, kid, you hungry?" With one hand he held out a large steaming plate stacked with meat. "In a minute!" Matej said, as he prepared to dive back under. "He can wait for his mom . . ." he heard his dad say before his ears filled with water.

The sky had grown pink by the time Yotso flicked on the pool lights that turned the water turquoise. Matej felt small and white. He saw Vlado and Yotso beginning to undress by to the patio table. Sandy and Beti had not yet returned. Yotso wiped his hands on his apron. Everything around the word

"MACEDONIA" was brown and greasy. He untied the apron and threw it on a chair, then stripped off his shirt and used it to wipe his forehead and neck. All he was wearing was a pair of dark-blue swimming trunks. "Whoa, Speedos!" Yotso said, jeering at Vlado. "They're back in fashion," Vlado replied defensively, tottering toward the pool, a glass of whiskey in one hand, and a burning cigar clenched between his teeth. "I don't know, maybe they're still wearing them in Greece," Yotso said, grabbing his own whiskey and cigar from the table.

"Enough with the wisecracks," Vlado murmured as he sat on the step at the shallow end of the pool, then blurted, "Shut your fucking hole, you faggot, and get me an ashtray." Matej felt relieved when his father plopped down into the water. In comparison to Yotso, he was much too naked. His bulging, greasy, shameful body was no longer so exposed.

"Still not hungry, son?" his father asked him. The corners of his mouth were covered with grease. As if he could read his son's thoughts, he dipped his hand into the pool and wiped his mouth off. Then he drew on the cigar. One of his eyes was slightly out of focus.

Matej shook his head and dove back under and would only come up for air, then swim right back to the bottom of the pool, his skin as white and smooth as the belly of a fish. He did not notice when Beti and Sandy, both in one-piece bathing suits, appeared and sat down in the shallow end. Sandy looked elegant and gentle in her swimsuit decorated with violets that seemed to dissolve into the turquoise water. "How well you dive! What a brave young man you are," she said, flashing a pearly smile.

"Come on honey, you've got to eat something," Beti said, putting a paper plate and a red cup next to the pool. "I got you a full plate, and some Sprite." Matej got out of the water and sat on the edge. He was hungry. There was a quarter of a burger patty, a fat sausage, a salad drenched in white dressing, and a chunk of bread. He bit into the sausage and something fat and stringy wedged itself between his teeth. He felt sick to his stomach and spit it back out on the plate.

"Can you believe this kid?" Yotso said. "This is the first time he got out of the water."

"Hey, you know how small our pool is," Vlado said. "And there're these two faggots who are always wallowing in it so he can't really swim around much."

"Come on now," Beti said, this time with a serious expression, "they're not faggots. They're just these two regular guys. And would you please speak English?" she added in a scolding voice. Vlado gazed at her, his eyes glazing over, and made a point of drawing fiercely on his cigar. Matej saw his cheeks and lips puff out and then collapse obscenely, the veins on his neck swelling. He put down his plate.

"Things like that are normal here," Yotso said, drawing on his cigar. "That's just how it is. Her sister has been living with her partner for more than ten years,' he said, not looking at Sandy, who began to swim toward the deep end of the pool, her head gliding above the water.

"You know I love lesbians," Vlado said. "Because I'm a lesbian too!" he guffawed. "It's just that I can't take those double-barreled bastards. Double-barreled shotguns for double-barreled bastards, that's what I say," he added, clenching the cigar with his teeth.

"You know they really do have guns here," Yotso said, trying to change the subject. Beti joined Sandy at the far end of the pool. Matej suddenly had to pee.

"Mom, I need to go to the bathroom," he said to her.

"Just take a right past the kitchen counter, honey, and you'll see a white door to your right," Sandy said, as if she had understood his Macedonian.

"Your towel's on the chair," his mother called out.

Matej slipped into the bathroom and plopped down on the toilet seat. For a long while he just sat there, staring at the dark-red Native American patterns on the wallpaper. "Cherokee red," he remembered, finally letting out a thin, fitful stream of urine that tinkled in the bowl of water below him. He continued to sit there for a long time as the moisture on his skin evaporated and his body grew cold. A little while later, there was a sharp rap on the door.

"Matej! We're leaving," his mother said, "Let's go!" He could hear the tension in her voice.

When he came out of the bathroom, he found her standing in the living room with Sandy. They were wearing their floral dresses, but their hair was wet. Beti was holding a Tupperware container filled with food. Sandy smiled at Matej. "OK, honey, I'm going to drive you home," she said with a tone of exaggerated kindness. His father and Yotso were nowhere to be seen. Beti and Sandy were making a great effort to talk as if nothing had happened during the time Matej had been in the bathroom.

"The drinking and driving laws here are super strict, we just found out," Beti told him with flat disinterest. "If the police catch you, you won't be able to drive for years or even get a job." She avoided his eyes as she impatiently watched him struggling to put his clothes on. "So Yotso's going to drive your dad home, and Sandy's going to take us back in our car."

"Your father needs the car so that he can go to work tomorrow," Sandy said, as if she had understood Beti's Macedonian.

A black SUV stood purring in the cul-de-sac. The windows were tinted, but Matej could make out Yotso behind the wheel.

"Now your father's going to chew my ass off about not having a license," Beti said under her breath as they clambered into the gold wreck of a car. "You see, we need to use both cars so that the two of them can come back home," she said, turning back to explain to Matej.

"This is for you," Sandy said, handing him a bag of potato chips. "Something for the road. You hardly ate a thing."

"Thank you," Matej mumbled.

The black vehicle in front of them moved soundlessly ahead. "Can you follow them, Sandy? I don't know the way," Beti said apologetically.

"No problem," Sandy said reassuringly. "Let's open the windows and let the breeze in. Good thing our hair is wet!" her eyes glittered in the rearview mirror.

Matej munched his chips, the crackling mixed with the roar of the warm wind that ruffled his hair. The murmuring of the women's voices made him sleepy. They were talking about trees, cactuses, neighborhoods, houses, homes.

Yotso's SUV pulled to a stop in front of the poolside sidewalk that led to their apartment. Sandy drove on into the parking lot, where the three of them got out and walked back to the SUV. Vlado stood leaning on the left front fender. "Let's go," he said, without so much as a "goodbye" to Sandy and stumbled toward the sidewalk. Sandy opened the passenger door and disappeared into the dark interior. The engine purred loudly as the clean, shiny car drove off, crunching the pebbles under its tires. Smoothing the road ahead, it vanished into the night like a big black cat.

Vlado swayed as he marched ahead; Beti followed, holding the Tupperware container in both hands; Matej came last. Like a raft of ducks, they passed the pool where, as usual, the two men were soaking in the water and drinking beer. "Hey!" they both said, but Vlado and Beti ignored them. Matej knew it was a mistake, but he couldn't help squeaking out "Suck dick" in Macedonian.

"You're starting that crap again?" Vlado stopped and looked at the boy as if he was about to hit him.

"Matej, I told you to stop with that kind of talk!" Beti hissed.

"What's that you're carrying?" Vlado suddenly stopped in his tracks and gave Beti the same glare he had given Matej.

"Nothing, I'll tell you inside," she answered, slipping past him, anxious to get into the apartment as quickly as possible. Vlado followed with determined fury.

"You telling me you took charity?"

"Stop yelling," Beti said as she hastened down the steps.

"Stop yelling?" Vlado was livid. "Is that what you said to me?" Beti unlocked the door and pulled him into the apartment.

"Matej!" she snapped. "Go to your room. Now!" and then stormed toward the kitchen. But the boy locked himself in the bathroom instead. There he heard the refrigerator door opening, and then an explosion of angry voices, his father shouting, his mother hissing.

"I don't see why you can't bring food home from the restaurant. Every dollar counts."

"Every dollar? Seriously?" Vlado yelled. "It's *me* who's working, remember? All *you* do is sit around on your ass leafing through your *stupid* magazines, you useless cunt!"

But Beti pressed on. "Look, all you have to do is take some food and, you know, put it in a container or something. No one's going to see you. Because, you know, we're pouring money down the drain here!"

"What, you want me to lose my job, you dumb cow?"

"Yeah, right! They're always throwing food out. You said so yourself!"

"I'm sick and tired of having to explain everything to you," Vlado yelled. "I'm sick and tired of having to be the man of steel, lugging you and your son on my back . . ." Matej flushed the toilet to drown out his father's words.

Then he heard his mother yelling, "Matej! Take out the trash! You hear me?"

His parents were sitting at the dining table. His mother's hair was disheveled from the long drive, while his father, bleary-eyed, was in an alcoholic sweat. She got up and shoved a black trash bag in Matej's hands, along with the keys to the pool and the little door that led to the alley.

"But it's dark out there," Matej said.

"Don't be such a fairy!" his father barked, slamming his fist on the table-top and rising, menacingly.

It was deserted outside. The only sound beside his parents' voices was the blaring of a television—perhaps the same one from a few days ago, Matej thought—and the droning of cicadas. The air hung heavy and hot. Matej trembled as he unlocked the wooden door and stepped into the deeper darkness of the narrow alleyway. The door slammed shut behind him. He stood there for a while, waiting for his eyes to adjust to the dark, where he could soon make out the three large garbage cans. A faint glow from the moon or the houses beyond the wall illuminated the garbage can lids and the gravel that crackled under every step. He remembered the house on the far side of the wall and his father's *I've seen them*. He lifted the lid off one of the cans to drop the black bag in, and an empty beer bottle—it was one of the ones with a Native American in headdress and the inscription "Cherokee" on it—fell out onto the gravel. Matej closed the lid, picked the bottle up and climbed atop the garbage can. He could see over the wall to the little yard and the living room of the men his father called "faggots." There were no windows, only large sliding doors through which Matej could see everything going on inside. In the right-hand side of a large room one of the men was chopping something green on a cutting board. On the counter next to him stood a glass of wine from which he occasionally took a sip. He was wearing a white T-shirt and cream-colored trousers. The other man sat comfortably in a dark-red armchair, his bare feet propped on a foot stool. He wore glasses and a thin white robe and was reading a book. He too had a glass of wine on the table beside him. He raised his eyes above the rim of his glasses and looked in Matej's direction, then turned to say something to his partner. They both laughed then stopped to savor the wine. Matej gripped the beer bottle in his hand and hurled it toward the house. It slammed the sliding door in front of the man reading, shattering the glass. The man jumped to his feet. Matej leapt from the garbage can. He crouched down beside it, wishing he could disappear into the darkness, wishing the dark earth would drink him up. Everything was still. Then he heard the wailing of a siren in the distance. He closed his eyes, waiting.

THE 8TH OF MARCH

(THE ACCORDION)

Vesna was quite pleased to discover an expensive-looking envelope in her pigeonhole. She liked opening letters because she enjoyed seeing her slender, manicured fingers wrestle with the crispy paper to reveal the prize inside. She rarely had this pleasure at home because her mail consisted mainly of bills, though every now and then she would receive an invitation to something or other at her work address.

"Ms. Vesna Stojchevska," read the front of the white envelope. Relishing the look of her fingers and the rustle of the paper, she drew out a smooth card:

The International Women's Community
invites you to a meet-and-greet of powerful women

Friday, February 15th
10 A.M.
US Ambassador's Residence
Skopje

"Powerful women?" she wondered. They consider me a powerful woman? "Hello, professor!" piped two students

walking by, but she was too distracted to respond. A powerful woman—how powerful that sounds! she thought, vaguely
recalling a similar expression she had heard somewhere, but
that this version of it didn't sound quite right. She wasn't sure
what "a meet-and-greet" meant. English was not her strong
point, but she could always ask her son, Vojdan. She would
be going to a meet-and-greet of powerful women together
with the International Women's Community—an organiza-
tion she'd never heard of—at the American ambassador's residence! She repeated the words with great pride, as if unable to
believe her luck. Who were these women? They must be very
important, she thought, if it's happening at the ambassador's
residence. Which surely means the American ambassador's
wife is part of this women's group, and who knows how many
other wives of ambassadors. diplomats or other members of
the international community, of whom she knew there were
quite a few.

It must be on account of the protest, she said to herself.
And, of course, my being a professor.

Every time she remembered the protest and the story
behind it, she felt an electric shock run up her left side, which
made her strike her heel against the floor like a mare shaking
off flies. To calm her nerves and restore her sense of balance,
she would take a few swigs from the flask she always kept in
her large leather purse.

It was this flask that was responsible for everything that
had happened, along with the fact that the winter had been
exceptionally cold and the conditions for protesting unfavor-
able. For when the students had gathered on the university
square and began blowing their whistles and vuvuzelas, shouting slogans in unison, the uproar they made reached the hall
where the faculty meeting was being held. A female professor
on the verge of retiring and thus unafraid of governmental

reprisals, interrupted the meeting with a long speech about how the professors were nothing without their students, that the time for solidarity was right now, that the very existence of the university depended on satisfying student needs, and that the new higher-education law which students were protesting against was disgraceful and would destroy the university and the careers of its professors.

"I'm retiring—and the future lies is in your hands!" the professor exclaimed, whereupon several of her colleagues nervously piped agreement, which in turn prompted a faint applause. Vesna was not quite certain what this higher-education law was all about. She wasn't the type to think she had to involve herself in every little thing, and was of the strong opinion that there was always someone else who knew more about whatever matter was being discussed than she did, who would step forward and seize the reins, someone who knew how to get things done. Besides, her father, now deceased, had always said: "Don't meddle in matters where it's not your place" and "He who keeps his mouth shut stays well out of trouble." Then she recalled another maxim he had invented: "The resourceful man is everyone's friend." The Dean was such a man. When the retiree finally finished declaiming, the Dean argued that, in light of the fact that the noise outside was hindering the meeting, and in view of his strong commitment to democratic principles, they should take up the rest of the agenda in a subsequent meeting, and asked, "Those in favor?" After a short pause, half a dozen professors raised their hands, and, one by one, the rest followed suit. "Those opposed or abstained—none!" he said and declared the meeting adjourned.

The professors poured into the university square uttering their customary babble. Vesna looked about for Aneta and Ellie, her colleagues, wondering if they would join the protest, because she decided she would do whatever they did. She found them smoking by a dried-up garden urn and stamping their feet to keep warm. It was so cold their every breath plumed like chimney smoke.

"So, we're joining, right?" Aneta asked Vesna as soon as she approached. Aneta was wrapped in a bulky brown shawl with Indian patterns, under which she wore a long brown coat, brown slacks, and brown boots, so the only thing that stood out besides her shock of curly hair—dyed bright orange—were her mouth and blue eyes, both outlined in brown, and a nose reddened from the cold. A faint trace of lipstick smudged her lips.

"I don't know, should we?" Vesna asked. "It's freezing."

"Well, I don't know how you're going to stay warm in those clothes," Ellie said, eyeing her up and down without moving her head. Ellie always stood bolt upright, thinking this gave her the aura of a lady. She took great care never to lower her head so as to prevent the wrinkles under her chin from showing. She smoked with a cigarette holder, with her head thrown back and an expression that suggested she was contemplating something important. Standing in her high-heeled boots, she gave the impression she was looking down on the world. Her hair was coiffed like an American first lady. "Your bottom will freeze, woman, if you don't mind my saying," she said to Vesna. Ellie suffered from insecurity because she was not from Skopje, so she pronounced the *tsch*, *dzh* ,and *zh* sounds as if she were Serbian, but still used the vernacular form of verbs.

Vesna had of late taken to wearing her short faux-fur winter coat because the long coat had gotten so threadbare under the armpits, and she could not afford to buy a new one. "Don't worry about me, I'm wearing thermal pantyhose," she lied, nearly freezing in her favorite gray lycra skirt and matching blazer. This was the only outfit she still owned that was elastic enough to fit. "Although it really *is* cold," she conceded, conscious of the fact that she was afraid to join the student protest and was pleased she could use the weather as an excuse.

"It looks like most everyone else is going," Aneta said, gesturing toward the professors standing with the students, some of whom were holding protest signs.

"Let's finish our cigarettes and then decide," Ellie said, leisurely inserting a fresh cigarette into her holder.

The square was filling up by the minute. As the whistling grew louder and louder, the large crowd that had gathered began loudly repeating the slogans a student shouted into a megaphone. The sound was deafening. Vesna, Ellie and Aneta felt like they were at a sports match at which their team had a strong chance of winning. An inexplicable wave of love and pride flowed through them each time the chorus of students bellowed their chant. Aneta mustered the courage to join the chant, but she came in late and lost the first word: ". . . justice, no peace!" Aneta's unsteady voice chirped. "There is no justice," Ellie smirked, as she donned her dark shades despite the cloudy sky, "There never was!"

The three of them noticed a commotion by the statue of Cyril and Methodius that dominated the square. Several people had climbed up onto its base and unrolled a large banner with a slogan the three of them could not make out. Other students raised their red student cards and began blowing whistles. Still others waved black flags bearing the inscription, "Student Plenum." She saw her son, Vojdan, standing next to Cyril. Or was it Methodius? Vesna thought, as she never could tell which was which. Her son was waving his student card and wearing a pair of John Lennons she had never seen on him before. Two girls had their arms around his waist. He turned and whispered to one of them, as he gently laid his hand on her shoulder. "Vojdancho!" Vesna yelped and pointed in his direction. "Where, where?" Ellie asked excitedly and even lowered her head a little so she could see above her shades.

"There, by the brothers!"

"Which brothers?" Aneta asked.

"Cyril and Methodius!" Vesna replied. "He's the one with the Lennon shades!"

"Oh, right!" was all Ellie and Aneta said, a little envious that their children weren't among the students who had gathered around the statue.

"Since my Vojdancho has joined the protest, so will I," Vesna declared.

"Filip must be here somewhere," Aneta said, referring to her son.

"And Simona said she'd come too," Ellie added, thinking of her daughter.

Vesna gazed at her son as he stood flirting and laughing with the girl. Thank God, Vesna thought. She had been tortured by the thought that her son might be gay, since he would go to parties and return in the morning with his male friends, where they sequestered themselves in his room from which she would then hear a *duh-ga-dug, duh-ga-dug, duh-ga-dug* of musical beats, with an occasional shout, peel of laughter, and finally, silence. These friends would sometimes sleep over, in Vojdan's room in the attic of the house that she and her husband, Ljubo, owned. He rarely had girls over. Almost never.

Vesna was also tortured by the fact that Vojdan had failed his first year in the pre-law program. She was so concerned about him that she called Professor Shemkov, a friend's brother-in-law she had met a few years back at a New Year's party. Vojdan, who claimed he had signed up to retake the exam, said the reason he had failed was that the professor was bad-tempered and held a personal grudge against him. "Vojdan

Stojchevski? I'm sorry, that name does not ring a bell," the professor had replied, clearly angry at the idea of someone calling him at home to ask a favor. Vesna had then pleaded with him to tell her how many times Vojdan had failed the exam. A few days later she received an arrogant email from his assistant, informing her that Vojdan had never taken the exam and had never once attended class.

Vojdan was still asleep when Vesna read the email. It was two in the afternoon. She went into his room. There was another boy sleeping beside him. But they were dressed and even had their sneakers on, much to Vesna's relief. "Vojdan! Vojdan!" she whispered urgently, but the boy refused to wake.

She pulled him by the leg. "Vojdan! Vojdancho!" his pet name slipped out. As one of his eyelids slowly unglued, he blurted, "What the fuck?" His friend started to stir. "I need to speak to you," she said and stepped outside the door. Vojdan skipped over his friend and came out of the room. "Who the hell do you think you are coming into my room when I'm with someone?" he growled. His breath reeked and there were black circles under his eyes.

"You never took Shemkov's exam!" she hissed. "He told me so himself!"

"Excuse me?" Vojdan snarled with the menacing look he had inherited from his father, sending a shudder of fear through Vesna. "But you didn't even go to *class!*" she shrieked.

"Get the fuck out of my face!" Vojdan snapped back. "Embarrassing me at the university! A mother calling a professor about her son! Barging into my room when I've got friends over. Don't *ever* speak to me again! You got that?" He gave her a little shove and slammed the door behind him.

From that day on he barely said a word to her. Vesna felt as though she didn't exist and had the sinking feeling that her son, perhaps, did not love her.

"I'm joining," Vesna resolutely said.

"Woman, you'll freeze to death," Ellie responded.

"Well," Aneta shrugged. "I guess it's okay to join. Look, our colleagues from the Psych Department are doing it," she said, pointing her chin toward a group of professors stamping their feet from the cold.

"Can you wait while I run to the bathroom?" Vesna asked, as she sidled toward the building entrance.

"Well, hurry up," Ellie said. "It looks like they're heading toward the government hall."

But Vesna had no intention of going to the bathroom. Instead, she went to the cafeteria, where she asked a waiter for a straw. Then she hurried to her office, took out a bottle of vodka she had hid in the cabinet by her computer ("just in case"), filled the flask to the brim, slid the straw in, and eased it into the inside pocket of her faux-fur coat. She figured that if the zipper slightly unzipped, she could drink from the straw, that is, if she got so cold she needed to tuck her face in to warm her nose. After all, I'm not dressed for this, she rationalized. I have to stay warm somehow. To test her theory, she went to the faculty bathroom, stood in front of the mirror, and took a swig. Then it occurred to her that the flask was probably too full and liable to spill over, so she took another swig, and then another. A warmth surged through her like a river. This is sure to improve my circulation, she thought as she hurried from the bathroom toward the main entrance.

The building was completely deserted and utterly still. In the empty hall she could barely hear the shouts of the students or the blaring of their vuvuzelas. Once outside, she saw the square had almost emptied. Aneta and Ellie were nowhere to be seen. Vesna followed on the heels of the departing procession, anxious not to be left behind, and suddenly became frantic at the thought of being alone with so many unfamiliar faces. She unzipped her coat and took several swigs from the flask, and just as suddenly felt a magical affection for all these beautiful young people. Several students flanking the procession, shouted slogans into megaphones to rile up the crowd: "You can't silence us!" and "No justice, no peace!"

These are my children! Vesna thought, uplifted by the sight of so many marching students waving flags and student cards. "My children! My beautiful children! You are the voice of the future!" she shouted, as she thrust herself among them, and added with a shriek that rose above the noise around her: "Enjoy your life and fight while you're still young!"

"Hey, professor," said a young girl who looked vaguely familiar, "let's take a picture together!"

"Yes!" Vesna shouted. "let's remember these moments!" They stopped to take a selfie with several other students, each of whom she embraced and said in a hoarse squeal, "You must fight, children, you must fight for us all!" She felt a wetness on her breast and realized the vodka had spilled on her blazer. She drew the zipper down and took several swigs, and when she finally looked up, all the warmth and affection she felt for these happy, determined youths marching toward the government hall was stronger, more glorious and moving than ever. Her eyes welled with tears. She was overcome by a feeling of grace she had only experienced once before. while boarding a little tour boat to the cliff-top church at Kaneo on the shore of Lake Ohrid after she had downed several gin and tonics. Propped against the bow, she had closed her eyes and let the wind and sun caress her face. She closed her eyes now, as well, and slowed her pace, thinking that she no doubt displayed great poise, almost as if she were floating.

"Oops! Watch your step there," a student said, grabbing her by the elbow. "You don't want to fall," he said to her.

She wrapped her arms around his neck and babbled, "You'll win! You'll win! I know you will!"

The crowd was gathering round a stage set up in front of the government hall. Still elated and tearful, Vesna noticed the scrubby thatch of orange that was Aneta's hair and the blonde backcombed ball that was Ellie's. She shouldered her way up to them.

"Yoohoo!" Vesna hooted as she squeezed in between them.

"What, you're here?" Aneta asked.

"We waited so long, we thought you'd left," Ellie said. "Aren't you freezing in that outfit?"

"How could you imagine I would leave! I wouldn't miss this for the world!" Vesna exclaimed, adding, "You guys ditched me!" For some time now Vesna had begun to harbor the suspicion that her work besties were avoiding her, that they only ever called her and asked her out for coffee when they needed her vote at a faculty meeting. Vesna consoled herself with the thought that she was needed, so she voted as they instructed.

"We had to," Aneta said. "Everyone was leaving and you were gone so long, we thought the cold had changed your mind."

"Ugh," Ellie said, wrinkling her nose. "Something smells weird, like nail polish remover or something."

"Isn't this just wonderful?" Vesna declared, trying to change the topic.

"Yes, I've never seen a protest this wonderful," Aneta said, as if she had ever attended a protest in her life.

"The students are teaching us a lesson," Ellie said, repeating a phrase she had heard someone else say.

"Just look at these bright, beautiful faces!" exclaimed Aneta, who, like Ellie, was still savoring the feeling that she was attending a winning game. Vesna too felt like she was floating on air.

"Have you seen my Vojdancho?" she asked.

"Yes!" Aneta said. "He was on the truck with all the music!"

"Oh, mommy's dearest!" Vesna said.

"He looked so handsome," Ellie said. "What a good-looking boy you have. And so brave, waving that flag! He looked just like a model in a magazine," and added, "I think he might be one of the organizers."

"He looks so much like Ljubo," Aneta said in a tone that left Vesna feeling that she had said this just to hurt her.

"Yeah, he's got daddy's looks and mommy's brains," she replied defensively, despite the fact that she had doubts that Vojdan was smart. Nor would she ever tell them that he had failed his first year, the thought of which so dampened her spirits that she tucked her face into her coat and took another swig.

"You're cold, huh?" Ellie asked, eyeing her suspiciously.

Swallowing the vodka, she peered up and said, "brrrrrr!"

"See, you're cold, and on top of that, you pulled your hair back," Aneta said. "Your ears and neck must be freezing. I can't even feel my feet," she said, hopping up and down.

"That's right," Ellie said, "Why don't you let your hair down?"

Vesna had pulled her hair back because it was greasy. Her hairdresser had once told her the more she washed it the greasier it would get, and so she put off washing her hair as much as she could, tightening it into a ponytail in the hope that no one would notice how oily it was.

"I'm not cold," she lied. "The students are keeping me warm!"

"I can tell. Your ears are burning red," Aneta sneered.

Just then a student climbed onto the makeshift stage and started shouting slogans into a microphone. The large crowd that had gathered stirred into life and repeated each slogan in unison. Aneta and Ellie forgot all about Vesna and began to chant and clap their leather-clad palms. Another student took the stage and held forth on the dreadful consequences of the higher education law.

Vesna tried to follow what the student was saying so that she could sound more informed in case Vojdan happened to talk to her about the protest. "That's right!" she shouted and clapped along with the rest of the crowd, but the sentences dissolved before she could grasp them, which also happened every time she tried to read a book.

"You know, with this law, they might just get rid of us," Ellie observed after the speech ended.

"Absolutley," Aneta added, "they're out to grab everything for themselves."

"What a time to be alive!" Ellie remarked. "You don't know whether to speak up or shut up."

"They'll do what they want anyway," Aneta said.

"That's how it's always been," Ellie said.

"It's just that this time they went too far," Aneta said.

"Yes!" Ellie said. "They'll turn us into beggars. We won't have any students or jobs. They'll make us teach in some god-forsaken village."

"But this isn't about us!" Vesna shouted, seizing the moment to finally outshine her colleagues. "This is about the students! About their future! What are we without them, huh? What *are* we?"

Ellie and Aneta exchanged glances, one of those hushed, mocking looks Vesna had learned to ignore.

"Would one of you like to talk on stage?" a student interrupted the uncomfortable silence. "Please, we need at least one professor up there."

"Oh, no, not me," Aneta and Ellie both said, shaking their heads, yet flattered they had been invited to do something important.

"Oh, come on, please, none of the other professors want to speak."

"Oh, no, I'm no good at public speaking," Aneta said.

"Same here," Ellie said. "I'm even worse than she is."

"How can that be when you're professors?" the student shot back, visibly annoyed. "It's incredible that none of you want to get up there and say something to defend the autonomy of the university."

"I'll do it," Vesna suddenly said.

"Hey, awesome," the student smiled. "Come with me then, quick."

Vesna did not have time to see Ellie and Aneta's jaws drop. She followed the girl, who led her toward the little stairs where Vojdan had stood. Defend the autonomy of the university, let's save the university's autonomy, Vesna repeated to herself as she made her way to the stage.

"Stay here," the girl said, "and when this speech is over, get up on stage." Before disappearing into the crowd, she signaled to the students who had been standing around Vojdan that she had finally found a professor willing to speak.

Vesna felt the same weakness in her knees as she had felt when she had seen Ljubo and Lilja strolling hand in hand down Macedonia Street. She plunged her face into her coat and sucked hard from the straw. She hid her head in her coat, savoring its warmth, trying not to think of how greasy her hair was, how she would be speaking in front of thousands of people, how she would probably wind up on TV, and how she hadn't the slightest clue what the higher education law was all about. She breathed deeply and thought of Vojdan and how they would finally be on the same side.

A young woman on the stage was waving her student card in the air. She wore a furious look, but her voice was calm and fluent. The crowd whistled and roared at the end of her every sentence, and booed each time she said *criminals, animals, dictatorship, mafia*. She raised her student card above her head, declaring that the higher education law would make it useless. She then threw it into the crowd and let her microphone drop. The crowd thundered as if this were a rock concert.

"Professor, it's your turn!" said the girl who had recruited her when she and several other students suddenly materialized from the crowd and gently edged her to the little staircase that led to the stage.

"Just don't go over five minutes," one of the students warned, as he guided her by the elbow. Vojdan was nowhere to be seen. "Come on, professor, let's go," the student urged.

"Where's Vojdan?" she asked, but he looked confused.

"Who?" he asked.

"Vojdan!" she shouted in his ear. The young man shrugged his shoulders.

"Please, the stage is empty," he said, giving her a little shove, "they're all waiting for you."

As she slowly mounted the stairs, unsteady as a newborn foal, Vesna felt her knees turn to water. But when she saw the sea of winter hats amid the grayness of the day, the bright red flags and vuvuzelas, she steeled herself and shouted, "Good evening, students of Macedonia!" but no one seemed to have heard her. She realized with alarm that the microphone was off. She looked helplessly around until a student clambered up onto the stage and turned it on for her. It's a good thing no one heard me, she thought to herself, since it's still day, not evening. Her eyes flared as she tried to focus.

What happened next was a blur. She remembered saying the word "Macedonia" a lot, and "wonderful students of our dear Macedonia," since the crowd rewarded her with a round of applause every time she mentioned the name of the country. She also remembered repeating the word "autonomy,"

having heard the previous speakers use it, as well as "crimi-
nal structures," a popular phrase in the press. She could also
remember a moment of panic when she realized she had no
idea why the students were protesting and so resorted to para-
phrasing the retired professor's speech from the faculty meeting: "You are the future of Macedonia! We exist for you! Fight
for us, oh you wonderful young people! Without you there
is no university, but there is also no life!" Here the applause
reached a crescendo that ended with whistles of approval.
Thinking of Vojdan, she boomed: "We are here to guide you,
we are here to show you the way. You are our children, and
we will never forsake you!"

She vaguely remembered ending her speech by blowing
kisses to the students and nearly tripping on the microphone
cable as she exited the stage. "Thank you, professor!" some of
the female students standing by the stairs chimed. Vojdan was
nowhere to be seen. "Have you seen Vojdan?" she asked one of
the girls who looked like she was part of the organizers. She,
too, shrugged her shoulders.

Vesna looked around for Aneta and Ellie as she pushed her
way through the crowd. Many of the protestors, especially the
older ones, congratulated her, saying: "You're so brave!" When
she reached the spot where she and her co-workers had been
standing, she saw that they were gone. She felt increasingly stifled by the crowd and rattled by the noise. A cold sweat washed
over her, leaving her chilled. She absent-mindedly made her
way toward the nearest taxi station. The crowd thinned as she
pressed on. Vesna tried breathing deeply and steadily, since she
had read in a magazine this is what you should do if you were
feeling poorly, but the filthy Skopje air only made her nauseous. She sat down on a concrete post and realized her butt
was completely numb. She had a sudden urge to call Vojdan
and took out her phone. Her fingers were so frozen she could

barely unlock the screen. She dialed his number, but there was no answer. She felt the need to call Ljubo, but she knew he was at Lilja's, which increased her nausea.

Vesna decided go home and lie down on the couch and wait for someone to show up. She thought Ljubo might come home if she appeared on TV. But it was Vojdan whom she longed to see. She called him again and again, but he never picked up. Then her phone started to ring like never before, one call after another from co-workers, unknown callers, relatives, friends from the past. And each time it rang, she hoped it was him.

"That was nonsense you were spewing," Vojdan said when he stepped in the door two days later. Vesna was still lying on the couch, huddled in blankets. She was burning with fever.

"I'm sick," she ventured, hoping to gain his sympathy. She had drifted in and out of sleep for two days running, praying that her speech at the protest was nothing but a bad dream.

"Sick in the head, you mean," Vojdan snarled.

Vesna burst into tears. She had run out of ways to make her son stop hating her.

"Poor baby,' he said, "stop your whining. I'll get you some rum. For your—you know—tea," he added and left the room, the house, and did not return for another two days.

"Brrrrrrrr," Vesna blubbered whenever she recalled what had happened. She would blurt this in the presence of other people, which invariably prompted odd looks. But even when she was able to suppress the "brrrrrrrr," she could not prevent herself from slamming her heel against the floor. *Bam, bam, bam*, she stomped, staring at the invitation in her hand as she regained her composure.

"Is everything alright?" she heard Aneta's voice behind her. They often ran into each other by their mailboxes in the library because their classes were scheduled at the same time.

"Yes! It's just this itch on my heel. You know the feeling when your foot itches and you can't scratch it?" Vesna said and stamped her foot again. Again she felt that tingling run up her side and again felt the flask in her purse, like a heavy, glowing object.

"Yeah, I know exactly what you mean!" Aneta replied. "You know, like, when your back really itches and you have to rub it against a doorknob or something? My kids are, like, 'Mom, what's wrong with you?'" and she burst into laughter as if she had said something incredibly funny.

"Ha-ha," Vesna replied politely, dying to let Aneta know that there were people who now thought of her as a "powerful woman."

"Oh, by the way, did you get this invitation, too?" she asked Aneta, who was still laughing over the hilarious incidents of her everyday life.

"Wow, what's this? 'Powerful woman!' Let me check my mail," she said and peered into her pigeonhole, only to find the stack of student papers she had let pile up. "Oh my God! Are you the only one who got this invitation? Well, then, bravo!" she said, in mock enthusiasm.

So, something good did come out of her protest speech. Her co-workers were envious, but also intimidated. When she encountered them in the hallway, they grinned when they greeted her, and when she spoke at faculty meetings, their voices fell into a respectful silence. She realized how jealous they were because of Ellie, who reproached her for describing herself as a professor of pedagogy in an interview. "You know, I'm the one who teaches pedagogy," she said, implying that the elective courses Vesna taught were irrelevant. "If you say you are a professor of pedagogy, it's like you're claiming you're teaching my subject. Just tell them the electives you teach. You've got bunch of little ones anyway."

Which was just one more reason why Vesna was pleased to see Aneta sucking up to her. Knowing that Aneta was the weaker of the two, Vesna seized this opportunity to taunt her.

"It's got to be because of my activism, this invitation. And did you know that I was also invited to the Professor's Plenum?"

"Oh really?" Aneta said, nodding as if she wanted to hear more.

"But I told them: I'm my own person. Individualism is where I'm at my best. But you have my full support. I'm here for you."

"Yes, yes, of course," Aneta said, struggling to give the appearance that she cared.

"But I'll go to this meeting," Vesna said, twirling the invitation between her slender fingers. "Who knows? It could open new horizons."

"You must tell me all about it over coffee! I'll give you a call. I have to go pick up Filip," she said as she scurried off.

What a pity, thought Vesna as she watched Aneta walk off, for she had hoped to mention Ljubo and make her think that everything was fine between them. She planned on saying: "Ljubo scolded me for speaking at the protest, said they would fire me! That it would've been better if I'd just kept quiet. But if we all kept quiet, where would we all be? Where will this get us? And, by the way, did anything happen to me? Noooo. They haven't fired me." And maybe she might have even said, "And just you watch me if they try!"

Ljubo had in fact come back from Lilja's shortly after Vojdan had left after telling her she was sick in the head. She had opened her eyes to find Ljubo sitting next to her. She wasn't sure if she was dreaming. She tried to speak, but nothing came out of her mouth except a croak.

"Jesus Christ," Ljubo said, "just look at you. I got you

some *Fervex*." He got up and went into the kitchen to check the kettle. "You know," he raised his voice so she could hear him in the living room, "I don't know what came over you, speaking at a protest like that. You know how dangerous it is? Why on earth would you get involved in something like that?" Vesna heard the kettle begin to whistle, the rustling and tearing of a paper bag, the clinking of a teaspoon on ceramic.

Ljubo came back into the living room with a steaming mug and set it on the coffee table.

"I'm serious," he went on. "You know how much it costs me to pay for this place?"

Vesna said nothing, thinking it was a rhetorical question.

"No, really," he insisted. "Do you?"

Vesna nodded. She didn't. It was Ljubo who paid all the bills and took care of their finances.

"All you do is waste your whole salary—that of a professor, mind you—and we all know how, right? But everything else, you know, comes out of my pocket. And I don't even live here full time." He paused, expecting Vesna to say something. But she stubbornly refused to admit that Ljubo did not live there all the time; in fact, he did not live there at all.

"What happens if they fire you? Huh? Who's gonna take care of you?"

Vesna took a sip form the mug and burned her upper lip. To keep herself busy she blew onto the surface of the hot drink.

"Alright. Forget about you. But what about your son? What about Vojdan? You think they won't take it out on him at the university, because of you?"

"But Vojdan was one of the protest organizers," Vesna plucked up the courage to say.

"That's irrelevant," Ljubo said.

"What do you mean, that's irrelevant," Vesna asked. "He

also thinks we should be speaking up about what's going on."

"That's not the topic of conversation," Ljubo said, as he always did when he was contradicted. "The topic is not 'what's going on.'. The topic is what's going to happen if you lose your job."

"Brrrrrrr," Vesna shuddered at the thought of being unemployed, or rather, of being without the salary she received for doing her job, if you could call it that. She only went in once or twice a week, and though she gave only four hours of class she clocked eight. Like most of her co-workers, she never held exams but simply asked her students to write papers she never read, and gave A's to everyone, which is why none of her students ever complained about her. In fact, she even taught a course called, "The Pedagogy of Free Time," so that when she failed to show up for class, she would tell the students that this was to give them time to do field work.

She glanced down at the invitation card, which restored her spirits. Say what you will, she reassured herself, but being liked by the Americans is no small thing. She felt that tingling in her side again and returned to her office to take a sip from her flask. Besides, she thought, if she ever found herself in distress, she might be in a position to turn to the Americans for help. But what she wished for most was for Vojdan to move to America, to get into a college there, somehow, or even receive a scholarship. Say what you will, she again reassured herself, but the education system there actually works and is stimulating for its students. She had seen this with her own eyes a few years back, when the American Embassy had given her a grant for a one-month stay at a university in Nevada.

Though she and the other grantees were housed in a seedy apartment complex off campus where shabby drunks roamed the parking lots, the sight of which left her trembling, especially if they were black, the splendor of the campus facilities astonished her. The restrooms were spotless. Not only did they have toilet paper, but soap, too. More surprising still, students and professors shared the same restrooms. Every professor had his or her own individual office, and every classroom was lavishly furnished with a digital board, a computer console, a projector, and a loudspeaker system. And they all had internet, too. There was a whole section of campus given over to leisure and entertainment activities, and was filled with restaurants and cafes, a rec center, and a club. Anyone could freely roam the library aisles. It was four stories tall and had computers on every floor. If the library didn't have a book you were looking for, they would borrow it from another college. Among the stacked shelves were study carrels filled with students who diligently attended class and were attentive. The teachers made lesson plans, never skipped class, and kept careful records of each student's progress. As she wandered the campus and saw the stream of students with heavy backpacks and earphones hurrying to class, she swore to herself that she would find a way to bring Vojdan here.

But that's when things began to go wrong with Ljubo. In fact, it was Ljubo's fault that Vojdan's life lacked vision. If they had only left the country, Lilja would not have happened, Vojdan would not be locking himself in his room all day listening to music or going to parties. He would not be failing school. Vojdan still had a chance in life—unlike herself. Unlike she and Ljubo, she thought, as she took a long swig from her flask. She glanced at the invitation again and realized the meet-and-greet was tomorrow.

* * *

Vesna knew she would be late because, standing in front of the open closet, she had no idea what she should wear. She had a vague recollection that wearing black to an official event was a definite no-no, but then again, she wasn't entirely sure if a "meet-and-greet" constituted an official event. Since Vojdan was not there to ask, she got online and gathered that a "meet-and-greet" was not expected to be terribly formal. There was nothing in her closet which both hid the fact that her belly had begun to sag like a half-deflated balloon and wasn't black. She decided to go with a pair of black slacks anyway, as it was the only pair she could still fit into, and a loose, black blouse that did not draw attention to her stomach, over which she wore a red blazer that matched her lipstick. Her only clean pair of panties were white and didn't match her black bra. It took all her strength to pull on the red ankle boots she had bought eight years ago when she and Ljubo went to Rome and had hardly ever worn since. She washed her hair and let it down. Perhaps she should have gone to the hair salon, she thought, looking in the mirror at the sad strands of dyed black hair hanging lifelessly along her cheeks. She hated looking at herself in the mirror. The sight disturbed her because the bags that had formed under her eyes the last few years were so puffy they made her look as if she hadn't slept for days. Her complexion also distressed her because of a sallow glow that peaked through regardless of how much foundation she packed on, giving off the impression that she was sweating.

"American ambassador's residence, please," she told the taxi driver, hoping he would know where it was. Once inside the cab, she broke into a smelly, cold sweat. I must be nervous, she thought, and though she vowed never to touch the flask before 2 p.m., she felt that the seriousness of the occasion demanded

it. She had another staunch principle, one which distinguished her from her female friends and colleagues, which
was to avoid Bromazepam, Diazepam, or Xanax as if they were
poison. "I would never touch that stuff," she would trumpet
whenever she saw Ellie pop a tablet in her mouth to cope with
what she called her "headaches." "That's all bad chemistry,"
Vesna would say. For the same reason she avoided analgesics,
arguing they were bad for the stomach. Alcohol, on the other
hand, she deemed natural. Vodka, in particular, as it was made
of potatoes, which was by far her favorite vegetable, and which
she felt compelled to consume in every form.

The taxi deposited her before an enormous iron gate. She
rang the intercom that had a camera above it and was surprised to hear a voice welcome her in Macedonian.

"Yes, hello," Vesna said in a shaky voice. I'm here for the
get-together."

"And you are?"

"Vesna Stojchevska," she replied, and the door buzzed
open.

She followed a cobblestone pathway lined with winter-
green shrubs that led to the entrance of the residence and saw
the front door opened by a middle-aged woman long before
she reached the doorbell.

"Hello! Hello!" Vesna cried out with exaggerated politeness on the assumption that the woman was the ambassador's wife. The woman did not flinch; she simply nodded.
Vesna extended her hand and received a grudging handshake
in return, whereupon the woman hurried to take Vesna's coat.

"No problem, I take vid me!" Vesna protested, but the
woman shook her head, slipped behind Vesna and grabbed
her coat by the collar, forcing her to relinquish it. "Tank you,
tank you," Vesna said submissively as the woman vanished
behind a door, leaving her alone in the spacious hallway. A

moment later the woman reappeared and silently pointed toward a doorway beyond which she could hear the chiming of women's voices. As Vesna stepped into the sprawling salon lined with tall windows draped with diaphanous white curtains, the woman disappeared again.

"*Zdravou, dobroudoydouvtey*," said a thin, bony woman with a thick American accent, approaching her. "*Vee-ey stay Vesna?*" she asked in Macedonian. She too was middle-aged but looked wonderfully fit and was elegantly dressed in beige slacks and a matching tweed blazer with three-quarter sleeves and a collarless jewel neckline. Delicate, oval earrings with what appeared to be semi-precious stones dangled from her earlobes. Her pastel makeup was nearly undetectable. The other women in the room were also dressed in clothes that seemed designed to blend in with the muted palette of the decor, which made Vesna acutely self-conscious of her appearance. Amid such elegance the colors she had chosen made her look like a roulette wheel. On top of everything, the sun was shining as it rarely did through the long Skopje winters.

"Yes, dat's me," Vesna replied, as if she were admitting to something terrible.

"*Yas soom Kelly Davis*," said the woman, introducing herself in Macedonian. So *this* is the ambassador's wife, Vesna realized. "*Ney zvorubam dobrow makedonkey*," Kelly added and flung her angular hands as if she were releasing fireworks.

"My English also not very good," Vesna said. She wasn't lying. English was not her forte. She was apt to say that though she had trouble expressing herself., she understood everything, which was simply not true. When she was in Nevada, for example, she always felt that Americans garbled their words as though they were chewing gum. So she would claim that her command of British English was much better, despite the fact that whenever she watched a British film she barely understood a thing.

"No, it's much better than my Macedonian!" Kelly said, flashing a grin. Her teeth were unnaturally white, whiter than any Vesna had seen since she had last been in the States.

"Hiiiiii," everyone said.

"Vesna," Kelly Davis announced, "is a professor of pedagogy at the University of Skopje."

"Pedagogy of free time," Vesna said.

"Ooo, sounds exciting!" Kelly said. "But as we're already running late, how about you make yourself comfortable, Vesna, and we all take turns introducing ourselves?"

Vesna looked about. Every chair and every spot on the sprawling sofa had been taken, and she was forced to sit on a cream-colored ottoman, where it took considerable effort for her to position herself so that her waistband did not cut painfully into her belly.

There were around ten women in the room. Most were in their thirties, but a few were younger. Vesna recognized some of them from television, but she couldn't remember who they were or what they did. I should have eaten something, Vesna thought, as she saw her vision begin to blur. Whatever she tried to focus on was little more than a smudge. This was not the first time this had happened, which she attributed to a change in blood pressure or blood sugar. This inability to focus on an object or a face left her even more disoriented. She lowered her head surreptitiously to see if her armpits smelled. The rank mixture of nervous sweat and the heavy perfume she had worn for the occasion, one called "Red," made her fear that here, too, she had made a mistake.

Kelly invited the other two women from the "international community" to introduce themselves. One was also the wife of an ambassador, but Vesna did not catch which one. Her name was Monica, and though she was a heavy-set woman she carried herself with pride. She introduced herself as an amateur gastronome. Vesna assumed the other woman was the wife of the Chinese or Japanese ambassador because she looked Asian, and was shocked to discover she was an American married to a diplomat "here on a mission." She introduced herself as "a wife and mother of two" who wrote plays in her spare time. Her name was Janice. Then the women in the room who were from Macedonia introduced themselves. Among them was an Albanian and a Roma who both ran nonprofit organizations. Here, too, like the foreigners, none of the Macedonian women failed to mention they were wives or mothers. One woman, Marija, was a journalist ("Marija has been the subject of many death threats!" Kelly announced proudly), while another appeared to be a lesbian and was into something called "social entrepreneurship," which Vesna had never heard of. Neither mentioned their marital status, and so, Vesna felt compelled to nod sympathetically and give them a patronizing smile. Also present were a writer, two businesswomen who referred to themselves as "entrepreneurs," two recent college graduates, a sportswoman, the editor of a fashion magazine, a lawyer, and a few women from NGOs who described themselves as "activists."

When it was Vesna's turn to introduce herself, she rose from her Ottoman, stuck her nose in the air and pretending she was Ellie, said: "I am professor at university in Skopje and I teach pedagogy of free time and metodology of yoots development. I am married and have son, he is twenty years. His name is Vojdan, means leader."

"A leader, wow!" Kelly exclaimed. "Leaders is what we all are here, too! And let me just add that Vesna," she said, extending an index finger bedecked with a jeweled band that matched her earrings, "is a big supporter of the student movement and has spoken out against the authoritarian practices of the government. Vesna is a powerful woman—isn't that what we all are here? Go, go, powerful women!" Kelly whooped, pumping her petite fist, as if she were rooting for a sports team. A few faint "Yay!"s followed. Their mini celebration was interrupted by the entrance of the woman who had greeted Vesna at the door. She held a large tray in her hands stacked with tiny sandwich wedges. She set it on the coffee table in the middle of the room and disappeared.

"O yay, our treats have arrived!" piped a diplomat's wife.

"I know we're not big on carbs, but see this is a healthy winter vegetarian snack," Kelly said with pride, as if she had prepared them herself. The woman, whom Vesna only now realized was a maid, returned with another tray of sandwiches, plates, and utensils. The maid went round to each person, obsequiously asking them what they would like to drink. "Water," Vesna said before the woman approached her, for she feared her body odor was noticeable.

"Before we dig in and continue our introductions, please don't forget to sign this sheet," Kelly said. "It's for communication purposes," she added. Printed at the top were the words: "Name / Institution / Email Address / Phone Number / Signature." Vesna filled it in while the others were wrapping up their introductions, then glanced at the sandwiches. Her stomach squealed like an unhappy puppy. She hadn't had breakfast that morning—like most mornings these past few years. The thought of food made her nauseous. That's because she always felt less than stellar in the mornings, until suddenly, she'd find herself famished. Then her appetite would accost her. Such was the case now.

When Kelly broke the ice and took a sandwich, holding her plate like a trophy, several other women followed suit. Unfortunately, the platter was well beyond Vesna's reach, which irritated her, because she would have to get up and cross the women's field of vision with her bumblebee body. When she had gingerly taken a sandwich and returned to her seat, she swallowed a bite and liked it so much—cream cheese and cucumber—she regretted not taking two.

As she chewed the sandwich, wondering how long she should wait before grabbing another, Kelly took the floor and began explaining why she had invited them all. She kept repeating the phrases "powerful women," "strong female voices," and "make a difference in the community." Which made Vesna wonder, what does "community" actually mean? It was one of those words like "discourse" she had trouble getting her head around. Then Kelly presented her plan.

"Back in college—oh my, that was a long time ago," Kelly said, "I took a couple of theater classes, because, you know, I was a very active member of our high school theater club. I've always treasured this experience in my life and now I can put it to use to honor our engagement as women in history and in this community," she went on, enunciating every word as if she were on television.

"Which is why I invited all you powerful women who've already contributed to making a difference during these very difficult times. Since International Women's Day is right around the corner, I thought it would be a good idea to stage a performance, you know, here, at our residence, which would be open to a select audience. And I would like to invite all of you brave women to take part in this performance, a performance with a cause."

One of the women choked on her sandwich. "Excuse me," she said, taking a sip of water in the attempt to suppress her cough.

Kelly elaborated her plan. She would be the director. Janice—the woman Vesna thought was the wife of an Asian ambassador—would dramatize the script. Monica, the other diplomatic wife, would organize the catering. Several other women who had been unable to join them today would handle the props and sound. The stage would be set at one end of the room where they were sitting, which, she assured them, could comfortably seat eighty people. The invitees would include esteemed friends of the American Embassy as well as human rights activists. Katerina, a piano accompanist who worked at the performance arts high school, would oversee the music, the announcement of which prompted a humpbacked woman with a frigid grin to wave her hand vigorously and nervously giggle.

The evening program would consist of several skits involving two, three, and possibly more people, said Kelly, expressing herself in the royal we, and she particularly recommended solo performances, such as the recitation of a feminist poem or brief essay. And she also encouraged, again in the royal we, musical performances in the spirit of the fight for women's rights.

Panic swept over Vesna. Though her vision had stopped blurring after the second sandwich, the thought of having to perform again suddenly squelched her appetite just as she stood poised to grab another wedge. Her English was pretty bad and she was consequently terrified at the idea of performing something in front of other people, but, on the other hand, she could hardly bow out now after appearing on stage at the student protests.

Kelly assured them that she would leave the choice of what to perform to them, but then added that she and Monica had already selected some skits and poems she hoped they would consider. "Do any of you have a preference in terms of what you would like to perform?" she asked.

A dead silence ensued, much like the silence that Vesna encountered whenever she asked a question in class.

"Elena," said Kelly, turning to the fashion magazine editor, "What do you think?"

"I'm okay with anything," Elena replied, with a shrug of her shoulders,

"Okay, let's put it this way. Is there anyone here who would like to do something related to music?" Kelly persisted.

Vesna felt a sudden urge to respond. Though she didn't know a thing about poetry and her English was hardly up to the task of performing a skit, she believed she had a musical talent that had long lain dormant. Years ago, when they were first married, she used to play the accordion and sing to Ljubo and he would gaze at her lovingly and coo, "Let me love those lips and those darling little fingers."

"Me!" Vesna shouted as she shot up her hand, then quickly brought it down as the smell of nervous sweat struck her in the face. "I can do musical performance."

"That's awesome!" Kelly said. "Do you have anything specific in mind?"

Vesna stopped to think. Having taken the initiative, she became infused with the feeling of creativity, vigor, and confidence she always experienced during those rare occasions when students responded positively to her teaching.

"You vant Macedonian or English song?" she asked.

Kelly was delighted, as it had not occurred to her that Macedonian songs might also be performed. "Both!" she screeched happily.

"What a great idea," several women chimed.

"Thank you for thinking of such a great thing," Janice said in a tone that was usually reserved for first graders.

"Sorry, my English . . ." Vesna stuttered. "In school I study Russian. My Serbian also—very good."

"No, please!" Kelly demurred, "That's two—oops, *three* more languages than what I can speak!" she exclaimed, laughing with exaggerated sincerity.

"For American song—I tink *Beetch*," Vesna said.

Silence fell.

"You know—Meredith Brooks," Vesna explained.

"Oh!" gasped Katerina, the musician. She then whistled the melody. The women's faces brightened as they recognized the song.

"Wow, that's risqué!" Kelly said. "But I love it!"

The women livened and began to stir. Inspired by Vesna's boldness they became less embarrassed to share their own ideas, but before they could say a word, they were interrupted by Vesna.

"And for Macedonian song . . . maybe 'Nazad, nazad, Kalino mome.' It is brutal song. Scandalous. Men lover says to vooman lover: Go avay, go avay. She don't vant to go avay! Men is married, has childrens. Kalina says him: I vill . . ."—at which point Vesna furrowed her brows and turned toward the fashion magazine editor and asked in Macedonian: "How do you say *chuma* in English?"

"Plague," the editor replied.

"I vill make myself black plack, I vill keell your vife, take care of your keeds, I vill be yours foreva," she concluded.

"Wow," Monica said.

"Wow. Just *wow*," Kelly added. "There's something about Macedonian folklore that's just so . . . *visceral*."

"So passionate and dark," Janice said. "So red and so black." Vesna stared at her for she could hardly believe it was possible for someone who looked so Asian to have an American accent.

Pride filled Vesna. Among all these women who were so accomplished in Macedonian society, all these powerful and independent women, she was the one who had mustered the courage to break the ice and share an idea. She rose to her feet and reached for another sandwich, but as she did, she heard a tearing sound and felt a slight release of pressure on her buttocks and realized with horror that her trousers had split. She dropped the sandwich on her plate in her haste to sit down and blushed from ear to ear. Everyone was staring at her.

"I would like to recite a poem," volunteered the woman Vesna believed to be the writer, but her thoughts fled elsewhere as she plotted her escape. Her underwear was white and would no doubt glare loudly through the rip in her slacks. She shifted to one side so she could discreetly feel if the hole was as big as she imagined, but several women had locked their eyes on her, as if they knew what she was up to. Her heart pounded in her ears. She felt an intense loathing for the maid who had taken her coat, for if she hadn't taken it, she could have covered the offending hole. Her plight deepened as she realized she needed to leave soon. She waited for a few minutes, nibbling the wretched sandwich that had cost her so dearly. Meanwhile, the women were chattering away, planning their roles in the performance, but Vesna was unable to follow the conversation.

"Oh, my Gad!" she cried, attracting their attention. "*Docnam na sostanok!* I'm late for meeting! May I go? I'm sorry," she said, as she quickly dialed up a cab.

"No problem," Kelly said. "Katerina will be in touch with you about the details regarding the music performance—and we'll call you about rehearsals. You know, we have less than a month left, so we'll all have to meet at least several times before D Day!"

"American ambassador's residence to Vlae," Vesna said to the taxi dispatcher who answered her call, nodding politely as Kelly spoke. Everyone remained silent as they waited for Vesna to finish the call and leave. When she hung up, Vesna rose to her feet and began walking backward toward the entrance, waving her hands and blowing kisses. "Bye everyone! *Prijatno! Blagodaram!* See you soon and tank you, tank you so much!" she called as she edged toward the doorway, where she curtsied slightly and gave them a namaste bow. As she waited for the maid to bring her coat, she reached back and felt the hole in her pants—it was as large as she had feared. Her loathing for the maid returned with even greater force. When the maid finally appeared, Vesna angrily demanded "Give me my coat!" and snatched it out of her hands as the woman tried to help her put it on. "I'm perfectly capable of putting on my own coat!" Vesna growled as she wrapped it about her and stormed out.

* * *

Over the next few days, Vesna lived with the torment of having suggested the idea of performing *"Nazad, nazad, Kalino mome,"* aware that she had only offered to sing this song to give the appearance of being a savvy feminist, although she would never profess to actually being one. The truth was that, in the cafeteria one day, she had overheard a woman from another department mention that it was the only Macedonian folk song that could possibly be construed as feminist. Vesna supposed this was owing to the stolid resolution of its protagonist, Kalina, who refused to end her affair with a married man. As she lay sprawled on the couch, chugging vodka straight from the plastic bottle she hid under the kitchen sink among the cleaning products, it occurred to Vesna that she identified with Kalina, despite the fact that she herself was no adulteress. She well knew that Ljubo belonged to Lilja now, and that, like Kalina, she consequently longed for something terrible to happen to the woman so she could get her husband back. In her fantasies, Vesna was even willing to raise Lilja's five-year old daughter. The child's age suspiciously coincided with the start of Ljubo's long and frequent absences from the house. Everyone knew what was going on, but they all pretended they didn't, as did Vesna, for it was important for her to retain some shred of dignity, which is why, whenever she felt insecure, she would reach for her flask or, like, Ellie, lift her chin to make the wrinkles on her neck less prominent. She would smile profusely, her lips smeared with red lipstick—the color of battle! she would say to herself. But for now, she felt helpless. She wallowed in the couch for several days, fearing the audience would imagine Kalina's words were Lilja's thoughts, that Lilja was summoning a plague on Vesna, that Lilja wanted Vesna dead and gone. Not only would Lilja have Ljubo, she would steal Vojdancho as well.

Vesna wracked her brain to come up with a way to cancel her performance, or at least change the song, but as soon as that impulse crossed her mind, she thought to herself: how can I even think of rejecting an honor bestowed by one of the most powerful women in the country? The American ambassador's wife, no less. No, it was simply out of the question. She was even afraid to change the song, knowing how thrilled Kelly Davis and her friends had been with her idea. Every email Kelly sent deeply troubled her. Vesna had received several, but replied to none; she was so paralyzed with fear, she could barely leave the couch.

"I'm not well," she told Vojdan when, two days later, he finally came out of his room and found her wrapped in a blanket, during which time Vesna had had to suffer the sound of muffled voices and the relentless beat of electronic music.

"Got any batteries?" was all he said.

"There're some in the second drawer under the utensils," she said, forcing a cough.

He disappeared into the kitchen from where Vesna heard clanking noises.

"What do you need them for?" she asked in the attempt to make conversation.

"For my joystick," he answered, setting the *Pelisterka* mineral water bottle full of Vesna's vodka on the table in front of her, and said, "Well if you're that ill, you should have some of your medicine," and left the room without bothering to close the door behind him.

Vesna burst into tears of self-pity. She cried because her son didn't love her, because her husband didn't love her, because she felt lost at work, because the country was a total mess and had no future, because her son was a total mess and had no future, because she didn't want to sing a song about a desperate adulteress, because she didn't want to perform at all. She dreaded the thought of going to rehearsals, where she would have to converse with those socially active, fluent English speakers, who wore such perfect smiles and were always in agreement with Kelly Davis and the other foreign wives. She cried because she had never learned English and was thus too embarrassed to respond to Kelly's emails regarding the rehearsal dates.

Her phone rang as she lay there whimpering.

"Hello, this is Katerina, we met at the American ambassador's residence?" a voice said.

"Oh, yes, hello," Vesna replied, collecting herself.

"Well, I'm calling about your performance," the woman said. "You know, you didn't come to the first rehearsal and never responded to the emails we sent you," she added with her signature laugh.

"I'm terribly sorry," Vesna said, no longer attempting to conceal her stuffy nose from all the crying, "but I've been horribly sick for almost a week. My eyes hurt so much I can't even read my emails." Lying to Katerina was not that difficult, Vesna realized. It would not have been as simple if the call came from one of the foreign wives.

"Will you be able to perform?" Katerina asked.

"Oh, by all means," Vesna said and then winced at the thought that she had thrown away a perfect opportunity to cancel.

"Will you also accompany yourself, as you mentioned?" Katerina asked.

"Yes, I'll play the accordion."

"Amazing," Katerina said and nervously giggled.

"It's just that I might not be able to come to rehearsals because, you know, I'm so very sick," Vesna lied, "I want to be healthy for the performance."

"Okay! I'll let them know," Katerina said.

Alright then, Vesna thought, recalling another of her father's home-made maxims "When God stops you in the middle of a bowel movement, you must be in the wrong." She reached for the bottle her son had set before her, raised her chin, wiped away her tears and took a long swig. Vojdan, she rationalized, only treated her so cruelly because he was unhappy, because he had no perspective, because the country gave him nothing, because the country had no future. That's why he locked himself up with his friends in his room day and night, listening to music and playing video games. As she raised the bottle for the third time, she fancied herself inviting the American ambassador and his wife over after the performance, a performance in which she would be nothing short of brilliant. She would serve them her legendary trout and new potatoes dish, treat them to a traditional Macedonian pie, salads to-die-for, and an exquisite selection of wine that would floor them. Ljubo and Vojdan would be there as well. "What a bright son you have!" Kelly would say and offer to do everything in her power to help Vojdan leave this shithole country. Tilting the bottle again, she barreled into the bedroom, dragged a chair up to the wardrobe and climbed up so she could reach the dusty accordion she had placed there five years earlier, when Ljubo started going missing from the house. She had inherited the old, heavy instrument from her father. She strapped it on her shoulders and pulled the bellows apart. The accordion inhaled deeply, all too ready to cry out. As Vesna fingered the buttons and keys, she realized she would have to trim her nails. They were still pretty, she thought. She took a deep breath and began to play. A rich sound filled the house. As Vesna sang, she moved toward the living room door, in the hope that Vojdan would hear her.

Dear Vesna,

Thank you for conveying your message to Katerina. I am disappointed that you weren't able to make it to any of our rehearsals. I do appreciate your commitment to our project, though I would also have appreciated a prompter warning regarding your situation. In any event, I am glad you are feeling better and that you will perform tomorrow. Just to remind you, though Katerina has assured me she has communicated this to you over the phone, your performances are after the first and second block of skits and/or readings. You perform right after the "I feel bad about my neck" reading and "The way to a woman's heart." At the end of the third block we're all participating in the collective skit. Since you didn't come to rehearsals, maybe you could just stand with us while we perform. Finally, I will wrap up the evening by honoring you all with my own poem "Power is in us."

Since we already held the final rehearsal for tomorrow's show, I invite you to join us for free snacks and drinks an hour before the performance, at 6.30 P.M.

With high hopes of seeing you tomorrow,

Kelly L. Davis

Kelly's email caused Vesna some distress, realizing the words "disappointed" and "I would have appreciated . . ." concealed an anger Kelly had only managed to suppress by virtue of good manners. This thought gnawed at her as she prepared for the event. She decided she would again put on the matching gray lycra skirt and blazer she had worn at the protest, hoping no one would recognize it. She had the illusion she had lost weight from lying in the couch so long and from playing the accordion—and from not having left the house, instead polishing off whatever little was left in the fridge—because there were no gaps in her buttoned-down shirt. She felt pleased with herself which diminished the anxiety that made beads of sweat freckle her upper lip and caused her knees to wobble and the accordion to slip from her hands as she clambered into the cab waiting to take her to the American residence. For once she wasn't late, but then she realized she had forgotten her flask. Although she had, like any other day, already downed a few screwdrivers beginning at 2 P.M., the feeling of elation and confidence that had filled her during the ten days she practiced for the event would not surface. I bet they'll have something there to help me unwind, she reassured herself, trying to imagine what Kelly's reference to "snacks and drinks" meant.

The same dour-faced maid took her coat, but this time Vesna did not shake the woman's hand. In return, the maid did not escort Vesna in, but just pointed her chin in the direction of the room.

"Welcome! *Dobroudoydouvtey!*" Kelly said as soon she saw Vesna. She extended her hand and leaned back to avoid the unpleasant traditional triple kiss on the cheek. "So nice to finally see you!" Kelly said, as they greeted each other with make-believe smiles. Kelly wore a pastel pink blazer and a skirt made of soft tweed. Her earrings and bracelet were adorned with opals. Most of the other women also wore some shade of pink. It must have been something they had agreed upon together, Vesna thought.

"*Dobro ve najdov!*" Vesna replied loudly in Macedonian.

"Are you feeling better?" Kelly asked.

"Yes, yes, not more sick, but it vas . . . someting terrible," Vesna lied, looking at the other women who were all politely smiling, each of whom she was compelled to extend her clammy hand.

All was set for the performance. There was a little stage with a projection screen at the back as well as two makeshift curtains that hid the props. Kelly pointed to the speakers set up around the room which was filled with eight rows of ten white plastic folding chairs. Three long tables were lined up near the flowing white curtains, two of which were empty, the other two topped with food, paper plates, plastic cups, and an assortment of beverages. A dark-skinned young woman in a white serving uniform stood vacantly behind the table.

"Why don't we relax with some refreshments first," Kelly offered, a suggestion Vesna had been desperately waiting for her host to make. "Over there you'll find some American sliders brought to us by *Hope*, a new company developed as part of our social entrepreneurship program for Roma women," Kelly added, throwing a glance at the young woman with the vacant stare. The women in the room nodded energetically and voiced loud exclamations of approval. "Emina over there will serve you whatever beverage you'd like," she continued. "I know I sure could use a glass of wine!" Kelly chuckled, and the whole room burst into laughter, as if she had said something hilarious. Emina looked at her shoes. "I think I may need something stronger!" chirped Janice, the wife of the American diplomat here on a mission. Everyone laughed again, as if they were part of some collective conspiracy.

Vesna felt the need to apologize to Kelly in order to keep

alive her fantasy of inviting her and her husband over for dinner so she could show them how well-rounded she was and how precious her son. "Pleeze, I apologize again, my seekness . . ." she blurted, edging herself closer to Kelly as they all moved toward the table with the drinks and sliders. "Oh, no, please!" Kelly said. "It's fine. I really appreciate your being here with us today. And I appreciate all you've done for your community."

That word again, "community." Vesna wondered if she was referring to her work at the university and nodded gratefully, but Kelly had already turned and was in a conversation with a tall woman with a booming voice. Suddenly she turned back and said, "Go ahead," motioning to Vesna that she was next in line.

Vesna found herself face to face with the silent Emina. She looked seventeen and lost.

"Got any hard liquor?" Vesna asked, getting straight to the point.

"There's rakija," Emina said.

"Fine, then, give me rakija," Vesna replied, swallowing her disappointment there was no vodka. "Better make it a double," she added as she watched the girl shakily pour the drink into a red plastic cup, which reminded her that her own hands were trembling, too.

"Please, have a burger!" someone said, approaching Vesna. It was Monica, the woman in charge of the catering. "We must fuel up before the show! Besides, they're delicious and loaded with American ingredients: cheddar cheese, jalapeno pepper sauce, and of course, iceberg lettuce." Vesna was not the least bit hungry, but she reached for a slider anyway and gobbled it down so she could get to the rakija as quickly as possible. "Mmm, very good!" she mumbled as she swallowed the last bite. Monika nodded, pointing toward Emina, whose gaze was still fixed on her shoes.

"Yes, thank you for reminding me, Monica!" Kelly piped and the women's voices faded into silence. "Please help yourselves to some food before the performance. And we'll be serving food to you and the audience after the performance as well. And thank you, Emina, for being such a great server!" Kelly added. Everyone turned to the girl an gave her a gracious smile.

Once served, the women slowly chattered their way back to their seats, bearing their burgers on paper plates. Vesna hurriedly ordered another double rakija before taking her seat. One of the performers Vesna believed to be the lawyer looked at her knowingly and raised her cup.

"Now that we're all refreshed," Kelly said as she handed out the program for the evening, "let's just make sure we're all on the same page." As with the invitation to the meet-and-greet, the program was lavishly printed on expensive-looking paper. It was mauve, decorated with dancing figures of women, and folded into three parts. Apart from having forgotten her reading glasses, Vesna saw the smudges had reappeared, blurring her vision. The letters on the page kept shuffling about. She closed her left eye in an effort to focus and spotted her name after the titles of the third and sixth numbers in the program, just as Kelly had said in her email.

SONG
"Bitch" by Meredith Brooks
Vesna Stojchevska (voice and accordion)

. . .

SONG
"Back off, oh Kalina" (traditional)
Vesna Stojchevska (voice and accordion)

The English translation of the folk song seemed a bit off, but she had no time to figure out why, as she was trying to follow the conversation of the half-blurred women around her.

"And where will you put your accordion, Vesna?" Kelly asked, standing in front of the women like a conductor. Vesna pointed toward the floor beside her chair.

"You'll have it with you all the time?"

Vesna nodded, finding the thought of speaking English unbearable.

It's from the stress, it's because I'm nervous, she said to herself as Kelly, Janice and Monica assigned the women seats. They placed Vesna at the far end of the second row where she would have room to lay the accordion on the floor. Kelly and Janice then informed them the first row was reserved for the diplomatic corps attending their International Women's Day event, and that the remaining seats were reserved for people who had "made a difference in their community." Shortly after they had arranged the seating and the order in which they would go on stage—"Be sure to take the stairs on your left, Vesna; remember, the left"—the guests began to arrive. Vesna recognized many public figures: several academics who were regulars on political talk shows, several fearless women she secretly admired who were always on the forefront of every protest, as well as actors, journalists, artists and other faces familiar from the press. Vesna's head began to spin. "I'm so nervous," she confessed to the lady sitting beside her, a middle-aged businesswoman whose beautiful figure belied her age.

"Ugh, me too," she said, fanning herself with the program. The woman's foundation had begun to melt around her eyebrows and nostrils.

"I don't know why I said yes to this," Vesna said in an outburst of sincerity.

"You gotta do what you gotta do," the businesswoman

replied, loosening the pink scarf around her neck and turning to inspect the people still filing into the room.

"The only thing you gotta do is die," Vesna said, looking down at her red booties. She noticed a hole on the knee of her pantyhose.

"Oh my God, everyone who's someone is here," the businesswoman enthused. She turned to Vesna with a triumphant look. "You know what kind of company we're in?"

"I do, and that's exactly why I'm nervous. I feel sick," Vesna said, taken aback by her honesty. She felt nauseous, desperate for help or sympathy.

"Look, if they told me to stand on my head, that's just what I'd do," the businesswoman spoke as if she was egging herself on. "You know what the Americans have done for me?" she asked. "If it weren't for the Americans, I could never have started my business. I would do anything they asked me to," she said, straightening her back and turning to Vesna with an air of confidence. Her chin was as sharp and forward as her question: "So what did they do for *you?*"

"What do you mean, what did they do for me?" Vesna asked in confusion, the blood draining from her face.

"Yes, what did they give you—a grant or something? Maybe sent you somewhere?"

Vesna stared at the woman, astonished that she hadn't realized until then the logic behind Kelly's invitations, the real reason why these strong women were all part of her little theater.

"So, what was it?" the businesswoman persisted.

"Yes, I was on a one-month fellowship in the US. They took us here and there. It was nice. I had a great time," Vesna said.

"See? Who does that?" the businesswoman gushed just as Kelly stepped onto the stage. The babel of voices tapered off.

Vesna reached under her chair for the plastic cup she had filled with the rakija. She took another sip, hoping her nerves would calm so she could focus on what Kelly was saying. She began with a warm welcome to her esteemed guests, telling them how happy she was they had all gathered there, and how humbled she was to have the opportunity to perform along- side such courageous women—and one man! she exclaimed, making the audience burst into laughter—who had made such a difference in their community. She said something about the title of the event, about how the word "empower- ing" held more than one meaning, but Vesna didn't under- stand that part. She rounded off her introduction by giving a little history of International Women's Day, explaining the importance it held for women around the globe.

"*Sreyken Ohsmee Mart!*" Kelly said, bungling the Macedonian for Eighth of March and then took her place in the first row beside her husband, the ambassador. The lights dimmed and soft music was heard from the speakers. The beam of the projector lit up the screen on the stage where the words "EMPOWERING WOMEN" glowed in large let- ters. Then the lights came back on, illuminating the audience. Someone sneezed. The young writer mounted the stage and everyone clapped.

This writer is quite ambitious, Vesna thought, sweating heavily, unable to follow the tenor of the performance, a poem Vesna was unfamiliar with in which the phrase "I rise, I rise" the writer repeatedly recited, and each time she did, she would rise on her toes. The work was awash with rhetorical ques- tions the young woman articulated with angry determination. Toward the end of the poem, she again repeated "I rise, I rise," but this time she extended her arms as if she was going to fly off the stage and, in the process, revealed large dark blotches under the armpits of her pink blouse. When she was done, she closed her eyes and twisted her face into a grimace as if she had had a sudden stomach cramp. The audience awarded her with thunderous applause, upon which the writer transformed from fearless actress to coy girl fumbling into her front row seat. Kelly and the other foreign wives mouthed "That was amazing!" and "Awesome!" Vesna grew dizzier than ever at the thought that Kelly would dislike her performance.

The lights dimmed again and a few people Vesna didn't know shuffled onto the stage and set up three rows of chairs and a six-foot sheet of cardboard cut in the shape of a bus's silhouette. This was the only part of the program Vesna recognized: Rosa Parks on the bus, something she had seen on TV. A recent graduate sat in the driver's seat. She was disguised as a man, had a fake handlebar moustache and a poor boy hat. The Roma woman who ran an NGO sat behind her. She was wrapped in an old-lady's shawl, had a pair of granny glasses perched on the tip of her nose and an old-fashioned handbag splayed on her lap. The third performer was the male Kelly had mentioned in her introduction. Tino was a real actor who hosted a satirical news show on a new independent TV channel and who now began a running speech. Vesna could not understand a word he was saying, since he was trying to sound like he was from the American South but his Macedonian accent kept getting in the way. Then he and the Roma activist began arguing but she refused to budge and only wagged her finger in his face as if it were a metronome. Vesna was not the only one in the audience who did not realize the skit had ended until several seconds after it was over. Then, they began to belatedly clap. Vesna again reached for the rakija: there was just enough to get her through the next performance, after which would be her own.

A woman stood on the stage who looked very much like Vesna: middle-aged, dark puffy bags under her eyes, sagging cheeks, a double-chin, hennaed hair—all the reasons why Vesna avoided looking at herself in the mirror, though none of these features bothered her in other people, especially men. The woman on the stage was trying to render a humorous performance of an essay referring to all those body parts that made Vesna feel redundant. The most frequently mentioned part was the neck, which Vesna's mother had once told her to always conceal with a scarf. The woman was clearly struggling to read the words with an air of pride and comedy, stopping now and then to throw the audience a meaningful glance over her reading glasses. But as she continued struggling through the English with her harsh Macedonian accent, the hand which held the paper trembled ever more violently, and she stopped looking at the audience. A strand of hair had loosened from her bun and was tremulously arching on the left side of her head. The woman's stammers noticeably increased. How perfect! Vesna thought, relieved that the high expectations set in motion by the first performer had completely evaporated. As she reached down for her cup, another bout of dizziness almost knocked her from her chair and she nearly fell on the accordion. Fortunately, no one noticed—the audience was busy giving the woman who had so adventitiously mocked her own aging a warm round of applause. Vesna downed the last of the rakija as the clapping subsided and saw Kelly's head turn toward her with a piercing look of suspicion, and, possibly, reproach.

As Vesna rose and went toward the stage, the heavy accordion slung from her shoulders, she had the same weak feeling in the knees that she had had when she mounted the stage at the protest. With every movement her vision grew cloudier until all she could see in the dark salon were vague blurry faces illuminated by cell phones. Then the lights went back on, the audience clapped and Vesna felt a bolt of electricity which instantly cleared her head and vision, and she could now make out all the famous faces who were celebrating Women's Day in Kelly Davis's theater. She closed her eyes and timidly played the opening chord as she squeezed the bellows.

The instrument wheezed like an asthmatic old man: one, two, three breaths for each chord. Vesna's plaintive voice followed the bronchial melody with its own complaint as she sang: "I hate the world today . . ." But when the voice and instrument finally came in sync, Vesna became elated by the wonder of harmony. She stood tall, never noticing that she had planted her feet apart, her muscles taut, but she was delightfully aware of her voice rising to a slow crescendo. "I really didn't know what I was doing," she had lied after her performance at the school festival in her sophomore year that had magically transformed her from a dour accordion player in a folk-dance group to a hippie who rapturously sang "White Rabbit" by Jefferson Airplane for no other reason than that she had a crush on Marko, a long-haired guitarist who claimed to have experimented with drugs. Then, too, she had closed her eyes and pumped the bellows so that the accordion thundered like a church organ. Her voice had boomed so loudly that the cleaning ladies could hear her all the way back to the janitor's room. In those days she had sung for Marko. Now she was singing for Ljubo, who, like Marko, was conspicuously absent from her performance. She prayed that Marko, or at least Ljubo, would not only hear of it, but deeply regret not having come, and, moreover, be proud of her. This fantasy emboldened her: *Ima beech, Ima lava, Ima chile, Ima mada* she belted, until every soul in the salon was now looking up from their cell phones. After the refrain, she muddled through the second verse, jazzing up the melody a bit and humming "m-m-m" or singing "na-na-na" whenever she had forgotten the words or thought they were irrelevant.

She rushed on to the refrain so she could tell all those present what she was and what she hoped to be. When she had finished, a few strands of hair clung to her sweaty face. "Pfffff," went the accordion, "Pfffff," went Vesna, as she tried to blow the strands of hair from her lips and mouth.

She opened the eyes and saw the audience sitting silent and open-mouthed in the light. Kelly's face was flushed a bright pink, pinker than her outfit. This time she didn't clap as she had when the writer concluded her performance. Then someone in the back row began a slow applause that spread here and there through the room like a handful of marbles. Only two or three people sitting in the far-right corner vigorously applauded, whistled and gave Vesna a "woo-hoo!" of approval.

As she returned to her seat, Vesna was certain she had outdone herself, that she had performed in the best spirit of the brave and powerful woman to whom Kelly Davis had dedicated the event. She was also convinced that not only had she surpassed the writer but would remain unexcelled all evening. She crossed paths with the businesswoman as the latter strode toward the stage. The woman gave her a tight-lipped smile, falsely cordial and full of unspoken thoughts. When Vesna sat down, the lights dimmed again, but people were now rustling and whispering. In the darkness, a suspicion sparked by the woman's tight smile began to rise in Vesna. All the passion, courage, pluck she had felt when she stepped down from the stage without taking a bow were sinking like a stone. When the room lit up again, she made out the name of the next skit in the program: "Jewelry Party."

Three women and the professional actor were sitting around a table heaped with jewelry. The businesswoman sat in the middle and pretended she was South American, while the other performers with their heavy Slavic accents pretended they didn't understand a word the woman was saying.

Vesna tried to concentrate on what was happening on stage but found it impossible. She realized that her clothes were drenched, her panties smelled of mold, her armpits gave off the sickly-sweet reek of nervous sweat. She glanced over her shoulder and saw that a famous journalist with a mocking smile was shaking her head and rubbing her eyes in disbelief. A law professor whose name Vesna couldn't remember squinted in disgust at the stage. Another woman Vesna recognized from television was pressing her temples. This, too, will pass, Vesna thought; I wasn't *that* bad, she said to herself as she tried to remember the triumph she had felt after her speech at the protest. She could only remember balancing her cold buttocks on a concrete post, and then Ljubo being so angry at her for getting up on stage. She imagined he would not be thrilled about her performance at this event, either.

Vesna felt sick to her stomach, as something churned inside her, making its way upward. She remembered her practice sessions, how she had sung loudly in the living room so Vojdan would hear her and tell Ljubo, so Ljubo would come, and ask her what she was practicing and if there was anything they could do to help; so she could have the pleasure of saying: No Ljubo, no, Vojdan, just come and be there for me. But it was only when Vesna saw the Macedonian bearers of change adorned with dime-store jewelry breaking their tongues on stage that she recalled several scenes from the week before; how Vojdan, for instance, had stomped down the stairs from the attic and shut the living room door as she stood tall, singing with her head thrown back. She could hear his angry footsteps were suddenly muted after another door slammed and a *toop-toop-toop* beat boomed from his room. In a cloud of dizzy haze she could see Ljubo's face floating above hers, saying: "Oh Vesna, Vesna dear . . ." turning her head to one side just as something sour seeped from her lips and dampened her pillow. "Oh, God," Ljubo said, and then everything disappeared.

Vesna suddenly realized her mouth was filling with saliva, as it always did when she fell asleep after a vodka binge. It must be the rakija, she thought, as she tried to swallow the saliva flooding her mouth. Breathe, she said to herself, just breathe, take deep breaths, breathe deeply through your nose, focus on something in front of you. She kept repeating the words to herself, the words of her father who was long gone and whose only memento was the huge and cumbersome accordion with which she had humiliated herself in front of the Skopje elite. Breathe, just breathe, just—Vesna covered her mouth and about to turn her head toward the empty seat beside her, but it was too late: a powerful force flung her chin forward like a slingshot as a jet of vomit sprayed through her fingers, showering the musician Katerina who was seated in front of her.

Someone screamed. Bright flecks of jalapeno pepper, cheddar cheese, and iceberg lettuce clung to the woman's hair as an orangey mix of rakija and water drizzled down the nape of her neck. Katerina reached back to see what it was, let out a hideous shriek, and then she, too, began retching. Meanwhile, the businesswoman on stage who was making a valiant effort to deliver her lines, stopped short at the sight of Katerina, who, despite having clapped a vomit-stained hand over her mouth, also spewed a fountain of half-digested food, some of which found its way onto Kelly's shoulder and lap. Her tweed skirt and blazer magically absorbed the fluid and acquired the bright hue of salmon gone bad. Kelly leapt to her feet with a piercing scream, whereupon the writer pulled out a packet of wet wipes from her purse and got down on her knees to clean Kelly's skirt. But then Kelly began to dry-heave and cry at the same time, and, a moment later, the writer threw up on Kelly's beige pumps. A few burly men with earpieces came forward and eased the ambassador back toward the wall from where he stared at the spectacle with his mouth agape. The eyes of the two security men nervously followed the growing number of people who were milling about the room and vomiting here and there. A man in an expensive suit was puking in the corner behind the buffet table. In the middle of the room a young woman with her head between her knees was spilling her guts. The sounds of screams, hurried footfalls and moaning filled the parlor. People were crowding the exit, where two guards tried to keep them from trampling each other.

Seeing that no one was looking at her anymore, Vesna allowed the last remnant of vomit to trickle from her mouth and land beside her red booties. She hadn't drunk or eaten much beside the rakija—a mini burger, a glass of water. Having emptied her stomach of the vile acid, she no longer felt ill. Her vision cleared, as did her mind. Deciding to leave, she reached for the accordion and accidentally struck a key that made the instrument moan with terror and despair. The whole room fell silent and turned their eyes toward Vesna. Her accordion wheezed and panted as she struggled to strap it on. Other sounds punctuated the stillness: Kelly's high-pitched whimpers; whispered ohmygods and whatthefucks; hacking coughs and retching. The air was filled with a sour stench like the reek of a toilet bowl in a nightclub.

Aware that all eyes were glued to her, Vesna wiped her mouth. The last remnants of lipstick striped the back of her hand red. It was as if everyone was waiting for her to say something. Instead, she shrugged her shoulders, laid one hand on her chest, and, with a twisted expression of pity pointed the other toward Emina, who stood motionless behind the plates stacked with mini burgers. Everyone stared at the Roma girl. A cloud of condemnation filled the room, an unsaid chorus of "Yeah, we all knew it was you . . ." Vesna made her way through this cloud to the exit, with people stepping back to let her pass. She said goodbye to no one, not even to Kelly, who stood whining in the puddle of Katerina's vomit; nor to the ambassador, who remained somewhat aloof from his wife, too disgusted to console her. The maid who had taken her coat was nowhere to be found, but Vesna had no intention of ever wearing that tattered old thing again. She stepped out into the night in her light gray outfit, the accordion strapped to her chest. A soft breeze heralding the end of winter caressed her face, and, light-footed, she descended the hill toward the city.

ACKNOWLEDGMENTS

This book was written in Skopje, Mavrovo, Split, Pazin, and Iowa City.

I would like to thank Traduki, the KURS association in Split, Croatia, the Writers' House in Pazin, Croatia, and the International Writing Program in Iowa City, USA for their generous support. My deepest gratitude goes to the people from the International Writing Program at the University of Iowa for letting me sit in their literary translation classes and workshops, where I met Steve Bradbury, the co-translator of this book. Thank you, Steve, for sticking with me throughout this journey.

Thank you, Magdalena Horvat and Vivian Eden for your invaluable and beautiful insight. And thank you my friends and family for all the love, stories and patience.

CPSIA information can be obtained
at www.ICGtesting.com
Printed in the USA
JSHW080529140223
37694JS00002B/2

9 781628 974546